PENGUI
THE MERLION A

Dipika Mukherjee was born in 1965. She is an Indian citizen and Malaysian permanent resident who has been living in Singapore since 1998, where she teaches at the Nanyang Technological University. She is a published poet and is working on her first novel.

Kirpal Singh has written and edited many books. His most recent book, *Monologue,* was launched at the First Hong Kong International Writers Festival in May 2001. He has been invited to some of the most important Writers Festivals internationally (Edinburgh, Toronto, Adelaide and Singapore). In 1997 he was Distinguished International Writer at the Iowa Writers Program. He currently teaches at the Singapore Management University where he is also Director of the Centre for Cross-Cultural Studies.

M.A. Quayum is Associate Professor of English in the Faculty of Modern Languages and Communication, Universiti Putra Malaysia. Books he has written/edited include *Colonial to Global: Malaysian Women's Writing in English 1940s-1990s, Dictionary of Literary Terms, Saul Bellow: The Man and His Work, Malaysian Literature in English: A Critical Reader, Diverse Voices: Readings in Languages, Literatures and Cultures, In Blue Silk Girdle: Stories from Malaysia and Singapore* and *Singaporean Literature in English: A Critical Reader* (forthcoming). Quayum's articles on American and post-colonial literatures have appeared in journals in the US, Australia, South Africa, Singapore, India, Bangladesh and Malaysia.

The Merlion and the Hibiscus

Contemporary Short Stories from Singapore and Malaysia

Edited by Dipika Mukherjee, Kirpal Singh and M.A. Quayum

PENGUIN BOOKS

Penguin Books India (P) Ltd., 11 Community Centre, Panchsheel Park, New Delhi 110 017, India
Penguin Books Ltd., 80 Strand, London WC2R 0RL, UK
Penguin Putnam Inc., 375 Hudson Street, New York, NY 10014, USA
Penguin Books Australia Ltd., 250 Camberwell Road, Camberwell, Victoria 3124, Australia
Penguin Books Canada Ltd., 10 Alcorn Avenue, Suite 300, Toronto, Ontario M4V 3B2, Canada
Penguin Books (NZ) Ltd., Cnr Rosedale & Airborne Roads, Albany, Auckland, New Zealand

First published by Penguin Books India 2002

Copyright © Penguin Books India 2002
Introduction copyright © M.A. Quayum, Kirpal Singh and Deepika Mukherjee
Copyright in the individual works vests with the respective contributors
Page vi is an extension of the copyright page

All rights reserved

10 9 8 7 6 5 4 3 2 1

Typeset in New Baskerville by Mantra Virtual Services, New Delhi
Printed at Chaman Offset Printers, New Delhi

This book is sold subject to the condition that it shall not, by way of trade or otherwise, be lent, resold, hired out, or otherwise circulated without the publisher's prior written consent in any form of binding or cover other than that in which it is published and without a similar condition including this condition being imposed on the subsequent purchaser and without limiting the rights under copyright reserved above, no part of this publication may be reproduced, stored in or introduced into a retrieval system, or transmitted in any form or by any means (electronic, mechanical, photocopying, recording or otherwise), without the prior written permission of both the copyright owner and the above-mentioned publisher of this book.

*To Our Loved Ones . . .
Prasanta, Arohan, Arush,
Sarah, Areta, Misha, Clarinda,
Lily, Jinney and Sasha*

Copyright Acknowledgements

Grateful acknowledgement is made to the following for permission to reprint copyright material:

CHE HUSNA AZHARI: *Mariah* © Faruda Publishing House, Bangi, Malaysia, 1993, reprinted by permission of the author and the publisher; GOPAL BARATHAM: *The Interview* © Gopal Baratham 1982, reprinted by permission of the author; UMEJ BHATIA: *AWOL* © Umej Bhatia 1995, reprinted by permission of the author; CHUAH GUAT ENG: *Seventh Uncle* © Chuah Guat Eng 1999, reprinted by permission of the author; LLOYD FERNANDO: *Surja Singh* © Lloyd Fernando 1999, reprinted by permission of the author; CATHERINE LIM: *'Write, Right, Rite'* © Catherine Lim 1989, reprinted by permission of the author; SHIRLEY GEOK-LIN LIM: *Mr Tang's Girls* © Times Editions Pte Ltd 1982, reprinted by permission of the author and the publisher; K.S. MANIAM: *Mala* © K.S. Maniam 1985, reprinted by permission of the author; KARIM RASLAN: *Neighbours* © Times Editions Pte Ltd 1996, reprinted by permission of the author and the publisher; ALFIAN SA'AT: *Bugis* © Alfian Sa'at 1999, reprinted by permission of the author; M. SHANMUGHALINGAM: *Victoria and Her Kimono* © M. Shanmughalingam 2001, reprinted by permission of the author; KIRPAL SINGH: *Monologue II* © Kirpal Singh 2001, reprinted by permission of the author; HWEE HWEE TAN: *Hungry Ghost* © Hwee Hwee Tan 1995, reprinted by permission of the author; SIMON TAY: *My Cousin Tim* © Landmark Books Singapore 1996, reprinted by permission of the author and the publisher; OVIDIA YU: *Kimmy* © Ovidia Yu 1986, reprinted by permission of the author.

Contents

Acknowledgements ix

Introduction xi

Alfian Sa'at *Bugis*		1
Catherine Lim *'Write, Right, Rite'*		12
Che Husna Azhari *Mariah*		18
Chuah Guat Eng *Seventh Uncle*		32
Gopal Baratham *The Interview*		51
Hwee Hwee Tan *Hungry Ghost*		60
K.S. Maniam *Mala*		67
Karim Raslan *Neighbours*		87
Kee Thuan Chye *A Sense of Home*		100
Kirpal Singh *Monologue II*		105
Lloyd Fernando *Surja Singh*		113
M. Shanmughalingam *Victoria and Her Kimono*		127
Ovidia Yu *Kimmy*		145

Shirley Geok-Lin Lim *Mr Tang's Girls*	156
Simon Tay *My Cousin Tim*	171
Suchen Christine Lim *Tragedy of My Third Eye*	194
Umej Bhatia *AWOL*	208
Wena Poon *The Move*	219
Zuraidah Ibrahim *Hamid and the Hand of Fate*	225
Notes on Authors	*237*

Acknowledgements

The editors would like to gratefully acknowledge the cooperation and assistance of the authors. The editors would also like to thank Robert Yeo for his sage advice, Neha Khoda, for help with scanning and typesetting and Natasha Chowdhury and Sunita Krishna for their proofreading skills. Our gratitude also goes to Theresa Manavalan and Lakshmy Bhaskar for crucial support at the launch of this project.

Introduction

When the Anglo-Dutch Treaty of 1824 made it clear that the Malayan Archipelago would be British while the Indonesian would be Dutch, few would have thought it possible that one day there would be natives from the Malayan peninsula and the small island of Singapore writing in the totally new language called English. This their colonial masters brought with them and taught them in order, in the words of the infamous Lord McCauley in his 1834 Minute to the House of Commons, to 'civilize these natives'. The Penang Free School had started teaching students fully in English in the late eighteenth century while the Singapore Institution (later better known as Raffles Institution) started teaching Singaporeans fully in English in 1823.

The students who gradually grew to think and express themselves best in this newly acquired foreign language called English had, from the very first, models from the great classics of Greece and Rome and the works of the masters of English literature. Apart from the old Bard himself, writers like Chaucer, Wordsworth, Milton, Samuel Richardson, Charles Dickens, D.H. Lawrence and James Joyce most influenced the new breed of hopefuls from Singapore and Malaya (as it was then called). The first time we were seriously exposed to a literary tradition other than that from the United Kingdom was in 1972-73, when, at the university, we were given an option to study American literature. Incidentally, masters was, indeed, an operative word since most writers studied were men.

Another statement which might be made here is the simple

observation that most natives of these two countries developed an inferiority complex vis-à-vis the writers whose works they studied. At best, they could only imitate and not truly create since their knowledge and mastery of English was going to be second-hand. Since their own teachers, even after the independence of Malaya in 1957 and Singapore in 1965, kowtowed to their own colonial masters (a legacy of colonialism everywhere), real creative efforts in English were considered naïve and silly radical experiments in a field thought to be beyond the grasp of the citizens. It is not surprising that the literatures of other post-colonial nations began to be taught in the universities in both countries only post-1984 or so . . . and even then (as now) sparingly.

The emphasis in the above is on denial; the Malaysian and Singaporean writers whose works appear in this wonderful anthology were constantly denied their real worth. Such a denial has come in myriad forms: from the difficulty of getting published to the near impossibility of getting their works established in schools and universities nationally (Harry Potter has more of a chance in becoming a school text in Singapore than has, say, Gopal Baratham's story 'The Interview') to the paltry sense of recognition accorded the writers. Though there have, of late, been signs of a change of heart in this respect, these signs remain very much precisely that: signs.

Thus it will not come as a major surprise that many of these stories are stories of complaint or lamentation or both. Beneath the veneer of subtle, even witty, writing is the clearly marked focus of emotional and psychological dislocation—whether represented as a fact of history (as in the stories of Chuah Guat Eng, Lloyd Fernando or Suchen Lim), a fact of rivalry/displacement in family life (as in the stories by Simon Tay, Kee Thuan Chye or Shirley Lim), a fact of racial/ethnic/religious/cultural diversity (as in the stories by K.S. Maniam, Hwee Hwee Tan or Alfian Sa'at) or a fact of private, individual perspectives (as in the stories of Umej Bhatia, Kirpal Singh or Ovidia Yu).

M. Shanmughalingam's beautifully crafted story, 'Victoria and Her Kimono', might serve as an example of the manner in which the writer chooses to parody both the inherited legacy of colonialism and the dramatic confrontations of this. Such confrontations clearly marked the dawning of a new age of literary sensibility, resulting in the creation of authentically relevant and appropriate responses to the living experiences of ordinary men and women, who went about their everyday affairs alienated from and yet near enough the centre of the political nerves to sense and be affected directly by its policies.

Much of the real creative talent in writing began to show itself after the Second World War. There is no readily available explanation for this, save to say that maybe the plight of thousands compelled writers to record their impressions and emotions in the newly acquired language, which would give their writings a broader base even within their own countries. As most readers will know, both Singapore and Malaysia are *multi* societies—multi-racial, multi-religious, multi-lingual, multi-cultural, etc. Given the richness of such a range of possible experiences even in the lived moment of a single second, how could writers not take to penning their wonderful feelings and thoughts about everything? The great war drew people together even as it made them suspicious of one another; it provided ample opportunities of intimacy as it did of enmity—a fact, by the way, which is only now becoming openly acknowledged. Whether it was the cruelty of the Japanese soldiers who butchered their way through the towns and the kampongs or whether it was the resolute assertion of power by the rather snooty colonial Englishmen and women who remained discriminatory of their local counterparts that made the natives behave in the ways they did will, probably, never be fully understood. Still it must be realized that time-passing (to echo T.S. Eliot) had profound effects on the psyche of time-future as lived. We, the natives, developed our own sensibility, a curious, complex blend of numerous histories and geographies which continues to baffle even us today.

Broadly, three generations of writers are represented here: the first, those who are above sixty and vividly remember the era of the Second World War and the notoriety of the Japanese occupation and the triumphant return of the British after the atomic bombing of Hiroshima and Nagasaki; the second, those between about forty-five and sixty, whose memories of these events are mainly vicariously obtained, through reading and listening to their parents retell stories; and the third, those between about thirty and forty-five who are still too young to bother about the fundamental lessons of historical contexts and who have their own, more immediately pressing, issues to explore. While it is always hard to say what informs a certain story's impulse, it can be pointed out, for purposes of discussion and understanding, that these three generations of writers overlap fractionally: they are all natives of Singapore and Malaysia. Beyond this, their writings reveal a dramatic individuality of voice which underlines the very genuine sentiments so daringly (in most instances) adventured upon in the crafting and realization of these stories.

An area of interest and one which has, of late, found a marked presence everywhere is the focus on women. Many stories here speak of the difficulties women have faced throughout their lives as mothers, sisters, wives and lovers. This is not an easy theme for writers to handle even though it might appear to be so; the sensitivities involved do not allow the usual comforts of simple exploration. The whole issue is complex and fraught with the sufferings that women have always been subjected to. Since the theme is nowadays so commonly written about and commented upon, the creative strengths of writers treating it are pushed to limits that defy ordinary analysis. The feminist movement has not sat upon comfortable bodies and minds in Asia. The women of Singapore and Malaysia have had to balance traditional value systems with the new impetus provided by their feminist sisters from the West. The result has frequently been a sense of non-belonging and yet having to perform the duties and roles culturally associated with the fairer sex.

Complaint and lamentation do not leave writers bereft because between them they encompass a wide world of conflicting, as well as complimenting, experiences. Thus the stories of writers like Simon Tay, Karim Raslan, Umej Bhatia and Wena Poon, though sounding as if they could have been written in any cosmopolitan situation, strike a deep chord in the minds and hearts of those of us who know Singapore and Malaysia and know what a convoluted history our nations have shared. The relationships among the various ethnic groups have sometimes led to conflicts which have left deep scars. But writers heal the wounds inflicted by irrational emotionalities, even as they expose the errors committed. The lessons learnt through the vividly realized dramatizations leave readers secure in the new knowledges obtained. The narratives remain etched in landscapes that will forever be alien to those of us who only read for the sake of reading, rather than actually intimately identifying with the depths of the ground of inner being. No reader can claim that any story here is only cerebral—our writers tend to keep away from mental preoccupations which do not have bodied accents! In a few of the stories, the English is markedly localized/indigenized in order to signal precisely the difference between English here and elsewhere in the world. Readers have frequently remarked just how glorious it is to see the establishment and growth of a new idiomatic English truly representing the national life of a country. Alas, in the great movements towards globalization, such idiomization might well be a memory not too long from now. A sad loss.

No single theme, issue, gender or age factor seems to have influenced the choice of the stories represented in this exciting anthology: the only feature throughout seems to have been excellence in storytelling. All the stories make for compelling reads and their intensities impel engagements which will, no doubt, go beyond the images of the printed texts. Beyond understanding there will be a learning and when the creative exchange between reader and text is complete the fusion is exquisite. None of the works here is so dense as to defy concentrated identification and understanding. None takes anyone for granted. However, they all do embody a complexity which will reveal itself through (dare we say it?) repeated readings. There is a little something for everyone and the free imagination which approaches these stories will be generously challenged and stimulated. In the end, there can only be freedom for both writer and reader.

We each have our own stories to tell. Those in this handsome book tell tales of anguish and despair, joy and sorrow, grief and healing, of men and women who have lived through experiences (real or imagined) which link their humanity to ours. Such is the nature of good literature. It works upon us. It finally makes us read it again.

Happy Reading!

Dipika Mukherjee
Kirpal Singh
M.A. Quayum

January 2002

Bugis
Alfian Sa'at

Salmah is wearing her tudung again.

For those who don't know, the tudung is this scarf that good Muslim girls wear. People like Salmah just want to action, act like good girl; but later in school, she will meet her boyfriend, and hold hands with him. This wearing tudung also, I don't know who teach her or where she learn. Last month she never used to wear, her hair was always tied at the back with a red scrungee. She would often take it off to wear at her wrist, like a bracelet.

Just one month and Salmah has found God.

I never saw her hair after that. Maybe it's now permed or dyed pink or itching with kutu, but if I know about most girls who wear tudung, it's that they don't care about their hair. They just care about looking like good girls and kissing their mother's hand at the front door and winning their mother's trust so they can later hold their boyfriend's hand in school. I have seen Salmah do it, and I have also seen her punch Sazalie's chest playfully. Action manja. Sazalie is her boyfriend, quite cute, but he cannot pronounce his r's properly. He says 'argh' instead and when I hear him talk I tell myself I must get a boyfriend whose tongue is not so short.

So here we are in the MRT on the way to the poly. Salmah is trying to revise her notes, using a pink highlighter that is almost dried up. I usually don't study in the MRT, so what I do is fan myself with a copy of *The New Paper* in my hands. (The headline today is: 'Will She Strip Again?') I do it not because it is hot, but because I want to ask Salmah if she is not hot wearing her tudung in the afternoon like this, but without opening my mouth. I don't know if she is getting the hint, but she is looking down at the opened file on her lap and mumbling to herself.

Salmah and Sazalie. They sound like a happy couple, the names would look good on a wedding invitation card, but I have seen them fight before. Salmah is terrible when they fight. She will make her blackest face, and turn it away from Sazalie. Her lips will pout. When Sazalie looks at her right, she will look left. When he looks to her left, she will look right. Their faces will be the two like poles on two magnets. That is why I think that all this girlfriend boyfriend business should start only after you finish school. So young, and wanting to find romance: my mother calls it 'cinta monyet' or 'monkeys in love'. I have tried talking to Salmah about it, but she will always ask me back, 'Why you so kaypoh? If I want to have a boyfriend, or ten boyfriends, it's my own business.' This coming from a girl who wears a tudung to school.

Suddenly I go, 'Yesterday my grandma made trouble again.'

Salmah looks up from her Particle Mechanics lecture notes. 'What did she do?' she asks.

'Don't know lah.' I always go 'don't know lah' before I start off telling a long story. I'm not sure where I picked the habit up from, but it has been pointed out to me by who else, but my best friend since primary school. For those who don't know, it's Salmah.

Then I continue, 'Yesterday, I was at the void deck with the guys. And then when I went up, that old woman started scolding me for nothing. She said I was grown up already, shouldn't be mixing so freely with guys, what will people say?'

'Who were you with?' Salmah asked.

'You know lah, the usual void deck people. Hisham, Firdaus, Omar.' Hisham is this really fat guy who wears baggy Cross

Color jeans. Firdaus is this guy who pierced his right eyebrow. And Omar is this half-Arab, half-Malay guy who has the biggest collection of dirty jokes ever. He never tells the same joke twice. I think the day Omar tells us a joke we've heard from him before will be the day he finally passes his 'O' levels. This year he is taking it as a private candidate, for the third time. The other guys like to tease Omar about it, and keep asking him when he's ever going to become a corporal. Once in a while they call him Private Omar, but the good thing about the guys is that they know just when to stop.

I first met the boys one day while walking home from school with Salmah. They were playing skateboard under my void deck. At that time, Salmah had her hair long and I must say she looked good with her two ponytails, one on each shoulder. Like a decent girl, hugging her file to her chest. When we were near the void deck I asked Salmah if she wanted to walk near the grass slopes, but she said, 'Don't care about them, we can walk wherever we want. Anyway, those boys all blind, cannot see the sign that said "No Skateboarding".'

So Salmah and I walked towards the void deck, and my heart was beating a little faster because I didn't like the sound of the skateboard wheels being dragged across the cement floor. I got the feeling that something was getting spoilt and worn out. Suddenly, one of the boys, Firdaus, the eyebrow-ring guy, glided up in front of us and very consciously arched his pierced eyebrow. He wiggled it up and down.

'Just got back from school?' he asked.

Salmah and I kept silent. We could have walked ahead but it seemed as if there were now three boys, poised on their skateboards, in front of us.

'Yah, unlike some people, we got school,' I replied. I didn't know what made me talk back to them.

'Wah, this one, so fierce,' the fat guy said.

I looked at Salmah. She was looking away, irritated. Then

she started placing her chin on the edge of her file. She sighed. She looked as if we were going to be there for a long time.

'Yah lah, a bit fierce,' said the third guy, the one in a singlet.

I knew it was all up to me. I knew how it worked, but the thought made me a little sad. Usually when two girls are confronted, the one who will speak up, who will defend both of them, the fierce one, is the less pretty one. The prettier girl gets to keep quiet, because if she opens her mouth then pearls will drop out, and their harassers will all scramble to pick them off the ground. Then the guys will never leave them alone, and they will do everything to hear their princess speak again.

'You all got nothing better to do ah?' I ask. 'Blind or what? Cannot see the sign over there, that picture, no skateboarding?'

'Eh, she's scolding us lah,' the singlet guy said. Then the eyebrow-ring guy spoke.

'Miss, you look at the sign again. What is there? This black person. One leg long, one leg short. He is riding a skateboard, OK, fine. But you see us. Which of us is black? Which of us is crippled? See, the sign only means: Black and crippled people cannot skateboard. Black people cannot, because at night, people cannot see. Crippled people also cannot because later fall down.'

I had never until then heard something more stupid in my whole life. I turned to my right and saw Salmah smiling slightly. She was going to sabotage my efforts. Suddenly I told the boys, in the rudest tone I could find, 'Hey, we all don't go for you Mats under the block. At our school got so many better people, people who can study, who don't waste time in the void deck. You all think, skateboard, very cool ah? Make noise only. Disturb others.' And then I tugged Salmah's sleeve and walked off with her, never turning to look back, whispering things in Salmah's ear. I left the boys behind us. I had a princess to safeguard. I also left my house behind me, to walk Salmah all the way to her home.

Three weeks after that, we were back again at the void deck.

Salmah had met a new member of the skateboarding group. He had dimples and his hair always had this wet look. He was the only one among all the skateboarding boys who had really clear skin. When he told Salmah that he was studying at the polytechnic I could see her eyes light up. I was wrong, there were some void deck Mats who went to school.

The boy's name was Sazalie.

Not long after, we would hang around regularly at the void deck, four guys and two girls, and one day I saw Sazalie's arm behind Salmah's back. At that time, I had one foot on a skateboard and I was pushing it back and forth, back and forth. And then it suddenly slipped from my sole and went off on its own. It hit a pillar, bounced off, stopped.

Soon, because I hung around so much with Salmah, I found myself hanging around with the boys too. And when Salmah and Sazalie decided to get together, Salmah left me at that void deck with the rest of them. One thing though, I never shook off that fierce image I had since the first day I met the boys. Sometimes I think, that wasn't even the real me; when I spoke so loudly on that day, my heart was actually beating very fast. I was trembling. But words still came out.

Nowadays I'm fiercer than ever, so the boys can call me what they want and give me nicknames. I sit around with them and sometimes I laugh like mad when one of them falls doing a skateboarding stunt. And then with that loud voice I've learnt to use, I'd go, 'Ha! Serves you right! Do again, I want to see!'

Salmah looks out of the window and watches the roofs of shophouses pass by, with their antennae, their circling crows. Suddenly the train shuttles into a tunnel and we hear the cavern-like whoosh surrounding the train. There is nothing but a rushing darkness outside, and the train passengers can all look at their reflections. I just take one glimpse at mine and then start unfolding my *New Paper*. Salmah is still looking at hers, adjusting her tudung.

'You're so good you're not living with your grandma,' I tell her.

'Both my grandmothers are dead,' Salmah replies. 'You're so lucky.'

The train stops at Lavender station and a group of Bangladeshi men walk in. I used to ask Salmah who gets off and on at Lavender, it was usually so deserted. Now the answer is: the whole world. The new Singapore Immigration Building was built next to it, and sometimes we would see groups of Filipinos, Thais and even Caucasians. The Bangladeshi men take a seat opposite us. Most of them are wearing white shirts, with pin stripes, tucked neatly into their trousers. All of them have moustaches. And all of them have combed their hair with oil.

'How are the guys?' Salmah suddenly asks me.

'Like devils,' I tell her.

'That's nothing new,' she says.

'I don't know why they can talk so much rubbish,' I tell her. 'There was this one day when I brought down my lecture notes, to see if I can study with them. I mean, if I get tired, I can joke around with them for a while. Five minutes. And then get back to work. I couldn't study in the house because my grandma was awake and she was nagging and nagging. She was telling me how when she was my age she knew how to cook, how to clean the house. So I sat with the guys. And I realized that I couldn't study at all. They're so funny. Everything they said was funny. I couldn't stop laughing. You should hang around more with us.'

The train stops at Bugis. People walk in and find seats. At this time of the afternoon, the train is not so crowded and everyone finds a seat. Some even have space to lean to one side and occupy two seats. A Malay woman walks in through the door on our left. She weaves her way towards us, holding on to the strap of her handbag with one hand. She is wearing high-heeled shoes, and she has to walk near the side of the aisles so her head does not knock into the horizontal handrails. She has high cheekbones, and she is wearing this white satin spaghetti strap dress that has a very high hemline. It shows off her thighs, her strong calves. She settles down two seats away from me. I take one look at her Adam's apple. The Malay lady is a man.

I look at the Bangladeshi men opposite me. Some of them are frowning, looking at her. The lady crosses one leg over another and leans forward, and then she rests her chin on her fist, her elbow on her knee. Her eyeballs swing from side to side, and then settle on an MRT poster. She is behaving as if she is an actress in a movie. She sucks in her cheeks for her best shot.

I wonder whether if this were their country, the Bangladeshi men might make wolf-whistle sounds at her. But they are quiet, and after a while, they start pretending that they didn't see her walking in, sashaying, and now tucking strands of hair with those big hands behind her ears. I steal a glance at this lady and wonder if she is wearing a wig. Her fingernails are painted a deep blood red. Suddenly I hear Salmah whispering into my ear.

'Transvestite,' she says. But she uses the Malay word for it, which has more sting, which makes one giggle. 'Pondan.'

'Isn't it funny,' Salmah then informs me, still whispering, 'that of all stations, she has to come in at Bugis?'

When I was small, my father used to tell me stories of how he used to go to Bugis Street with my mother for a laugh. I thought it was strange, to go and see pondans on your date, but I supposed that was how courtship was for them at that time. My father used to say that some of them were really gutsy, wearing tight clothes, miniskirts, flirting around with the Caucasian sailors. He said he once saw one climb a table top with her high heels and then a striptease show. When she took off her bra people applauded; she had a flat male chest, shaven to smoothness. She threw the bra upwards and it hooked on to a lamp post. It was scenes like these that kept my mother and father occupied and amused when they went out on dates. But nowadays, Bugis has been cleaned up, dolled up decently for the tourists. There's nothing there but a shopping mall. The transvestites are gone. But somehow this one, with her biceps and lipstick, has found her way into our train.

The lady starts to yawn, and she uses that coarse hand to cover her mouth. But her fingers are bent delicately, in defiance of its design. I have seen the way the fingers of transvestites work. They touch everything as if it carried germs. They only use their fingertips, which is what the lady is using to wipe the sides of her eyes. Then she turns to me, and smiles.

'Eh,' she exclaims, softly. She places her fingertips on her chest. Her voice is deep. She has it under control though, she tunes it soft so instead of gruff she can keep it sultry.

'You look like Ziana Zain!' she suddenly exclaims. Ziana Zain is a Malaysian singer hysterically famous among the Malays. She sings ballads with titles like *The peak of love*. Her eyebrows are very arched, and when she sings, her mouth is very wide, such that my mother always says, 'She's going to swallow the microphone.' But she has many fans. When she had her wedding, the 10,000 guests who turned up caused a tent to collapse, and months after that, Malay weddings had the bride in a green baju kurung because that was what Ziana had worn. But I look nothing like Ziana Zain. Salmah, who knew this, giggled by my side.

'No lah, kak,' I tell the lady. This is crazy, I think. I'm actually calling her kak. Kak is Malay for sister. I wouldn't want a sister like that. Maybe I should have called her abang instead, abang for brother. What would she say to that?

'No, just now when I walked in, I thought, eh, this is Ziana Zain. What is Ziana Zain doing in Singapore? I was thinking of telling my friends I saw Ziana Zain inside the MRT!'

I shake my head and still say no. I'm also wondering what kind of friends she has. Salmah on my left is pretending not to have heard a single thing, but I know inside she is kicking up her legs and laughing like mad. Salmah keeps looking at her

Particle Mechanics notes, the same page, and although there is nothing funny with her notes she has this fixed smile on her face.

'Really, you know, you look just like her.' At this point, the lady gives me a concerned look, as if she is aware of all the possibilities of being a Ziana Zain lookalike. 'Except for the specs. But you still look like Ziana Zain if she puts on specs. Hey, why don't you take off your specs, let me take a good look at you?'

I look at what I am wearing. A Billabong-shirt, and jeans. I have a haversack on my side. The Bangladeshi workers are all looking at me. This woman is crazy, I think. This woman is out to humiliate me. If there is one thing worse than sitting beside a pondan, it is sitting beside a pondan who is out of her mind.

I remove my spectacles and I look at the transvestite. I have nothing more to lose. Without my specs, she looks more like a woman. Her mouth doesn't appear so big anymore, and when she smiles, it is less of a leer. Her hair is more natural, and I suddenly realize that she has quite a good figure, broad shoulders and a full chest. But I put my specs on again and I see him, his fake fingernails, fake wig, fake breasts, fake shaven shins. The only thing real about him is the surprise on his face, coupled with what looks like satisfaction from being the only one in the world who is able to see that I look like Ziana Zain. He has the expression of someone who is about to groom a star.

And then just as suddenly, he leaves his seat and tells me, 'I get off here. My station.'

The station is Outram Park. If he walks out, he will wander smack into the heart of Chinatown. I wonder what it will be like, this tall Malay transvestite walking around in Chinatown, past the medicinal halls smelling of dried herbs, the dumpling stalls, the pirated VCD shops with prices black-markered on fluorescent stars. This pondan and his fine fingertips.

Before he goes, he smiles at me. It is a mischievous smile. He then waves, still with his fingertips, and flicks his hair. It doesn't fall off, the wig. It stays firm on his head. He says, 'Bye Ziana, see you in concert!' And then he says to Salmah, 'Bye Ziana's friend, from just now so shy!'

When he leaves, Salmah breaks out laughing. She laughs until there are tears in her eyes. When she finishes she is almost breathless.

'Ow,' Salmah says, 'stomach pain.'

'Salmah,' I ask her, 'Salmah, if you are my friend, you will not tell this to anyone.'

Salmah snorts as if suppressing another round of laughter.

'Salmah,' I say again. 'I don't want the whole school to call me Ziana. That pondan was crazy.'

'See how,' was all Salmah could say. And she returned, smiling, to her notes.

On the walk to school, I find it hard to have any conversation with Salmah. Nothing seems to displace the one idea in her head. I try to talk about deadlines, homework, which lecturers are boring, which ones are cute but married to ugly wives, which ones drive what cars, which ones cycle and wear tight, tight bicycle shorts. But she doesn't want to speak about any of it.

When we reach the polytechnic, we find that it is crowded; it appears that they are selling things in the foyer. Valentine's Day is in one week's time. There are photo frames, Forever Friends T-shirts, cards with hearts, even a booth selling healing crystals with names like 'amethyst' and 'hawkeye', but they have to be bought in pairs. They are even selling inflatable sofas. Salmah has arranged to meet Sazalie near this noticeboard where lovers can write down messages on a red paper heart to be pinned on it. I had read some of them, really nonsense stuff like 'I hope that our love will forever burn like an eternal flame' and 'I was lost until I found you. It was fate that brought us together, and fate that will never keep us apart.'

'Eat already?' Sazalie asks Salmah.

'Not yet, want to go for lunch?' Salmah asks. 'OK.' Sazalie is smiling, his two dimples coming out from hiding.

'You won't believe what happened to our friend here just now,' Salmah goes.

I stop suddenly behind the two of them. 'Salmah,' I say. 'Salmah.'

'What?' she asks. She is smiling. 'What?' she asks again, in a higher voice.

At that moment I ask myself why the whole world has to pretend. That pondan, with his broad face, his rough skin, who does he think he can fool? And Salmah, all of a sudden, becoming very religious, wearing that tudung of hers. And Bugis Street pretending not to be the place it once was, full of wolf-whistles and bras swinging from lampposts. And the Bangladeshi workers pretending not to have seen the pondan, pretending it is none of their business! I start feeling sick of pretending. I reach out and pull Salmah's tudung from her head. I pull it all the way as if I were pulling the wig off the pondan's head. Salmah screams and people look in our direction.

'What are you doing?' she shouts.

Salmah's hair is tied up in a bun at the back of her head. Sazalie looks at me with an expression that could be angry or puzzled or both. I look back at him. I want to tell him that I am doing all this for him, but he wouldn't be able to understand. I want to tell him that ever since that first day I saw him in the void deck I could never stop thinking about him. But Salmah's tudung is crumpled and silent in my hands.

'Write, Right, Rite'

Catherine Lim

'It is the acme of my career as a writer in Singapore,' says Catherine Lim with profound gratitude, 'to be chosen to represent Singapore at the International Writers' Conference in Oslo. Far more important than the joy of meeting fellow writers from as far away as Peru, Paraguay, Paris and Papua New Guinea is the opportunity to project the image of Singapore as a country with a distinct cultural identity of which it is so justifiably proud. I shall therefore try my very utmost to do my country proud by presenting a story that will enhance the very . . .' and here the writer casts about in her mind for an original turn of phrase, *'positive* image that the world already has of us.'

Further dredging in the mine of her vocabulary is necessary to throw up more glistening nuggets of laudation, and by the time the writer has finished writing the reply to the Ministry of Cultural Development, typed it and sealed it for posting, it is replete with the most profuse thanks for the signal honour.

The writer spends the next month working on the story to be presented. It is the most demanding task she has yet set herself, but the result is something she is extremely satisfied with. She has succeeded in writing *the* story that is uniquely Singaporean, the story against which all future attempts at Singapore writing will be judged for inculcation of national pride and fervour.

But some quarters are not pleased. The writer receives letters, the tone of which ranges from mild admonition to distinct displeasure.

The Unit for the Revitalisation of Mother Tongues (URMT) writes:

'Dear Catherine Lim,

'We have read your story and are pleased to note that all the characters speak Mandarin. This reflects well on the efforts of URMT. However, we note that the parrot on page 3 speaks dialect, i.e. Hokkien. It is described as sitting in its cage in the sitting room squawking Hokkien proverbs, idioms and some obscenities. This may be construed as the Xiu family being insincere in their efforts to speak Mandarin at all times, secretly speaking their dialect at home; how otherwise could the bird have picked up Hokkien? Therefore, we would be pleased if you could make the necessary correction.'

Catherine Lim replies:

'Dear Sir,

'I am in full agreement with you that the reference to the parrot speaking Hokkien will give people the wrong impression that dialect is still being spoken at home. I shall accordingly make the parrot curse in Mandarin. There will be the consequent loss of colour and flavour, for Hokkien curses cannot be matched in their virulence and power. But in the national interest, this literary advantage will be willingly foregone.'

The writer receives the following letter from the Department for the Enhancement of True Asian Culture (DETAC):

'Dear Catherine Lim,

'We would like to draw your attention to a certain detail in your story, of which you may not be aware. There is a vivid description of a spittoon on page 11-13. Moreover, you describe, in equally vivid detail, the early morning ablutions of the Old Patriarch, in which there is much loud and laboured gathering of phlegm in the throat prior to emission into the spittoon. We would like to suggest to you that the spittoon is not an artefact that one would select for the projection of Asian cultural refinement. Could you not think of some other artefact?'

Catherine Lim replies:

'Dear Sir,

I'm sorry that you do not like the spittoon in my story. I have to beg your understanding for its retention, as it is central to the plot of the story.

The removal of the spittoon, together with all the activities of the Old Patriarch connected with it, will irreparably destroy the unity of the story and cause it to lose its focus. I did indeed try to replace the spittoon with the French commode, this being the only other portable artefact I could think of (portability being an absolutely essential ingredient in the plot), but I had to abandon the device, as I think the intrusion of a foreign contraption would harm the Asianness of the story. Therefore I would be most grateful if you would let me retain my spittoon.

On your point that a spittoon may be a demeaning reference to Asian culture, may I make bold to point out, Sir, that at a recent Christie's auction in London, a spittoon from an imperial bedchamber was sold for $1.2 million. It was described as exemplifying the finest in the art of that period.'

DETAC replies:

'Dear Catherine Lim,

We accept your explanation for wishing to retain the spittoon in your story. However, we would insist that instead of making it a cheap enamel spittoon, you upgrade it to porcelain.'

Catherine Lim replies:

'Dear Sir,

I am very happy with your suggestion that I upgrade my spittoon. I have made the necessary revision, and the spittoon is now no longer cheap enamel but fine porcelain. Moreover, the inside rim is inlaid with mother-of-pearl.'

The Department of the Inculcation of True Moral Values (DITMOV) writes:

'Dear Catherine Lim,

'We have just fine-combed your story and found, to our satisfaction, that the Asian value of Filial Piety is dominant. May we congratulate you on your awareness of this important Asian value. It is precisely because it is so important that the examples and illustrations provided must have maximum impact. We have found that the examples in your stories are too weak. May we suggest that you bring in the well-known Confucian story of "The Young Man and the Mosquitoes". In case you are not aware of the tale (and clearly you are not, otherwise you would not have omitted it in your story in the first place), may we briefly tell it:

'"There was a young farmer who was extremely filial to his old mother. He was so filial that every evening he would take off his shirt and, exposing his bare body, call out in a loud voice, 'Oh, mosquitoes, oh, mosquitoes, please come and bite me. Bite me all you want, have your fill of me!'

'"Now when the mosquitoes had had their fill of him, they left his mother alone, so that every night she could sleep undisturbed."

'We suggest that you take note of this most inspiring anecdote, give it a Singapore context, and incorporate it in your story.'

Catherine Lim replies:

'Dear Sir,

'What a wonderful story that was. It was a serious omission on my part, but now I have made up for my negligence by incorporating the anecdote fully into my story. I have described in detail the swarm of mosquitoes, and the vicious bites and welts they left on the filial young man's body. I have also taken the liberty to add a detail that was not found in the original Confucian tale, namely, that the young man slept with a cherubic smile on his face, which reflected the deep satisfaction and peace experienced as a result of filial piety.'

DITMOV writes back:

'Dear Catherine Lim,

'A cherub belongs to Western culture. Please delete the reference from your story.'

Catherine Lim replies:

'Dear Sir,

'I have replaced "cherubic" with "fairy-like". Fairies belong to *both* Western and Asian cultures.'

Catherine Lim then gets a letter from the Ministry of Environment:

'Dear Catherine Lim,

'We are not happy with the reference to swarms of mosquitoes in your story. This is a gross inaccuracy. There are hardly any mosquitoes in Singapore today, owing to the assiduous cleaning up operations of our Ministry. We would therefore urge you to remove that anecdote from your story; otherwise Singapore will have a very poor image as a dumping ground.'

Catherine Lim replies:

'Dear Sir,

'I am really at a loss about what to do. Could you please liaise with the Department for the Inculcation of True Moral Values and let me know of your joint decision? Needless to say, I will go by that joint decision.'

The Ministry of Environment and DITMOV reply:

'Dear Catherine Lim,

'After much discussion, we have both agreed on a compromise. The anecdote may be retained but "mosquitoes" should be replaced by any insect whose presence, even in swarms, does not reflect poorly on the hygiene of a country. Needless to say, flies, lice, bugs, ticks, fleas, leeches and chiggers are OUT.'

Catherine Lim replies:

'Dear Sir,

'Will bees do? There are some Chinese legends which show bees in a very favourable light. In fact, there is one in which the Queen Bee is a reincarnation of a most august warrior princess.'

The Ministry of Environment and DITMOV reply:

'Dear Catherine Lim,
'Bees are OK.'

Catherine Lim sighs with relief. The story is finished at last. With much trepidation, it is presented at the International Writers' Conference in Oslo. Alas, to Catherine Lim's intense disappointment, it receives no prize. Indeed, it is not even deemed fit for the Honourable Mention list. The writer is crestfallen and is about to rush out to send a telegram home, apologizing for failing her country, when her attention is suddenly drawn to the words of the chief judge on the flower-bedecked, light-filled stage.

'We must make special mention of the entry from Singapore. Although it has not been placed, we must congratulate the writer for a story that was so unique as to defy all easy categorization for judgement. It makes use of disparate elements, so disparate and opposed that it has required a feat of imagination to pull them together into a story. The concrete and the abstract, the real and the imaginary, myth and fact, the arcane and the ordinary—all these have been brought together in a narrative mode that fits no existing category. For instance, there is a reference to a spittoon, mysteriously crafted so that while it serves some mundane purpose, its interior remains pure inlaid mother-of-pearl. And there is a strange bird that is a mixture of earthiness and ethereality, of the crude sounds of the earth as well as the brooding silences of heaven. The symbolism is tantalizing, and has so far eluded the judges. We would like to say that the fact that the Singapore entry has not been placed does not reflect on its quality; it simply reflects the judges' inability to comprehend its full meaning. Therefore, it is our pleasure to award a special prize to the Singapore participant, a prize for creating a new genre of the short story, and for opening up new vistas for creative exploration which we hope other writers will be inspired to emulate!'

Mariah

Che Husna Azhari

It was seven in the morning on a typical day in the small village town of Molo. The main trunk road from Pasir Puteh to Kota Bharu was already choked with the bicycle traffic from school children wending their way to the three main schools in the village. Long past subuh time, the mosque was empty. The hub of activity was now the market square where men congregate to have breakfast. Breakfast could be the various nasi, roti canai or the myriad Kelantan breakfast tepung.

That particular morning, though, most of the men were not eating their breakfasts but instead their gaze was fixed on the main entrance to the square. Seven a.m. was a bit late for breakfast; already the first slant of sunlight was filtering through the eaves of the blinds in the market. The men were getting restless. They were definitely waiting for something to appear. Very soon after, however, there was much excitement. All eyes were transfixed on a figure coming through the entrance. It was the figure of a woman. She was delicately balancing two huge basins on her head, her hips swaying gaily to and fro with the rhythm of the balancing. That particular gyrating seemed to mesmerize the men and glue them to their places.

There was much to mesmerize as far as Mariah was concerned, for that was the name of the lady with the two basins on her head. Mariah was a nasi seller in Molo, in fact the nasi seller in Molo. Every morning at seven sharp she would walk past the market entrance into the village square and mesmerize the men with her swaying hips as well as her nasi: nasi kerabu, nasi belauk and nasi dagang. Rumour had it (started by the womenfolk) that her nasi wasn't much to crow about, but it was a combination of Mariah's swaying as well as her easy smile that made all the men flock to the village square. Many a nasi belauk breakfast remained cold and uneaten in the houses as men ignored their wives' cooking and paid tribute to Mariah's instead.

Mariah also had another asset. She was without a husband. Note that I didn't say either divorced or widowed. It would not have mattered either way in Kelantan. The most important thing was she was not with a husband. This was not to imply that she was not decorous in her manners . . . on the contrary, she was very much so . . . but men seem to want to partake of her nasi more because of her unmarried state.

Mariah had been married once, but her husband had passed away soon after. There had been many suitors after her husband's untimely demise, but Mariah had seemed singularly uninterested. Rumour too (also spread by the womenfolk) had it that it was our Mariah who drove her husband to an early grave. This rumour was never corroborated by medical evidence, so we will never be able to confirm this allegation. Fifteen years after her husband's death, which would make her fortyish, Mariah could easily pass for a beauty in her late twenties. Mariah was tall and well-proportioned and moved gracefully. No, not gracefully, but sensuously. Her face was unlined, her complexion fair and her very dark, very black eyes appeared to glow. Mariah always had on a short kebaya, which accentuated her well-proportioned curves. As a concession to propriety she used to cover her head and part of her torso with a kain lepas, a two-metre traditional head and body cover much favoured by the working womenfolk of Kelantan. The Kota Bharu Nickies or the more modern women prefer either a sliver of a scarf or go bareheaded, but in Molo one does not go about without a kain lepas. To do so would be to incur the wrath of the village Imam, who was the guardian of modesty and propriety and enforcer of stringent mores.

On that particular morning, the Imam was with the men, falling on Mariah's nasi belauk with much relish. His wife's own nasi belauk was still waiting for him on his kitchen table under the tudung saji, getting very cold indeed. The Imam's wife was pottering about in her spotless kitchen, muttering about the Imam's lateness for breakfast. It wasn't like the Imam at all to be late for breakfast. The Imam liked his nasi belauk, and his wife took great care in the preparation. Her culinary skills were not her only attribute; her housekeeping was also a model to be followed by other womenfolk in the village. One could always call at the Imam's house at any time of the day, guaranteed to be greeted by a well-turned-out wife, hot tepung and fragrant surroundings. The Imam's wife was somewhat assisted in this respect by not having grubby children who would mess things up. It was the only flaw in an otherwise perfect marriage.

Quarrelsome couples who called at the Imam's place for arbitration would be sobered by the domestic serenity of the Imam's abode. They would all gape enviously at the surroundings and forget to quarrel. They would listen attentively to the Imam's sermon and exhortations to peace, hang their heads in shame and make new resolutions, but promptly quarrel again as soon as they got home. Their own domestic atmospheres were just not congenial enough for peace. But enough said about the Imam's exemplary household, more important events were unfolding.

As the Imam's wife was vigorously scrubbing at an already spotless sink, there were salutations from the front door. It was a delegation of womenfolk from the village headed by Cik Gu Nab, one of the local women leaders. She was a teacher at a local primary school. Cik Yam wiped her hands and bade the visitors in. They were unexpected but not unwelcome. Cik Gu Nab made small talk for a while, commenting first on Cik Yam's exquisitely appliquéd safrah before launching into the matter at hand. The matter at hand turned out to be none other than Mariah.

'Cik Yam,' began Cik Gu Nab, trying to put the matter across as delicately as possible, 'we mean our sisters no harm; in fact we are very happy if each one of us goes about doing her own thing. As we often say, each woman to their own rizq. In fact, we feel very bad about having to come to you. We don't like to backbite our own sister.'

Cik Gu Nab cleared her throat and looked at the others for assent. Having got it in the form of gravely nodding heads, Cik Gu Nab continued: 'Cik Yam, the problem now is that one of our own sisters is not doing her own thing at all, but instead meddling with other people's.'

The Imam's wife, Cik Yam, listened attentively.

'Who do you mean, Cik Gu Nab?' Cik Yam asked, 'er . . . this troublemaker?', wondering what this meandering of Cik Gu Nab's was leading up to. Cik Gu Nab was known to favour a touch of melodrama and to use it to maximum effect always.

'Why, Cik Yam, we mean Mariah, of course, the nasi seller! Don't tell me you don't know what she's been up to!' Cik Gu Nab looked peeved at Cik Yam's ignorance of important village matters.

What can Mariah possibly be up to, thought Cik Yam. Mariah was apt to go around in her short and loud kebaya, but she was always properly covered by her kain lepas. If she hadn't been so, the Iman would have reminded Cik Yam to pay her a visit. So it couldn't have been the kain lepas.

'No, I don't know, Cik Gu Nab. What has she been up to?' Cik Yam smiled sweetly. Cik Yam knew about most village matters, but not quick enough, it would seem. She was always too busy with housework to gossip. Besides, it was not considered proper for the Imam's wife to be caught gossiping.

'Cik Yam,' continued Cik Gu Nab, 'Mariah has been enticing our men to abandon their homes for her kedai merpati. You know her nasi cannot be that special. Why, I am sure for one she cannot beat your nasi belauk.' (Cik Yam readily agreed.) 'But why do all these men seem hell bent on eating breakfast at her place? I reckon, I mean we reckon she has put "something" (Cik Gu Nab put heavy emphasis on the word *something*) in her nasi.' Cik Gu Nab paused for breath.

'I can't believe that, Cik Gu Nab! God forbid!' Cik Yam considered her next words carefully. 'We cannot accuse Mariah of something so grave without any concrete evidence. That's terribly unfair, you know, Cik Gu Nab. Perhaps that "something" you alleged she put in the nasi is just plain skill, Allah knows.'

Cik Gu Nab started. She felt she was being reproached. She did not like this allusion to her cooking skills either. Certainly, it was not her forte, still Cik Yam need not have referred to it in such a manner. Cik Yam was being very malicious, she thought.

'I didn't say "it" enticed all the men, Cik Yam. My Cik Gu Leh (Cik Gu Nab's husband), for instance, would never dream of having breakfast anywhere but at home. Some men do get easily enticed, some don't. Speaking of which, I saw the sainted Tok Imam himself having breakfast at Mariah's.' Having delivered this stinging repartee, Cik Gu Nab stood and left in a huff. In a pointed rebuff, she did not even say a proper farewell.

Cik Yam went a deep shade of crimson. Cik Gu Nab's last retort was as good as a slap on the face. Cik Yam, incidentally, was a seasoned politician. The words stung her, surely, but she did not flinch. She was unnerved, but she quickly regained enough composure to smile at the rest of the delegates, served them her beautiful tepung and indulged in the social niceties required. Replete with Cik Yam's tepung and fortified with the latest gossip, the ladies then left. Only then did Cik Yam sit down to think of a way to settle the issue with the Imam. He was not going to escape unscathed, that she was going to make sure of!

The Imam went about his usual business and came home at twelve-thirty to have his lunch. Cik Yam was there to greet him;

she took off his kuffiyah and gave him a clean sarong to change into. The Imam looked at his wife with obvious pride. There was not a living man in Molo who did not envy him for having such a devoted wife. But then, quick as lightning, as always he would look around at his empty house and let out a sigh. Why couldn't his wife bear children like other women? Some women, it seemed, have the fecundity of rabbits, but not his wife. Like all men of his generation, it never occurred to him he could be the culprit in his wife's supposed inability to bear children. As far as he was concerned, bearing children was a woman's job, and if she didn't there was something wrong with her. Fertility had nothing to do with men.

'Is lunch ready, Yam?' asked the Imam.

'Why, yes, Abang, it's under the tudung saji,' replied Cik Yam. The Imam picked up the tudung saji for his lunch, but much to his surprise it turned out to be the morning's nasi belauk. He was stunned into silence for a good few minutes and Cik Yam took the opportunity to confront him.

'I thought you would still like to finish off my nasi belauk after you breakfasted at Mariah's. After all, I have to prove that my nasi belauk is still edible compared to Mariah's, *especially* since the whole village saw you eating away, behaving as if your wife has never prepared nasi belauk for you! And Abang, I had to learn of it through someone else too!'

Cik Yam threw the tudung saji on the floor, narrowly missing the Imam's foot, then ran sobbing to their bedroom. What the hell is happening, thought the Imam. How did she know I had breakfast at Mariah's. It must have been one of the womenfolk.

'Oh . . . women! They are so impossible; why do they have to go around making life difficult for men? Beats the hell out of me,' muttered the Imam in vexation.

It was the only time he had ever gone to Mariah's. And he had done so only at that Cik Gu Leh's insistence. Cik Gu Leh had been extolling the virtues of Mariah's nasi belauk, but really Cik Gu Leh was no authority on the subject as his wife Cik Gu

Nab, as everybody knew, was a hopeless cook. The Imam begged to be excused, but Cik Gu Leh was most persistent. So finally, the Imam relented. The nasi belauk was, as he had expected, passable, but no more. It did not surprise him in the least. The thing that did surprise him was Mariah herself. At the thought of Mariah the Imam smiled dreamily to himself. What a woman she was! The Imam became transported to another time: his youth.

When the Imam was a young man of fifteen his father had voiced his wish for his son to be sent to Pattani in southern Thailand to learn under the tutelage of a well-known sheikh. His father had spent a few years there himself but had not progressed very much. He had always nursed a secret ambition for his son to be the scholar he could not be and in doing so exculpate himself. The Imam had protested, full of other plans. He had no stamina for the arduous task of being a scholar. He feigned delicate health, but his father had decreed. The Imam, under protest and under duress, was sent to Pattani. The Imam was miserable in Pattani, moping for his mother and his friends rather than studying. But Allah is great and the Imam's misery was soon alleviated.

One day when he had been in Pattani about three months, the Imam took his water pot to go to the communal well for his ablutions. It was around two or three in the afternoon when there were not many people about. The Imam saw from a distance a young lady drawing water from the well. Perhaps she thought there was no one about so her head was not covered. The Imam saw her tresses in their full silken glory. The white of her skin on her bare throat was blinding. The Imam stopped in his tracks, then took full flight. He ran trembling to his hut, panting and breathless. He took a drink of water and reflected upon the event. Who could that beautiful creature be? 'I love her,' he said to himself. 'I love her and I shall make her mine. I want no one else,' he vowed. He felt his head. It was throbbing as hard as his heart, as hot and feverish as his passion. Then he learnt that the object of his ardour was the daughter of the Sheikh himself.

The Imam kept the burning secret to himself. Even his housemates never knew of this love. The Imam's behaviour was nothing but exemplary. His manners were extremely correct, especially to the ladies. He was punctilious in the performance of his duties. If the Imam was consumed with love, the Sheikh was the last person to know. The Sheikh thought that the Imam stayed for the love of the Deen. It is true that as the years passed the Imam grew to love the Deen and the Sheikh, but so too did his love for the Sheikh's daughter grow. In the Imam's final year, the Sheikh was entrusting more and more of his duties to his model pupil, the Imam. The Imam was conducting kulliyahs, performing prayers and sometimes even paying courtesy calls on the Sheikh's behalf.

He is grooming me to take his place and to be his son-in-law, thought the Imam. How full of hope he was! How sweet were the days as they passed for the Imam! How he patiently waited for the day when the Sheikh would broach the subject to him, but it was not to be. The Sheikh did broach the subject of his daughter to him but only to invite him to his daughter's wedding to a cousin. The Imam was shattered. His world crashed around him. Pattani was nothing but a cauldron of smouldering embers. The Imam packed his books and bade goodbye to his Sheikh. He was really very fond of the old man and also very grateful for the tutelage, but he had to go. The Sheikh begged him to stay to look after his mosque for him, but the Imam gently refused. If it were not for the agony of having to see his beloved as somebody else's wife, he would have stayed.

The Imam came home grieving to Kelantan. His mother understood the grieving and in a few months found him Cik Yam. Cik Yam, though no raving beauty, was an accomplished cook as well as being modest and extremely virtuous. She had been an obedient and excellent wife, but she was not the Sheikh's daughter. The Imam had been happy with Cik Yam and gradually as he grew older the hurt had eased. He had not thought again of the Sheikh's daughter for a long time . . . that is, until that morning, when, by the fate of God, Cik Gu Leh had dragged him to Mariah's kedai merpati.

'Oh Mariah . . . ' sighed the Imam. 'Why do you have to be so like her . . . my long-lost love, the Passion of My Youth? Oh Mariah, why do you have to look like her from your toes right up to your eyebrows! It's a test. By Allah! It's a test.'

The Imam became very frightened. He left the table, took his ablutions and quickly went to the mosque.

'Let me find refuge there,' he thought. 'Save me, oh God.'

What had his Sheikh always said in times like this? He quickly recollected.

Abase Yourself to the One You Love. Passion is Not Easy. Indeed, passion is not easy. 'I have dispensed with thee, oh Passion. I have divorced thee thrice.'

The Imam kept repeating this litany as if in prayer. After the afternoon prayer the Imam stayed long in prostration. He dallied in the mosque. He came out but went in again. Finally he went in and fell into a troubled sleep, something which he had never done before.

The days passed. Things appeared normal. The Imam was punctual in his prayers and diligent in his duties, but his heart was in turmoil. He remembered a verse from his Pattani days.

> O lady of excess who strips away my
> acts of devotion in every state.
> There is no kindness in my wound
> Either it is by abasement and it is
> attached to passion, or it is by
> might and it is attached to Kingdom.
> If you're in your immunity, it
> protects us and if you're in the sea,
> you come in the boat.

It was either from Fusus Al-Hakam or the Knowledge of Man, the Imam could not be certain, but it certainly seemed apt now.

The Imam tried to go home to Cik Yam after subuh prayers, but every time somehow, in spite of himself, he would be by Cik Gu Leh's side going to Mariah's for breakfast. Mariah saw nothing amiss. She treated the Imam with reverence and courtesy, befitting his station and stature. She served him the choicest morsels on her best cutlery. He was, after all, the village imam.

The Imam would take the nasi belauk without averting his gaze from the plate in accordance with the Koranic injunction for men to lower their gazes. He would tremble slightly, but the men in the kedai merpati attributed that to extreme modesty. 'The Imam is an extremely modest man,' thought the other men, 'not used to the company of women.' Every time he took the nasi belauk from Mariah he would feel a pang of guilt, remembering his wife's nasi belauk under the tudung saji.

'Forgive me, oh God, for men are weak,' supplicated the Imam silently, spooning nasi belauk into his mouth. After the nasi belauk the Imam would still tarry, nursing a cup of coffee with Cik Gu Leh. At least, that was how it looked on the surface. That was the time the Imam would use to steal long lingering glances at Mariah. His heart ached with the pent-up longing for the Sheikh's daughter. Oh Mariah! . . .

Things would never be the same again for the Imam. He spent the nights in supplication, asking God for succour. He was frightened of the emotions stirred up by his unintentional meeting with Mariah. It was too colossal for him to handle. And yet he felt elated. He believed it was fated, a part of a grand design by God to heal his heart; but on the account of a woman? Can a beautiful, alluring woman be a part of a healing process? It seemed so profane to the Imam. But why should a woman be more profane than a man? Did not the Prophet himself say that three things are pleasing to him: prayers, women and perfume? There you are! Proof, exoneration for the Imam. He felt resolved to do what he had to do. Cik Gu Leh would be his emissary.

The Imam chose the occasion well. It had to be on a Thursday night, the eve of Friday. After prayers and long supplication, the Imam went to his bedroom. Cik Yam was sitting on the bed waiting for him to finish. He knelt by the bed and kissed Cik Yam's hands. Cik Yam was surprised by this reverent show of affection but did not say anything. Cik Yam waited. The Imam kissed Cik Yam's knees and then placed his head on Cik Yam's lap. Cik Yam stroked his head lovingly. Immediately as if released by a valve the Imam's hot tears fell on Cik Yam's sarong. Cik Yam felt the hot tears on her skin as they seeped through the sarong. Cik Yam lifted the Imam's head and looked at him questioningly. Fifteen years of marital bliss had left their mark. Love and understanding shone through Cik Yam's also tear-filled eyes.

'Tell me what grieves you, my husband, and I will make it better for you,' Cik Yam whispered to the Imam. At these words the Imam felt himself choke, but he steeled himself. He told Cik Yam of his unrequited love for the Sheikh's daughter. He told Cik Yam of his pain and longing. He then told Cik Yam of Mariah, how he had fought his emotions and how he had lost. He begged Cik Yam's forgiveness, kissed the hem of Cik Yam's sarong and asked for her permission to take Mariah as his second wife!

Cik Yam jumped up as if struck by a bolt of lightning. Can that dreaded thing most feared by women be real, happening to her? Please God, let it not be true, she prayed. Why couldn't it have happened to that lazy Cik Gu Nab, who couldn't even fry an egg properly? Why her? The loving, devoted wife, the model housewife? Why? Why? Despair and humiliation all came and passed through Cik Yam's heart. She threw herself on the bed and wept piteously.

'O wretched, wretched self!'

By then Cik Yam was racked by despairing sobs. The Imam tried to hold her, but she pushed him away. Finally the Imam managed to capture her in his embrace and placated her with promises of his love and continuing devotion.

'I love you and will always love you, Yam. Nothing can change that. I will always be your husband. I will care for you, Yam . . .' said in between kisses on Cik Yam's forehead, hands and finally, in the final act of submission, on Cik Yam's feet. Thus the night passed and in the morning with the first rays of sunlight, Cik Yam said 'Yes' to the Imam's request, on condition of equality. The Imam had breakfast at home with Cik Yam and he himself spooned the nasi belauk into Cik Yam's mouth.

Three days after this event, the whole town of Molo was rife with speculations. Word got around the village that the Imam was taking a second wife, and that person was none other than Mariah!

'Isn't that rather odd?' gossiped the villagers. 'The Imam and Cik Yam have been married for fifteen years and Cik Yam is a model of virtue.'

'Then of course Cik Yam is childless. . .' voices trailed away.

The men in the village were all excitedly handling this issue in their own ways. They had all at some time or other in their lives fantasized about having second wives, but, sadly, neither their wives nor their budgets were accommodating enough. Cik Yam became a paragon of virtue. Women wondered how she could have easily succumbed to the whole arrangement. The men, on the other hand, wondered what Koranic ayats the Imam blew on Cik Yam's face to subdue her. Perhaps he knew something they didn't. It was difficult for everyone to agree upon one common reason. There was, however, something that everybody definitely agreed upon and that was . . . Cik Yam would certainly be found sheltering in the shade of the Umbrella of Siti Fatimah (the Prophet's daughter) on the Day of Judgement. 'Mashallah!' they all whispered reverently in awe of Cik Yam's virtue and steadfastness; would that they were as strong as Cik Yam!

But what of Mariah, the object of all this commotion? She continued, serenely unaffected, with her nasi belauk selling until the very day she married the Imam. When Cik Gu Leh, the Imam's emissary, came to her house asking for her hand, she had been surprised, to say the least. The Imam was not on her list of prospective suitors. Initially, she had thought Cik Gu Leh had come on his own behalf: Cik Gu Leh had been most partial to her nasi. Cik Gu Nab had even begun sending threatening messages. But Cik Gu Leh had come for the Imam. Mariah only dithered for a day, then said 'Yes.' The Imam was the man to marry, if she would ever wish to marry. A man of religion would be the only person worth marrying after all those years of self-imposed celibacy. She wondered why the Imam had ever considered marrying her. Cik Yam was a model wife. Mariah was, in fact, slightly in awe of the pious Cik Yam. Mariah felt like a harlot in her short orange kebaya, sitting beside the robed Cik Yam. Cik Yam had been kind to her and allayed her fears. Truly Cik Yam was an angel, to willingly share her husband with her, Mariah the blousy lady, untutored in religion, in fact untutored in everything except nasi belauk selling!

'It's all Allah's decree,' sighed Mariah. 'So be it.'

Mariah's wedding surpassed even her own expectations. Her relatives, in deference to the stature of the new husband-to-be, organized the wedding with particular zealousness. She took out her savings from nasi belauk selling and prepared a bridal chamber grander than that of her first wedding. In an uncharacteristic show of flamboyance and extravagance, Mariah had her wedding finery tailored in Kota Bharu, no less. Her first husband had not been an imam; there had been no need for such fuss. Guests streamed into the house compound from sunrise till sundown, heaping compliments upon her and congratulating her.

'Well, at least they harbour no ill feelings towards me,' she noted.

After isha' prayers, with the guests finally departed, she sighed with obvious relief that it was all over. Mariah found herself alone in the bridal chamber, ready to again begin life anew as a married woman. The Imam saluted at the door, and she replied, giving him permission to enter. The Imam was dressed in a white jubah and white serban, looking resplendent. Mariah noticed that the serban was held in place with the ends fashionably tied back. She suddenly realized how physically attractive the Imam was: tall, well-built and with measured movements. Mariah quickly averted her eyes from his piercing gaze and looked demurely at her hennaed hand. He came forward, took Mariah's hand in his own and kissed it fervently and long, inhaling the heady scent of Mariah's Tabu perfume. His eyes closed, his dream realized, the Imam managed a hoarse 'Thank You, God, for Your Bounty,' before Mariah's perfume completely enveloped him and his senses.

Seventh Uncle

Chuah Guat Eng

The yellowness of his skin took Siew Hoon by surprise. And the waxen sheen. For one horrifying moment she thought she saw beads of perspiration on his upper lip and was startled enough to try to look more closely. Peering through the glass window of the coffin lid, she moved her gaze slowly from his chest to his nostrils to his eyelids. Just in case. Silly of her, of course. He'd been dead for three days. They were waiting for Betty, his only child, to come home for the funeral. So even if there had been a mistake . . .

Siew Hoon had always thought of him as a handsome man, this uncle of hers, husband of her seventh and youngest aunt. When she was a child, she used to think of him as the second handsomest man in the world, the handsomest being of course her father. Not too surprising, really. Until she was thirteen, Seventh Uncle was the second most important man in her life.

She and her cousin Betty were born into the family almost as soon as the war was over, the youngest in their generation; carried by their mothers through those final difficult months of the Japanese occupation like talismans against death and despair. To her sister and her other cousins, all born before the war, they were 'The Babies' and still were, even though they were now middle-aged and menopausal. True, some of their pre-war cousins were old enough to be their parents. But Siew Hoon often thought that the real reason they would always be 'babies' was that they never knew war, never had their education interrupted, never had to learn Japanese and never had to eat tapioca every day. For their innocence of those particular hardships, they would undoubtedly be treated by their elders with protective kindliness until they died.

Siew Hoon spent many of her school holidays with Betty. She loved those holidays: eating out almost every day at different restaurants, each one chosen for a particular speciality; endless supplies of comic books; and movies almost every day because Seventh Aunt had a job with a local movie magazine and received an endless flow of complimentary cinema tickets. Strangely enough, she never grew particularly close to the family, and, in the way relatives have of slipping out of one's life, they slipped out of hers. Betty went off to boarding school in Ireland after Form Three. Her parents must have expected her to go on to university, but she got married instead and moved to Canada where she settled down. Siew Hoon joined the Diplomatic Corps soon after graduating from university, never got married and never settled anywhere. And so they lost touch.

It was not until many years later that she saw her Seventh Aunt and Uncle again. It was 1990, and she was forty-five. She remembered the year because it struck her then as somehow significant that the century was exactly twice as old as she was. Throughout Europe, the Perestroika thaw was just beginning to set in. In South-East Asia, the new 'Tigers' were beginning to roar into action. Malaysia too was moving out of a recession into a new age of industrialization. As for her, she was at a crossroads in her life: old enough to opt for early retirement, but not too old to hope that she might start her own small business, maybe even get married and settle down. The future had seemed so unusually bright at that particular point in time.

On coming home, her sister Didi told her that Seventh Aunt had been unwell and suggested that they called on her. Didi had always been very good about keeping in touch with relatives. During that visit, they learned that Betty hardly ever wrote to her parents and had come home to see them only once in all those years. Having recently lost her own parents, Siew Hoon began calling on them whenever she could, trying to make up for Betty's absence by assuming the role of surrogate daughter.

By that time the old couple were in their sixties, and Seventh Uncle in particular had not aged well. There were heavy, distended bags under his eyes and liver spots on his face, hands and forearms. He kept his hair trimmed almost to the scalp, no doubt to camouflage the sparseness on top. Age and something else—arthritis? degeneration of the bones?—had pushed his head and neck forward from his shoulders into that permanent, painful-looking stoop that reminded Siew Hoon of drawings of the Neanderthal man. Yet the childhood impression remained. She continued to think of him as a handsome man. Maybe because of his own perception of himself.

He was a man very aware of style. Her aunt told her once, in the kitchen out of his hearing, how terribly upset he had been when the children of a new neighbour addressed him—quite properly and respectfully—as 'Grandfather'. *Are their eyes covered with dog turd?* he had raged as he stomped in from the garden, his sixty-odd-year-old face red with exasperation. And only a few months before his death, he had told her with great pride how much weight he had lost; why, he could even put on his trousers from ten years ago. *But cannot lah,* he had added with a grin, *too out of date now, the cut.*

There was about him a certain glamour, an aura Siew Hoon associated with Hong Kong film stars. Another time, her aunt showed her his wardrobe. It was a congestion of handmade shirts and trousers. Most of them had not even been looked at for a decade or more, but they hung there as if waiting to be pulled into service any day now. All of them were in almost-new condition. *Never wore these more than half a dozen times, but he won't let me give a single thing away—not even to the gardener or the church,* her aunt had grumbled. Now, Siew Hoon thought, there's nothing to stop her from giving everything away, except maybe sentimentality.

It was during those visits as an adult that she saw what a man of the world her uncle was. Like most Cantonese people he knew and loved his food. Every meal with him was an occasion, and it was amusing to hear his views on gustatory matters. On wine: *Never drink wine in this country. If you can afford it, it's not worth drinking; if you can't, it's overpriced.* On the common practice of having a little dish of fresh-cut chilli soaking in soy sauce beside one's plate at every meal: *If the food's any good, you won't need additional sauce. If it's no good, no amount of sauce or chilli is going to help.* And on the vulgar use of expensive cognac as a status symbol: *If people had any sense at all, they'd offer their friends VSOP and keep the XO for themselves.*

The aphoristic way he expressed himself gave those statements the weight of universal truths. He uttered them with an arch glance in Siew Hoon's direction so that she could never be sure whether he really believed them or was merely trying to show her, his globetrotting niece, what a sophisticate he was. Yet she could never consider buying a bottle of wine or cognac, or even watch people fill their side dishes with cut chilli and soy sauce, without hearing his voice and seeing that glance. It was true that she hardly ever bought wine and cognac since coming home for good. But whether that had to do with Seventh Uncle's dicta, the exorbitant price of alcoholic drinks in the country or her own meanness, she could never be sure. Probably a bit of everything.

Seventh Uncle drank a great deal more than he should have, and, in the beginning, Siew Hoon assumed that that was the reason for her aunt's perpetual air of subtle disgruntlement, of bearing him some deep, unspoken grudge. But shortly after she began to see them on a regular basis, she became aware of other possible causes. One evening her aunt made one of her rare phone calls to her and spoke at incoherent length about some woman she accused of having designs on him. As Seventh Uncle was by then seventy-two, Siew Hoon did not take her aunt too seriously. It did occur to her, however, that that was probably why Seventh Aunt had always insisted on retaining her financial independence by working as a badly paid secretary, even though Seventh Uncle was obviously able to provide her with a comfortable life. Whatever the truth of it, that was one thing less for Seventh Aunt to worry about now that he was dead.

Lying on his back, Seventh Uncle's upper dentures sank into his skull, way behind his lower jaw, so that his own teeth—suddenly too long, too solid and too yellow—jutted out in a grotesque underbite. Someone had placed a grey felt hat on his head. She had never seen him with a hat on while he was alive, unless she counted the photographs taken during a holiday in some mildly temperate country, Australia, probably. Whoever did it must have thought he should make his final exit the way he had lived—in style. But they had only succeeded in making him look like a parody of himself. And that caused the tears to spring to her eyes.

She felt a light touch on her shoulder and turned. It was Betty, her eyes red-rimmed, a little smile of greeting on her tired face, but otherwise composed, cool, correctly dressed, as Siew Hoon remembered her.

'Baby,' she said, using the nickname Siew Hoon had refused to answer to since she was sixteen, 'thank you for coming.' They exchanged a quick, polite hug.

'You OK?' Siew Hoon asked.

'Yes, it's my mother . . .'

'I know. I'll go and talk to her in a minute,' Siew Hoon said.

'Thanks.' But Betty's eyes had already slid past Siew Hoon to Didi, who was standing behind her. Suddenly unsure whom Betty was thanking, or for what, Siew Hoon was sharply reminded of the reason they had never got very close in spite of the amount of time spent together: *she never liked me, it's as simple as that.* When Siew Hoon was younger, she used to wonder why. Was it because she always did better at school? Was it because Betty thought her parents paid her too much attention? But even as a child, Siew Hoon knew she could never ask anyone in the family those questions; she would have been told off for being silly or unkind. In any case, once Betty went away, the questions became unimportant.

Seventh Aunt, hair uncombed and face unpowdered, was standing by the coffin directly opposite her. She was bending over her dead husband, engaging him in an earnest monologue. She was usually so taciturn and well groomed that Siew Hoon wondered if the pointless murmuring and neglected appearance were part of the role expected of a newly bereaved Chinese widow. She found she had to look away.

Next to Seventh Aunt was a woman about Siew Hoon's own age, maybe a bit older. She was dressed in black, which surprised her a little. Siew Hoon had always thought that only the children of the deceased were allowed to wear black at a funeral. A blouse of some silky material and a gathered skirt accentuated the overwhelming fullness of the woman's breasts and hips. Her hair, dyed an unnatural black, fell to her shoulders in loose waves. She had too much foundation on her face, her eyebrows were too well shaped and her eyes too distinctly outlined. But her lips bore only the merest touch of a discreet shade of coral. She looked familiar but Siew Hoon could not place her, that is, not until she looked up and straight at her. And then there was no mistaking that look of vacant good nature. It was Noneh. Siew Hoon smiled, and Noneh smiled back, uncertainly.

Siew Hoon had forgotten all about Third Aunt's daughter. No-brain Noneh, they used to call her behind her back. Noneh was neither a pre-war nor a post-war baby. She was born right in the middle of those difficult, unsettling years, while her father was languishing in Pudu Jail. A rich man's son, Third Uncle was unused to deprivation, and food, especially meat, was scarce. So when a neighbour's chicken wandered into his backyard one day, he did not stop to think about the pros and cons of having that bird for dinner. Unfortunately for him, the occupying forces took a very dim view of his un-Bushido-like lack of self-control and he was summarily hauled off to prison. But the real victim was Noneh. As a result of his absence during much of Third Aunt's pregnancy and subsequent delivery, it was often whispered, albeit only within the family, that Noneh's real father was not Third Uncle at all, but a medical officer in the Japanese army. Hence, so the story went, her nickname. It was supposedly a shortening of *anoneh,* one of the few words the older cousins still remembered from their war-time efforts to master Japanese. Siew Hoon never found out what the word really meant.

Neither could she remember which of her siblings or cousins was relating that story of Noneh's paternity when she overheard it. As the youngest child in the extended family, the only way she ever learned about things like that was by eavesdropping; no one ever told her anything. But thinking about it now, Siew Hoon could not give the story credence, for one very simple reason: Noneh's father—her Third Uncle, that is—was from all accounts a being quite devoid of brains. Even the way he died suggested a total lack of common sense. He had not been tortured to death or anything like that; he'd survived his miserable, unheroic incarceration, right up to the day the British troops finally arrived. The soldiers brought freedom, food and a warning not to eat too much all at once. But Third Uncle brainlessly ignored the warning and gorged himself to death. Literally.

Now here, if further proof were needed, was his daughter, looking every bit the gourmand he was, wobbling towards her like a black Jell-O, working her way round the coffin without so much as a glance at the dear departed in it.

'Eh, who are you?' Noneh asked when she was maybe a yard away. Her words tumbled out, drenched in that little throaty laugh Siew Hoon remembered so well: nervous, apologetic, self-depreciating. The laugh of a woman who had long accepted her role as the family's near-idiot.

'You look so familiar . . . I feel I should know you . . . but I can't seem to . . .' and she brought her right hand up to her temple with a fluttering motion startlingly reminiscent of Third Aunt's during her last days, before she died of the brain tumour discovered too late for anything to be done.

'I'm Baby,' Siew Hoon said, using the nickname she knew Noneh would remember her by.

'Oh my goodness! If you hadn't told me . . . My goodness! If I were to see you on the street I would never . . . Oh my! When was the last time . . . ?' And before Siew Hoon knew it, she was being bustled out to the garden where an assortment of metal and wooden folding chairs had been arranged in rows for the friends and relatives expected to come and pay their last respects.

It was true they had not seen each other for many years. Siew Hoon was still a schoolgirl when she overheard her mother telling her father that No-brain Noneh had eloped with a Eurasian soldier. In those days it was unheard of for nice, well-brought-up, middle-class, Straits-born Chinese girls to get involved with men of a different race, leave alone soldiers. So she heard no more of Noneh. Now, forty years later, she learned for the first time that Noneh had four sons, all grown, all professionals, all married, and two grandchildren, both girls.

'And your husband, is he . . . ?' Siew Hoon asked, uncertain if he was still alive.

'Who? My old man? Oh, he's around. No, no, not here. He's at home, looking after my younger granddaughter. Eh,' a sudden, barely controlled giggle, 'you remember how we used to exchange songs?'

Until Noneh reminded her, she had forgotten. As children, they had lived in the same town, gone to the same school and travelled in the same schoolbus. Every afternoon as the bus wended its long, circuitous way all over town dropping the girls off practically at their doorsteps, the older ones at the back would start a sing-song of the latest pop hits. Didi was too serious to indulge in this 'silliness', as she called it. But Noneh and

Siew Hoon, then fifteen and twelve, were caught in its fever. They tuned in to every single request programme on the radio; sat with their ears glued to the speaker, paper and pencil ready in hand to take down the lyrics of the latest pop hits; and they compared notes and exchanged lyrics every day during recess or in the bus.

It so happened that at about the same time their mothers were going through a mahjong fever. In spite of his disapproval, Siew Hoon's father had no choice but to drive her mother to her mahjong session every Sunday, on the way picking up Third Aunt and dropping her, Siew Hoon, off to spend the day with Noneh. So for a stretch of several months they became quite close.

By then Noneh's mother had remarried, and the new Third Uncle was a round-faced, jolly-looking man who loved having Siew Hoon visit, never tired of making her cups of hot Bournvita chocolate and delighted in feeding her all kinds of cakes and puddings that he had made himself. He was a very home-loving sort of man, that Third Uncle, always smiling and always busy—cleaning, sweeping, splitting thin bamboo for crab traps, tatting fishing nets and, of course, baking and cooking. In that way he was the ideal husband for Third Aunt, who never quite got used to the idea that she was no longer the socialite wife of a rich man's son.

Noneh suddenly said, 'Do you like dancing? I love it, you know. I don't know why, but I just love to dance. Maybe my mother danced too much when she was carrying me. They used to call her the Tango Queen, you know. Do you know the Hard Rock Café? I go there every Friday and Saturday evening.'

The Hard Rock Café? Noneh? Every Friday? And Saturday?

'What do you do there?' Siew Hoon asked with a small laugh, hearing in her own voice that tone of patient indulgence one adopts with near-idiots.

'Oh, dance a bit, drink a bit, listen to the music. I just love the music.' She started humming, then, remembering where they were and why they were there, looked restlessly around before leaning over to whisper in Siew Hoon's ear, 'What say you we get out of here?'

'Where to?'

'There's a coffee shop at the end of the road, remember? Come lah.' Her voice ended on the cajoling note of a little girl.

Siew Hoon took in the carelessly applied foundation collecting in the creases of Noneh's skin, the teeth too perfect to be natural, the old-fashioned eyeliner painted on with an upward stroke at the outer end of each eyelid, the blue-black of the tattooed eyebrows. And she was overcome by—protective kindliness, she supposed.

'All right,' she said, 'but just a while, OK? They're leaving for the cemetery soon.'

'Don't worry. We have plenty of time.'

At the coffee shop Noneh ordered kopi-o-kau and roast-pork rice for herself. Since Siew Hoon was still full from the laksa she had eaten on her way to the funeral, she asked for a Nescafé Ice. While waiting for the rice to come, Noneh began spooning great dollops of ginger-chilli sauce on to her side dish.

'The sauce here is very good, you know. You should try it one day.'

'How can you taste anything else after all that hot stuff?' Siew Hoon asked, eyeing the side dish with disapproval.

'Don't be such an orang puteh celup lah, you. It's the sauce that makes everything taste better. That's why we have different sauces for different things. See, with konlo mee, you eat green chilli pickled in vinegar. With hokkien mee, you eat fresh red chilli and raw garlic in thick soy sauce, although some people like it with sambal belacan . . .' And she rattled on.

When her plate of roast-pork rice finally appeared, she said, with one of her little throaty laughs, 'Actually I'm not supposed to eat any fatty meat you know, but don't care lah, eat first, die later, ha?'

'Aiyo,' she continued between relished mouthfuls, 'if my hubby were to see me now, he'd kill me, man. Actually he's quite OK, but to tell you the truth, I don't know how I came to marry him. All the time I wanted to marry a gwailo, you know. That time there were so many soldiers around, remember? But maybe you were too young. Ya, I used to go out with the British soldiers those days. But of all people I go and marry a Eurasian. Fate, all fate.'

'But he's been good to you?'

'Cannot complain lah. You see, like now, he's looking after our granddaughter for me. When I go to the Hard Rock Café also.'

'You mean he doesn't go with you?'

'No lah,' Noneh said dismissively. 'That fella hates going out. Old already, you know. Prefers to stay at home and play with the granddaughter. He can lah, but I can't, I simply got to go out. I'll die man, if you ask me to stay at home day in and day out like that. Why, I also don't know. From the time I was small you know, could never stay at home. That's how I got my accident lah, driving that stupid school bus.'

Siew Hoon stared. A cousin of hers, a member of her family, a blood relation, driving a school bus. She fought down the urge to laugh out loud.

'So who do you dance with when you're at the Hard Rock Café?' she asked, instead.

'My boyfriend.'

Now she could laugh, and did. 'Oh-ho, so you've got a boyfriend on the side ha?'

'Not to say boyfriend, but he's always at the Hard Rock Café when I go, so we dance a bit, drink a bit, talk a bit. Old already, no more nonsense lah.' A burst of throaty laughter.

'So how old is he?'

'Don't know, about sixty I think. Gwailo. I've always liked gwailo you know. But see? I ended up with a Eurasian fellow. But Betty married a gwailo, you know?'

The mention of Betty reminded Siew Hoon of the funeral. She looked at her watch.

'We'd better be going back,' she said, 'what time are they leaving for the cemetery, do you know?'

'Don't worry, there's plenty of time.' A slight pause, and then, 'Actually, I don't feel like following you all to the cemetery, man.'

'Why?'

'Why should I go for that old fool?'

'You mean Seventh Uncle?'

'Ya lah, who else. The old fart.'

Perhaps taking Siew Hoon's stunned silence for disapproval, she went on, 'I know, I'm not supposed to speak ill of the dead, but you don't know what happened man, you were too young. You know he . . . ? Ahh! don't want to talk about it lah. All past and gone.'

Noneh had finished her rice by now and, picking up the little, short-handled china spoon, began vigorously to stir up the sugar at the bottom of her kopi-o-kau. Not knowing what to say, Siew Hoon watched her in silence. All of a sudden, Noneh let go of the spoon so that it slithered all the way into the coffee, and began to knead the bridge of her nose with her thumb and forefinger. Her eyes were tightly shut but that did not stop the tears from seeping out. Impulsively Siew Hoon took hold of her other hand, now twitching rather alarmingly where it rested on the table.

At her touch Noneh looked up and tried to smile.

'I know, you know. I know you all call me No-brain Noneh behind my back.'

Siew Hoon opened her mouth, realized that to protest would be adding insult to injury, and closed it again without speaking. But Noneh did not seem to be expecting any kind of reply.

'Just don't think I don't know, OK?' Then, after a brief pause filled with heavy breathing, 'That's the whole trouble. Just because I have big breasts,' and she thumped her chest most violently, making her breasts jiggle, 'just because of these big, stupid tits, people think I have no brains, cannot feel pain, cannot feel shame, cannot feel anything, cannot cry, cannot speak up, cannot tell the truth!'

Siew Hoon tightened her hold on Noneh's captive hand and tried to stop the violent twitching. This was alarming. True, they did call her No-brain Noneh behind her back, but she had never heard anyone using it in a malicious way. On the contrary, the name was always used with a great deal of affection, paradoxical though it seemed. In any case, no one had called her that for years; it was a phase they had gone through when they were in their teens. And she was sure that none of them would have been so unkind as to call her that to her face.

'You know how I know? You know how I know?' The words came out almost aggressively. Siew Hoon said nothing, waited for Noneh to answer her own question.

'It was that bastard, that ugly bastard lying in that stupid coffin! He thought I would never tell Seventh Aunt, but I did. Then he tried to deny it, said she shouldn't believe anything I say because everyone knows I have no brains, that's why all my cousins call me No-brain Noneh, that my father also had no brains, and my mother, that no one even knows for sure who my father was, that I'm a bastard and—oh my god, I'm so glad he's dead!'

Quickly pulling her chair closer, Siew Hoon put an arm around Noneh's shoulders, as much to shush her up as to comfort her. They were the only customers in the little coffee shop, but Noneh's voice had risen to such a pitch that it had drawn the proprietress from out of the depths of her kitchen. She now hovered about, trying not to look as if she was watching them. Siew Hoon did not think she would have enough English to understand everything that was being said, but the violence of Noneh's distress transcended language.

'Come, Noneh, this isn't the place to talk of such things. Let me drive you home. Wait. I'll get my car.'

So that was how Noneh and Siew Hoon missed their Seventh Uncle's funeral.

'When and how did all this happen?' she asked Noneh in the car.

'You remember that time when my mother went mad over mahjong? She and your mother used to go and play every Sunday, remember? What you don't know is that on weekdays too she would go off and play and leave me alone with my stepfather. That was when it all began.'

Good heavens, Siew Hoon said to herself, not Third Uncle as well. It was difficult for her to imagine that her Third Uncle, who looked like a Laughing Buddha, could have done what Noneh seemed to be suggesting.

'That stupid fat old fool. When he died I didn't even bother to go to his bloody funeral. After all, by that time my mother was already dead. Ya, he too thought I wouldn't tell my mother, but I did. And she threatened him. She said if it ever happened again she was going to tell the whole family. But to be on the safe side, she made me go and stay with Seventh Aunt, thinking I'll be OK there. But men, they're all the same. So the same thing happened. Once, when Seventh Aunt was working late. That bastard came into my room.'

'And you told Seventh Aunt.'

'Ya,' she sounded angry, 'but what could she do. She had to work, sometimes late. So I started going out every night. Tried to find a nice gwailo to marry. And then what happens? I end up with a Eurasian chap. Only half a gwailo!' She burst into a peal of near-hysterical laughter.

Siew Hoon suddenly found herself wondering about Betty. Betty who never let her guard down and never allowed her to get close, who was sent off to school abroad at the age of fifteen and who hardly ever came home after she found her gwailo.

It wasn't until she had dropped Noneh off at the block of

low-cost flats where she lived that Siew Hoon remembered Didi, who was depending on her to drive her home. When she got to Seventh Uncle's house, everybody had left for the cemetery except for Didi and a couple of distant relatives. It was clear that she was furious over Siew Hoon's unexplained absence, but since she was not allowed to lose her temper on account of her blood pressure, she resorted to a stiff silence as they drove home. Siew Hoon did not particularly mind. She had a lot of thinking to do.

'So which one of you lot started this business of calling Noneh "No-brain Noneh", anyway?' she burst out at last as they turned into the road to Didi's house.

'What are you talking about?'

'Come on, Didi. You know that you and the older cousins used to talk about her as No-brain Noneh. Don't deny it because I overheard you people laughing over it. I just want to know which was the wise guy who started it.'

'Why? Did you go and tell her?'

'I didn't. But someone else did. And it's been hurting her all these years. Did you know that?'

Didi fell silent after a little click of the tongue. Siew Hoon could guess what was going on in her mind. They were dealing with a breach of the family tradition, of showing protective kindliness in front of one another, never mind how cruel one might be behind the person's back.

'Actually,' she finally said, 'I don't think it was any of us, I mean the cousins. If I remember correctly, it was Seventh Uncle. Who started it, I mean.'

'Seventh Uncle! When was this?'

'You remember the time Noneh went to stay with them after failing Form Four for the second time? She was supposed to be looking for a job. Instead she spent all her time hanging about with British soldiers, coming home late and all that. He was upset. Naturally. I mean, I would be too, if I had the responsibility of looking after someone else's daughter but had no authority to control her. That's what he told some of us when he invited us to dinner. It was at Lee Wong Kee restaurant, I remember, and it was in honour of me, because I had just graduated. You weren't there; you were at home with Mama. And Noneh wasn't there either; she'd gone out on a date. With a soldier, I expect. And I think that was what made him so angry.'

'You mean it all began as late as that?'

'Ya. You don't think we could have thought up such a name for Noneh when we were kids? We weren't as smart as children are these days. Besides, Noneh was . . . Well, before you and Betty were born, during the war, when we were all staying with Granny in the big house, she was everyone's darling. Even the Japanese doctor who came to give her her smallpox vaccination adored her—Hey, watch it!'

With a start, Siew Hoon realized that she had taken both her hands off the steering wheel and was rubbing her palms on her skirt.

'Listen,' said Didi outside her house, 'if you're not doing anything, why don't you come in? Stay for dinner? I only need to put the chicken in the microwave.'

'I'll come for dinner, but there are a few things I must do first,' Siew Hoon said. 'I'll come by around six-thirty. All right?'

While driving home, quite unbidden a scene flashed through her mind: a hot, still afternoon; she in a room with Seventh Uncle, Betty outside banging on the door, shouting to come in, and Seventh Uncle putting one finger up to his lips and holding her hand tightly to stop her from going to the door. *Did I, though? Did I open the door for Betty?* She could not remember. Another scene: the three of them in a room playing Snakes and Ladders. *But was it the same room? And the same afternoon? Did I open that door?* She willed herself to remember, to see herself wrenching her hand free, getting up from the floor, running to the door, opening it and seeing Betty there—an angry Betty, a Betty declaring that she didn't want to be her friend any more. But her mind remained stubbornly blank.

Why couldn't she remember? Why that mental block? How old was she then? Could it be that there was in fact nothing to remember? Was this merely a figment of her imagination, suggested into existence by Noneh's story? Then why the wordless panic?

Once back in her condominium apartment, she changed and went down to the swimming pool which, she knew, would be deserted at that time of day. She swam until she thought her lungs would burst. Then she had a long, thorough shower, switched on the air-conditioner in the bedroom, set the alarm for five o' clock, drew the curtains, and crawled into bed. All the time a mantra she had learned as a child repeated itself in her head: *Om mani padme hum, om mani padme hum*—hail the dew upon the lotus, hail the dew upon the lotus. She had no idea what it meant.

She was late arriving at Didi's.

'What's this?' said her brother-in-law, Ben, as he relieved her of the bottles in her hands while she slipped off her shoes at the door. 'Wine. And XO! Have you struck a lottery or something? What happened to all those famous rules about not drinking wine in this country and keeping the best cognac for yourself?'

'Just shut up, enjoy, and count yourself lucky, OK?'

In the kitchen she got some fresh chilli out of the fridge, sliced them, put them in a small side dish, drowned them in soy sauce and set the dish in the middle of the dining table. Didi watched with a bemused expression on her face but said nothing.

What with Didi's cooking, her wine and Ben's near-legendary accomplishments as a raconteur, dinner was a happy, if somewhat noisy, affair. No one looking at them would have suspected that the two women had that very morning just missed burying their Seventh Uncle. Then Siew Hoon's hand-phone began to bleat.

It was Noneh, sounding very far away, very puzzled and nervous.

'Hallo. Who is this? Can I speak to . . . ?' A pause before she said uncertainly, 'Siew Hoon?'

'Speaking,' Siew Hoon replied. 'Is that you, Noneh? Is anything the matter?'

'Ya, ya, I'm fine, but who are you? I found this business card in my purse . . .' Siew Hoon remembered the name card she had pressed into Noneh's hand just before saying goodbye to her, '. . . but I don't know anyone by this name.'

'This is Baby, Noneh. That's my Chinese name.' Siew Hoon was not surprised that Noneh did not know her Chinese name. She did not know Noneh's Chinese name either. As with most Straits Chinese of their generation, their Chinese names were on the birth certificate for official purposes only, never used by the family.

'Oh, then you must be Second Aunty's daughter. When did we meet ah? Aiyo, I can't seem to remember anything these days . . .' Siew Hoon could almost see Noneh's right hand fluttering up to her temple.

'That was Noneh,' Siew Hoon said at the end of the most disjointed telephone conversation she had ever had. It was strangely exhausting, as if she had spent a few hours trying to throw a lifeline out to a drowning person buffeted about by the waves of a great stormy ocean of forgetfulness, always slightly out of reach. She turned to Ben, the doctor in the family.

'Do you think Noneh might be losing her sanity?' she asked.

'What do you mean?'

'Well, you know. Her mother died of a brain tumour, didn't she? What if she—'

'Nonsense. She's always been a bit of a scatterbrain, you know that.'

'Ya, but—well, she doesn't even seem to remember that we met at Seventh Uncle's funeral, that we had a chat and that I drove her home. And this morning while we were talking she kept rambling on about . . .' Siew Hoon stopped. How much, if anything, did Ben and Didi know? 'Or do you think it's Alzheimer's?'

'Rubbish!' barked Didi. In recent years, she had become less and less ready to believe that people younger than her could be capable of suffering from the diseases of old age. 'It was that accident of hers!'

'She did mention an accident, but what happened actually?'

'She almost died man. That was the time she was driving a school bus. So silly. Why she had to go and work as a school bus driver I'll never know. It's not as though Cyril couldn't support her. Apparently she lost control of the bus and it crashed through a road divider and overturned. Fortunately there were no children in the bus. I only knew about it because Cyril phoned to ask us to donate blood. I went to see her in hospital and my god she was a mess. Did you notice she's wearing dentures? Lost all her teeth. I wouldn't be surprised if the impact has affected her brain as well.'

'So you've met her husband,' Siew Hoon said. 'What's he like?'

'Cyril's an angel lah, I tell you. He was there day and night. Practically lived in the ward, looking after her. I tell you, in his place, I would have left her years ago. She's darn lucky to have married him, if you ask me. Mad, she was, running away from home and all that before she'd even finished school.'

'You know why she ran away from home?'

'Ah! You know Noneh. Never thinks twice before doing anything. It's not as if her life was so terrible at home. Third Uncle was always so nice to her. So much so I once heard Third Aunty complaining to Mama that he had spoilt her.'

Spoilt her? What did she mean, *spoilt* her.

'But wait, wait. She didn't run away from home in the usual sense, did she? She went to live with Seventh Aunty, right?'

'Ya, and you know something? Of all the nieces and nephews, she was the one Seventh Uncle loved the most. But I guess you were far too young to remember, huh?'

The Interview

Gopal Baratham

It was my father who suggested I interview Brigadier Mason. This did not surprise me. Like other Eurasians of his generation he had a deep-rooted admiration for the English, especially Englishmen with military designations. Paradoxically his approbation for them was based on what they themselves would have considered a debacle: the fall of Singapore. My father was particularly naïve about military matters and regarded the fall of Singapore and its recapture proof of the kind of tenacity which the unsavoury features of Mr Winston Churchill epitomized. The Japanese victories he considered not only temporary but also necessary to provide the English with an occasion to demonstrate their indomitable spirit. The whole episode was to him living evidence of the correctness of Kipling's injunction to treat triumph and disaster with parity. He did not see his attitude as an old man's nostalgia, justifiable but having little relevance to the present world. On the contrary, he managed by a bewildering process of intellectual alchemy to attribute all the problems of my generation of Singaporeans to the fact that we did not subscribe to his views.

'The trouble with you people,' he frequently said, 'is that you did not live through the war. You haven't seen enough change and suffering to value solid principles.'

Those like me born in the post-war years he styled pleasure-pursuing pragmatists. Protesting that the timing of my birth was dependent entirely on action initiated by him in no way exonerated me. 'Principles,' he would intone, 'lie buried under high-rise buildings.' He was particularly prone to alliteration, intoning and extravagant imagery when he sat drinking with his old cronies who had, as he put it, 'suffered and seen the war through' with him.

I have no doubt that it was one of his old friends who informed him of Brigadier Mason's brief visit to Singapore, as my father rarely read the newspapers—they only consolidated his opinion of the contemporary world. The media as such was anathema to him and he regarded anyone connected with it as 'a pimp and purveyor of profligacy'. He disregarded my hard-won job with Singapore Television to the point of denying it altogether. If his friends inquired about the nature of my work he would mutter vaguely about my being 'in government service'. Even when he suggested the interview with Brigadier Mason he could not bring himself to mention television.

'I hear Brigadier Mason will be in Singapore for a day or so. Perhaps you should interview him for your "thing",' he said, before he went on to eulogize over how the man's 'honour, courage, pride and steadfast principles' had withstood the 'unmentionable atrocities' of the Japanese.

'You think I am intolerant,' he continued, 'but talk to him and you will realize that what you call tolerance is merely the acceptance of your own and your generation's desire for self-indulgence.'

My own motives for the interview were mixed. I had not done any interviews lately. An interview with Brigadier Mason would certainly provide nostalgia for older viewers who were rapidly discovering that memory lane had been replaced by a six-lane highway. It might also amuse younger viewers who had never been exposed to a real-life Colonel Blimp and whose chances of meeting a specimen of this rapidly disappearing species were remote.

I contacted Brigadier Mason with some difficulty. He was

busy meeting old friends and extremely pressed for time, but agreed to the interview if I could arrange it literally on his way to the airport. This suited me ideally. I had no intention of wasting my time with an anachronism whose only redeeming feature was his potential for ridicule.

Mason proved to be somewhat different from what I had pictured.

He was very tall and lean, stooped slightly and had exuberant grey hair. His blue eyes were bleached by the sun but his complexion hadn't the coarse redness which so many Englishmen carry as a stigma of service in the tropics. Time had marked his skin but the wrinkles at the corners of his mouth and eyes were more a legacy of laughter than of anguish. He spoke in a low unmilitary voice without the faintest trace of the slightly nasal intonation which some Englishmen affect as an insignia of their class.

I began the interview by asking him what it was like to have been a Japanese prisoner of war.

'Mainly it was boring. We spent hours devising ways of killing time.'

Mason smiled apologetically at his weak attempt at humour.

'Were you not deprived of the essentials of life?'

'Well, deprivation is largely an attitude of mind. One comes to expect certain privileges without recognizing them as privileges. We assume a certain amount of food and drink, a way of dress, a way of life, what do you call it nowadays . . . ?'

'A lifestyle?'

'Yes. A lifestyle. We assume these things are absolute prerequisites for living but they appear not to be. In prison I realized how little is really absolutely necessary for life and even happiness. I doubt if you have been really hungry, but if you have, hunger becomes not just an unpleasant sensation but almost a companion. It was so constant and familiar while I was in prison that in the immediate post-war period I used to actually miss being hungry.'

'Isn't that masochistic?'

'I suppose you'd call it that today, perhaps even have me sent to a psychiatrist.' He smiled even as he spoke to remove any injustice his words may have implied. 'But it's not quite like that. The familiar somehow becomes valuable on its own account. Can I make a small confession?'

'Please do. There's nothing interviewers like more.'

'Even today, particularly when I am a little lonely, I deliberately go hungry just to be in the company of a well-known friend.'

'I guess that helps you keep slim.'

'I suppose it does, though I am not particularly concerned about my health or my appearance.'

'Would you tell us about the atrocities committed in Japanese prison camps?'

'*Atrocities* is not a word I would choose. It's a shade too suggestive and damning. By their own rules the Japanese treated us justly. But quite simply, their methods differed from ours.'

'And you feel this even though you were yourself tortured?'

'Yes, but please don't let that confirm your suspicions that I am a masochist or, even worse, an apologist for cruelty.'

'Are you prepared to tell us about your experiences in the torture chamber or are they too private?'

'They are private but I am prepared to talk about them.' For a while, Mason stared at the tips of his fingers as my mind filled with visions of nail extractions, electric shock, water treatments, genital mutilation and a hundred other excruciating images supplied by my father. When Mason started speaking again I decided I should not interrupt him.

'The whole business of my being tortured was the result of a rather silly mistake. Certain strategic installations had been bombed by B-29s and the Japanese were convinced that the bombings were the result of information the Americans had received from someone in Singapore. Why I was suspected, I still don't know, though it's possible that some poor wretch, probably one of our own men, had under torture or the threat of it volunteered my name.'

Mason paused and smiled to himself. His smile was benign, slightly amused, and did not reveal the slightest trace of bitterness.

'For the purpose of the interrogation I was moved into a room by myself. Every morning at exactly the same time I was visited by my interrogator. We saluted each other with a formal bow. Not the casual nod that passes for a greeting in the West but a gesture which required precise coordination of the entire body. We bowed from the hips, hovering for a moment with both upper and lower parts of the body held rigid, then, as though some telepathic signal had been exchanged, rose simultaneously. Masahiro, or Hiro as he preferred to be called, got down to business as soon as the greetings were over.'

I was getting increasingly agitated by his calm voice and placid face. I knew of the proverbial British stiff upper lip and of their flair for understatement, but this serenity while contemplating what must have been sheer hell disconcerted me to such an extent that I was forced to interrupt.

'Tell us the details?'

'The details are so unimportant that I barely remember them myself. Descriptions of torture are, like pornography, a self-limiting process. Ingenuity fails after a bit because the end point of the exercise is pre-determined. Hiro, who incidentally had studied English in Japan, told me at the outset that his duty was to obtain from me the method by which we had passed information to the Americans and the names of the people involved in the transaction. He smilingly dismissed my protest that I was ignorant of the bombings and did not have the information he required. Although I was telling the truth he was quite right to disbelieve me because an admission of guilt would have resulted in immediate execution.'

'What did you feel while you were being tortured?' My question sounded so silly even before I had completed it that I quickly followed with, 'What did you think of?'

'At first I used to try and think of England. The soft green country of the south, my family, my schooldays, believing that happy visions of the past would smother the disagreeable present.'

'But the trick didn't work?'

'No. The juxtaposition of the past with the present only made the present less bearable. So I decided to face the pain and even accept it an intrinsic part of my everyday life. I cannot say that this approach miraculously removed all suffering but I was certainly able to cope with it better.'

'How long did this "interrogation" last?'

'Oh, for three, perhaps four weeks. I must say I got a little hazy about time towards the end. Though Hiro's English was not very good, we developed a kind of intimacy which you might find difficult to understand. We got to know each other extremely well and this is not altogether surprising. We were both involved in something of greater intensity than most people ever experience. I suppose lovers, at the height of their passion, might feel the same.'

'Isn't that a little sick?'

'Sick?'

I searched for an equivalent word. 'Perverse?'

'I am sorry. You must forgive an old man's unfamiliarity with the modern idiom.' Mason looked suitably contrite. 'No, it wasn't . . . sick. Neither Hiro nor I had wished this upon ourselves. I think we both found the whole episode extremely distasteful. He was doing his duty, unpleasant as he found it, just as he knew I would have done mine. I think we both appreciated this. Our intimacy was based not on anything physical but on this appreciation which bred mutual respect.'

'What happened when he failed to break . . . I'm sorry, obtain the information he required?'

'When physical methods failed he added psychological ones. Hiro was really very good at his job and he was prepared to go quite far. He tempted me with what I wished to believe. He told me that Japan was on the verge of surrender and any information I might divulge could not affect the outcome of the war. I persuaded myself he was lying, and lying cleverly, for he must have known that, while all of us in prison had snippets of information about Allied victories, none of us believed the end of the war was in sight. Subsequent events proved, however, that he was telling the truth.'

Mason paused to look at his fingers again.

'Then one day he returned my watch which had been confiscated when I was first imprisoned. He confessed that he had failed in what he had set out to do and that this was the first time he had ever failed. The Japanese had no alternative but to execute me. This had been arranged for the morrow and he would come at eight in the morning to take me to the place of execution. The watch, he said, would allow me to apportion my last few hours to the thoughts I considered important and thus prepare myself properly for my death. He would arrange for me to have a bath if I wished. Then he did something he had never done before. He shook my hand—very gently, mind you, so as not to hurt my damaged fingers—and said it had been an honour to meet such a brave man. My remonstrations that I was not brave but merely innocent he brushed aside with a tiny sceptical smile, as though he wished to show that he appreciated my modesty as well as my courage. We then bowed formally to each and he left.'

'But you were not executed?' In my agitation I had made it a question rather than a statement.

'I believe not,' Mason replied. There was for the first time a hint of mischief in his eyes. 'I still don't know why. I waited expectantly the whole of the next day, checking and frequently winding my watch, and nothing happened.'

'How did you feel when nothing happened?'

'Distinctly disappointed.'

Noticing my look, Mason quickly explained.

'When death is inevitable and imminent one looks towards it more with curiosity than anything else. Lest you again label me "sick", I must say that I am not unique in experiencing disappointment when I cheated, or more correctly, perhaps, was cheated of death. Mountaineers falling great heights and expecting to die have felt similarly disappointed at finding themselves alive.'

'How do you, Brigadier Mason, view all the cruelty the war produced?'

'War is, at best, a rather unpleasant business. I don't use the word "cruel" because it implies that suffering was purposeful and an end in itself. Like so many other Japanese, Hiro did to the best of his ability what he saw as his duty. When you come to think of it, it is hard to match the sheer callousness of our side who dropped not just one but two atomic bombs on the civilian population of a nation that was already defeated.'

Time had run out. I concluded the interview and drove Mason to the airport. There were several questions I would have liked to ask him, but what he had already said left me so confused that my questions foundered at the tip of my tongue. Mason himself was perfectly composed during the drive. While we were waiting for his boarding call in the lounge he gave me a strange look and said, 'There's something else I should tell you.'

I was still a little disappointed that the interview had not gone the way I had planned and was annoyed with myself for being so obviously nonplussed by what he had said. Wishing to forestall any further disquieting revelations the man might have, I said, 'Don't tell me you are going to Japan to spend a golfing weekend with your . . . "interrogator"?'

'Alas, that will not be possible. Hiro was tried and executed for war crimes shortly after the Japanese surrendered. He wrote to me shortly before he died, however.'

'He did?' The stridency of my voice betrayed my surprise.

'Yes. He asked if I would condescend to be present at his execution. He said I was probably the bravest man he had met and that he would be honoured if he could in a small way reciprocate the display of courage I had shown. Unpleasant though I knew I would find the experience, I realized that I had no choice in the matter. Protesting that my so-called courage was based on a misunderstanding would serve no purpose. So I replied saying that I would be honoured to attend.'

'And did you?'

'Of course.'

'But why didn't you tell me all this during the interview?' I was disgusted at having failed to record the most dramatic part of his story.

'It would be unfair to say that you never asked. Moreover it would be dishonest. The real reason is that I consider it rather private.'

'Then why tell me now?'

'Simply because I feel that you ought to know the end of the story. I realize that my views are probably vastly different from your own and you appeared so disturbed, even distressed, by what I said that I couldn't really leave you without giving you all the facts.'

The public address system announced his boarding call. Mason picked up his briefcase and shook my hand.

'Goodbye,' he said, 'and good luck.'

Being an exceptionally tall man, Mason tended to lean forward as he talked, and I am still uncertain as to whether there was a hint of a formal Japanese bow in his gesture of farewell.

Hungry Ghost

Hwee Hwee Tan

When I die, I'm not going to have a funeral like my gong gong's. My funeral will be a quick and simple affair. People would arrive at three, say nice things about me, then leave at five.

When my gong gong died, his funeral lasted forty-nine (seven x seven) days. Priests and nuns gathered outside my grandfather's house, a small army whose rituals supposedly rescued him from the clutches of the demonic Yuen Thou Wong and lead him across the bridge to Heaven. During the afternoon, I drank Fanta orange while the saffron-robed monks beat their gongs under the red canopy. The tock-tock-tock of their gongs mingled with the background music—the Bee Gees singing *Staying alive*. To this day, I don't know who chooses the music for funerals. The only thing I know is that the same inappropriate music is played in public functions in Singapore all the time—I've yet to attend a wedding where they *haven't* played, *Please release me, let me go* . . .

The damp, heavy air sat on my shoulders. Sweat flowed with its own tangible life down my body as if someone had squeezed a dripping towel on my neck. I hid under the red canopy, because on a hot day like this five minutes under the sun and my black hair would be hot enough to fry an egg on. We tried that at a Brownies' camp once but that's another story.

I coughed. There was smoke everywhere—grey smoke from

the joss sticks, black smoke from the cars and trucks that whined past and puffs of cigarette smoke from the monks having their tea break in the corner. I finished my twelfth glass of Fanta orange. The Chinese have a thing about Fanta orange—orange is a lucky colour, so it's the only drink, apart from Chinese tea, that they serve at public functions. The water vapour condensed, ran down my glass and left a rim of liquid on the table. A cluster of ants scurried across the wooden table and waded into the wet rim, looking for sugar. A few ants scrambled up my glass, but I squashed them with my thumb. Though sick of Fanta, I asked for yet another glass of orange soda because there was nothing a kid of eleven could do at funerals apart from drink, choke on smoke, murder innocent ants and wonder which level of hell the deceased had descended to.

There was no doubt my grandfather was in hell and that I was going to hell too. These two facts were established when he took me to Haw Par Villa last year. Haw Par Villa is the garden of the gods, a real tourist-magnet because you got to see the statues of the Golden Buddha, the Prosperity Buddha, the Health Buddha, the Longevity Buddha—well, you get the idea.

The statues didn't interest my grandfather. No, instead he made a beeline for the cave that housed the 'Ten Levels of Hell'. My grandfather pointed at the first statue, a man whose tongue was being gnawed off by rats.

'That is what happens to liars,' my grandfather said.

I knew then that we were going to hell, for my grandfather lied about my age at the box office, shaving three years off my actual age to get me into Haw Par Villa for free.

'What did he do?' I pointed at a man whose nails were being yanked off by the demons.

'He stole,' my grandfather said.

I stuck my hands in my pockets. The number of Snicker bars I had stolen!

A drop of water fell from the ceiling on to my nose and trickled to my lips. What did hell taste like? I licked the droplet.

I tasted nothing.

My grandfather gripped my hand. 'There are tortures Haw Par Villa dares not show. Tortures like the Exploding Water Torture. The demons stick a hose into your mouth, then pump you full of water. When your body is bloated, they jump on you and—boom!'

I saw my heart, kidney and intestines sprayed across the walls of hell.

'This torture is the punishment for children who are disrespectful and forgetful of their elders and ancestors,' my grandfather said.

Thus began my quest to shorten my stay in hell. Months before his death, when he brought me to the coffee shop for lunch after he picked me up from school, my grandfather would repeat this lunch-time story (in different versions) that served as a guide, a sort of 'How to Reduce Your Time in Hell' story. It went like this:

Once upon a time, there was a boy who lived with his widowed (of course) mother. He slogged all day planting rice, but his earnings only enabled him to buy a single bowl of rice. The conversation at the dinner table usually went like this:

'Mother, take this single and only and last bowl of rice that we might ever get for the next two months.'

'No son, I'm not hungry,' she lies. 'You need the rice to give you strength to plant rice.'

'Mother, I'm not hungry.' But his stomach growls.

'But son, you're so thin.'

'But Mother . . .'

You get the idea. Of course the mother gets the rice in the end. That night, a thunderstorm wakes the mother. She screams. The boy rushes into the room and hugs her all night until the storm dies.

After a few weeks, the mother snuffs it (tuberculosis would be an appropriate agent of death). So, after his mother is in the grave, whenever there is a thunderstorm, the son would run to the graveyard and hug the grave, crying, 'Don't be fearful, Mother, I'm here to protect you.'

It was a touching story the first time round, but it got boring after the hundredth telling. It was always the same, my grandfather telling me the story at the coffee shop while he drank his Guinness, back in the time when it was still advertised as a tough working man's drink instead of a surrealistic mark of 'Pure Genius'. When he finished his story, he stubbed out his Marlboro and said, 'You know what you'll have to do for grandfather after he dies, don't you?'

My grandfather planted a hell phobia in me. I was a voracious reader and replaced the many 'Hardy Boys' and 'Choose Your Own Adventure' books that I usually read for pamphlets on Buddhism, Islam and Christianity.

So a year later, when I was at my grandfather's funeral, I wanted to read the Bible but I couldn't because books were frowned on at funerals. Books were bad luck because the Chinese word for 'book', 'shu', was a pun on the Chinese word for 'loss'.

I looked for a place where I could hide and read the Bible secretly. In the corner, two monks were dozing at a table, the area round their neck and armpits wet with sweat.

I crawled under the table from behind them. I opened my Bible, confident that the yellow tablecloth hid my activities. Outside, a monk wailed his mourning song.

I flipped to the Gospel of Matthew. Digging my fingers into my socks, I took out a Snickers bar I had stolen from the Econ Mini-Mart. Every bite of that chocolate bar meant an extra fingernail pulled off when I was in hell, but I chewed on. My fear of hell couldn't stop me from evil; it only clouded my life with a sense of doom. I tried to stop, honest, but after two weeks without Snickers I would hear the Snickers siren call—'Caramel and nuts covered with a delicious milk chocolate' and my hand would reach for that forbidden bar.

I'm not sure what happened while I was under the table during the funeral. Maybe I dozed off but I can't see how that could have happened, what with all the clanging and wailing around me, the tumult of noise that was necessary to scare off the demons that wanted to disrupt my grandfather's funeral. I was reading the Sermon on the Mount when suddenly, I was transported elsewhere. I saw Someone—not a face, a form or a colour—what I saw was a presence. I knew it was Christ. I can't explain why I knew. I just knew.

I can't describe the experience so I won't. I might say it was like running in the hellish desert for days when suddenly the desert—sand and sky—disappeared, and I laid down to rest. Or I might say that it was like climbing a hill, away from a valley of fire. The flames flicked at my heels, the mud dragged my steps, but I reached the top and stepped into a world where there was no hills, no flames, no earthly things. I might say all that but I won't. There are no earthly parallels to unearthly things.

When I opened my eyes, I was back under the table at the funeral. One of the monks stirred. His hand went under his robe, pushing it aside. Before this incident, I always wondered what monk underwear looked like. Was it spotless? Was it holy? The monk's robe fell aside, revealing—jeans. He scratched his thigh.

That night, after the funeral, I told my mother that I had become a Christian. My mother shook her head.

'Thank heavens your grandfather isn't alive to see this,' she said.

I went to my room and took my piggy bank. I emptied the coins from my piggy bank into an envelope addressed to the Econ Mini-Mart, as a restitution for my theft. The encounter under the table had filled me with an inexplicable goodness, so that I couldn't steal anymore. I don't know why.

Every August the Chinese celebrated the Hungry Ghost Festival, which, according to my mother, was the time when my grandfather was released from hell to enjoy himself on earth for a month. My mother would prepare my grandfather's favourite food—Bee Hoon: hard-boiled eggs soaked in soy sauce, Kentucky Fried Chicken, Guinness Stout—and place the food on the altar for my grandfather to eat.

My mother also bought packets of ghost money from the temple. They were square sheets of paper the size of a handkerchief with red and gold patterns printed in the middle. My mother would light each sheet of ghost money one by one, then drop the burning paper into an empty Graham Crackers tin. Each sheet burnt meant extra money for my grandfather to spend during his vacation on earth. My mother burnt enough money for my grandfather to buy new clothes, a car and a condominium.

During one particular Hungry Ghost Festival, three years after my grandfather's death, my mother reminisced about my grandfather's final days. 'The doctors told me your grandfather didn't have long to live. A heart attack could kill him suddenly. I never told him about that. I'm glad: he died suddenly, free from worries during his last days.'

It was then that the pieces fell together. My mother's words reminded me of the time, months before he died, when my grandfather gave the waiter at the coffee shop a hundred dollars for a bottle of Guinness. 'Keep the money,' he shouted. 'I can't take it with me.'

Before my mother told me about his illness, I always thought that the trip to Haw Par Villa and the endless retelling of story about the grave-hugging boy were just typical manifestations of senile sadism. Now I saw that in those last months, my grandfather's fear had rubbed off me. We were both searching for the same thing, me through my books, and him . . . I guess he wanted me to relieve him from the agony of hell by offering him food, hugging his grave and burning money for him to spend.

My mother burnt the ghost money and prayed that the flames would lick the money to my grandfather. I coughed and waved the smoke away.

It's been eight years since my grandfather died. I rarely visited my grandfather's grave—I only went last summer because my mother insisted that ever since I left Singapore to study in America my grandfather had missed me.

'Why don't you pray to your grandfather?' my mother said.

I did nothing.

'You've spent so much money flying in, you might as well talk to him.' My mother pointed at my grandfather's photograph. 'Look! I've been to your grandfather's grave so many times and I swear this time he looks happier in the photo than he's ever looked. He's so happy to see you. Why won't you talk to him?'

I stared at my shoes.

'Tell him that you're at university,' my mother said. 'In New York. Tell him where New York is.'

My mother lit a joss stick and waved it three times towards my grandfather's photo. 'Your turn.'

I shook my head. All that was in front of me was a photo stuck to a piece of rock. There was a lot to say to my grandfather—like how I knew why he took me to Haw Par Villa, why he told me those stories about the grave hugger—but I couldn't say all that to a slab of stone.

My mother stuck the joss stick in the red metal holder. The amber glow burnt down the brown stick, leaving a trail of grey ash that teetered in its wake. The wisp of smoke brushed my face. My mother began to pray, 'My dear father . . .' but her breath blew the ash away. The ash floated, stayed still in the sky for a moment. But then the wind dropped, and the grey flecks fell to our feet.

Mala

K.S. Maniam

When Malati left school she came into full encounter with her family. Having dreamed and drifted through her education, she came to roost in her home. The neighbour woman soon branded her lazy and called her 'Mala', an abbreviation of the Malay word 'malas'. The neighbour repeated it with the relish of an insult the more she saw the girl idle and happy. She was stuck with the name when her family began calling her Mala. There was an ugly sound to it whenever they were angry with her.

That was often enough. For some reason they felt offended if Mala hummed a tune in the bathroom or sat in the doorway reading a magazine. The father was a thin, tall man who only straightened from his stoop to deliver some unctuous reprimand. His colleagues at work never knew this side of him for he was always smiling. Mala's mother clattered through her housework with a solemnity that made desecration of a temple seem like a prayer. Her two brothers, constantly running errands for their stout mother, looked at Mala with a sense of achievement.

Parental love pursued a twisted path here: it was expressed through a terrifying ritual of silence. Her indifference grated on their self-gratifying sense of diligence. The boys spent their afternoons desultorily digging at an unyielding plot of ground. Mala, watching them, noticed how the handles of the changkul flew away from them. There was a dull thud as the changkul bit the ground. Their bodies were covered with a lacklustre glow. Mala's father clucked at the chickens; they squabbled restlessly, refusing to be housed for the night. Mala's mother, looking on, gave some silverware a shine where none was necessary.

The punishment began the day they learned she had failed her final school examination. There was no show of anger or of disappointment. They withdrew into silence that froze her movements and her spirit. No talk passed between them. If they saw her they turned their heads away. Meals were swallowed in utter silence, beds made in rustling quiet. Outside the house they resumed interrupted conversations with their neighbours as if nothing had happened.

'Have I done something wrong?' Mala asked, unable to bear the cemetery quietness in the house.

They only placed their fingers on their lips and rolled their eyes in the direction of the family niche. Here resided not only pictures of gods and goddesses but also photographs of a pantheon of dead relatives. Even on ordinary days the sight of these photographs revolted her. Now they produced a darkness in her mind. Not a day passed without their genuflecting before the staring, vacant eyes. Garlands, a week old, bordered the picture frames of these departed men and women. Mala had never helped the family string the flowers.

Mala began her own rituals. Getting up before the others did, she took a cold bath and went out into the unfenced compound. The dawn air hit her then, causing a shiver to course through a body that had just risen from sleep. The skin on her face seemed to peel away and reveal a new self. She stood under the mango tree and watched the sun rise over the hills. As the land emerged from the darkness and mist she felt herself torn up and rushed toward the brightening clumps of trees and hill slopes. Perhaps to replace the stinging silence of the family there rose, beyond, a resonant clamour. She turned abruptly— a door had slammed inside—towards the house.

That morning she sat in the doorway, her eyes blinking at the mystery the trees were losing. The leaves slowly turned a flat green as voices from the neighbouring houses reached her in monotonous waves. A breeze stirred the loose skirt she wore. She felt a gentle slap of coolness on her calves and thighs. Her mother came out with a bucket of washing, her lips twisted in perpetual scorn. The neighbour woman appeared at the door and whooped with delight.

'Ah, showing your legs to the world, Mala!' she screamed with unrepressed pleasure.

Mala rose and went into her room.

The silence deepened. Her brothers sat in the cubicle-like living room, afraid of making the slightest movement. Mala's mother was a squatting, impassive statue on the kitchen floor. A scrappy, cold lunch, garnished by the intolerable gloom of the house, had been eaten. The afternoon passed and brought Mala's father back from his work. Her parents had a whispered conversation under a tree outside the house. The boys sat on, knees held together, biting their nails.

Mala's mother stomped back, thrust the door of the room open and tore off Mala's clothes. She wrapped a white sari in suffocating folds around Mala's well-fleshed body. As she was dragged to the bathroom, she saw her brothers cleaning the tray and lamps at the family niche. Inside the bathroom her mother poured pail after pail of water over her loosened hair. The water came so fast, the woman held her so tightly, Mala could not breathe. But her mother didn't stop. She grunted and bent and slammed the water against Mala's hair, eyes, face, breasts and legs until the girl was thoroughly numb. She had been reduced to a nerveless, confused girl when her mother pulled her back to the niche. A lamp had been lighted. Mala's mother pushed her down before the colony of deceased. Her father placed his hand on her head so that she would remain on her knees. Her mother branded her forehead with a streak of the holy ash.

At last, when he was tired, Mala's father removed his hand. Mala moved in a daze to her room. The sari, having wrung the heat off her body, had almost dried. Mala changed and sat on the bed. Her immersion in the punishing waters had ended the silence. There was an unnatural gaiety as the family laughed at the talk of the father. A chicken was slaughtered, a feast prepared to which Mala's father invited her with some cajolery. She remained in her room.

A fury broke upon her in the night. The snores of the well-fed and contented roused a rebellious anger within her. She wanted to get out but the thought of bodies in various postures of sleep confined her to the bed. In her restlessness she tossed and turned and then lay rigid, waiting for the dawn. At the first cockerel's crow, she stumbled towards the bathroom. She stood there, unclothed, letting the chill prick her body. Then she splashed water on herself and soaped and rubbed her body so that the blood flowed again. And she recalled the red-tinged sky of the previous dawn opening upon a landscape, miraculous and fresh. She went out into the compound and let her warm breath thaw the dew and mist around her face.

'Mad Mala,' the neighbour woman said, 'standing like a ghost under the mango tree!'

The word spread. 'She rubs her bad blood on her body! Stands naked in the mist!' The squat and ugly neighbour woman returned from the town, where she was believed and made its spokeswoman. The town gathered about her as if she carried in the marketing bag on her arm colourful bundles of mysteries. She did possess strange powers and ways of knowing, sometimes accompanied by prophetic pronouncements.

'Mangoes are ripening,' she said, referring to Mala's breasts. 'Keep them covered with sacking. Hands may reach out.'

The warning was not heeded. Mala walked to her friend's house beyond the bridge. She had felt stifled, closeted in her room. For an hour or so Susi, her friend, talked of Kuala Lumpur. Her brother who had a small business there had told her of the freedom, lights and wealth of the city.

'Nobody knows you there,' Susi said. 'Here everyone knows the colour of your shit!'

The ugliness of Susi's words didn't jolt Mala out of the trance into which she had fallen. Had she not herself escaped, for a brief spell, from the daily torment, imprisonment, boredom and slow dying? She returned home late to an angry mother.

'I'll burn your legs!' she screamed. 'Who heard of a young girl wandering wherever her feelings took her? Haven't you brought the family enough shame?'

'Tame the goat or the rams will bristle,' the neighbour woman called sagely.

There was a whispered consultation that night between Mala's parents.

A priest came to the house, when it had been washed and sprinkled with saffron water, to purify it. He sat in the living room and chanted until it was assumed that evil spirits had been cast away. Then he rose to go saying, 'The dead came freely into the house.' He accepted a few dollars on a sireh leaf and departed, mumbling, 'Friday would be an auspicious day.'

Preparations were begun on Thursday itself. Flowers were gathered from bush-like plants in the compound, strung together, and left overnight to be moistened by the dew. The two boys wiped the picture frames free from cobwebs and dust the following morning. Highly honoured among the deceased was Mala's great-grandfather. Her father often recounted the story of his life, dwelling on his hunting activities.

'He was a wild man when he was young,' Mala's father said. 'Many women threw him glances until your mother's mother showed him the good life.'

'Tell us about how he went into the jungle,' one of Mala's brothers said.

'He disappeared for two or three nights. When he came back he carried the best wild boar meat slung on a pole across his shoulder.'

'No one helped him?' the other boy said.

'There was no need,' Mala's father said. 'He could carry two wild boars on his thigh unaided.'

'He was never frightened of the tigers and elephants he saw out there,' Mala's mother said.

'Not one word about jungles or wild boars after his marriage,' Mala's father said. 'He could change at the blink of the eye.'

'But he never did,' Mala said. 'He died of the wasting disease, you told us.'

'Pull your tongue out!' Mala's mother said. 'That was God's great test of patience. And your great-grandfather went like a warrior to Him.'

The great-grandfather's virtues were extolled again that evening. The vegetarian meal they had had in the afternoon made them particularly receptive. Laughter had been banished for the whole day. Mala's father slaughtered three toughened cockerels that evening with sacrificial zeal. The boys caught the blood, the woman plucked the feathers and the man chopped the meat into chunky pieces. Mala had been told to remain in her room, closeted with holy thoughts.

The cooking nearing its completion, the boys took their baths—short spurts of water thrown over their bodies. The parents wore clean, white garments for the purification. Mala was made to stand in a white sarong knotted at her breast while her mother repeated the punishing bath ritual. Mala's initiation into the world of the dead had been made.

Mala waited in her wet sarong watching her mother lay out the feast for the dead: large scoops of rice, drumsticks, vegetables, chicken curry, a bottle of stout (opened), cigars (for the deceased ladies) and cigarettes (for the dead men and striplings). The boys made the gestures first, bringing their camphor tray and incense brazier thrice around the closet of the dead. Mala's mother followed. She rubbed the holy ash at the base of her throat and struck her forehead until tears started.

Mala's father made the full obeisance before the pantheon of the good, undistracted life, now dead. He took a garland that had been lying on a tray in the middle of the niche. He put it around Mala's neck and thrust her forward. She performed the ritual with brief gestures. The father then led them in favour-asking from the dead.

'May you grant us sobriety,' he called to the ancestors.

The others repeated the words solemnly, Mala with distaste.

'May you grant us the strength not to take the crooked path.'

'May you grant us the swiftness with which to stop the blood rising in anger, lust and bestiality.'

'May you grant us patience.'

'May you grant us long life.'

'May you grant that this girl, now your daughter too, does not shorten that life.'

They took turns placing kumkum and oil and holy ash on the part in Mala's hair. She was led to her room, where she barely succeeded in keeping down the bile that rose to her mouth. For the whole week she hardly left her room, suffering a depression that left her convinced she really belonged to the dead. One evening she escaped to Susi's house, where she listened to Sanker who had come on a holiday from Kuala Lumpur.

'O! O! The mangoes want to fall into some man's hands!' the neighbour woman remarked loudly.

She had laughed over their method of 'taming' Mala. Her father reported that he heard the town laughing at him the minute he turned his back.

'Better put an end to it all,' Mala's mother told him with a certain look in her eyes.

A different kind of word passed around this time. The neighbour woman was then at the peak of her career: no men came to Mala's house although it had been recurtained, redecorated, refurnished and, in some other ways, restored. A fresh string of mango leaves hung over the front doorway.

Weeks passed. The mango leaves had curled and turned brown when a man, accompanied by his son, called at the house. Mala's father hurriedly put on a shirt and ushered them in.

'Is there anyone else coming?' Mala's mother asked, noticing the absence of women.

The man looked around him unhurriedly and shook his head.

'Aren't we enough?' he said.

His son, clothed in tight pants, a broad belt and tapering-collar shirt, examined the various articles in the room. He paused a long while at the collection of tapes, scratched his head as he read the titles and then turned, with a puzzled expression on his face, to Mala's father.

'No modern songs?' he asked.

'We don't sell records here,' Mala's father said.

The young man sat down and laughed. The proceedings were conducted to the accompaniment of his laughter.

'As you can see, my son is educated,' the older man said. 'Good music makes him go mad. Now what about your daughter?'

'She has been to school,' Mala's father said.

'Come, come. Even a donkey can be led by the neck to school,' the man said. 'Let's go to other things. Jewellery?'

'I can only afford a chain,' Mala's father said.

'A mare with jingling bells!' the man said, rising to go. 'I was foolish to come after hearing so much about your girl.'

The next suitor came alone. From the minute he stepped into the house he would not sit down. His face was pockmarked, his eyes red and his hair bristled like the back of an unruly bull.

'I'm a widower,' he said. 'I've three children. I've a lot of money. The children need a mother and I want a woman. I know all about your girl. She needs someone like me to tame her.'

'Go and join a circus!' Mala's father shouted, thinking of the whole town turned out to see his daughter the mother of three children on the marriage day itself.

Mala heard the negotiations and, humiliated, thought of suicide. The eyes of the ancestors seemed to stare at her. She saw herself pinned between glass and wood, withered flowers garlanding her memory—a monument to sacrifice for the good name of the family. In that cold, hazy hour between night and morning, she let herself be peeled and revealed. She lived again, fiercely, stubbornly, in the light that spread over the country, knowing instinctively that there could be no greater darkness than despair.

'I'm going out,' she said firmly when she left that evening to visit Susi.

'Don't you know about the auspicious period you've entered?' her mother asked.

'You can auction me off on the name I've got from this town,' Mala said.

Susi was in a thoughtful mood. She laid aside a letter from her brother.

'Sanker is thinking of marriage,' she said. 'He has asked me to look for a girl.'

'There must be plenty of girls in Kuala Lumpur,' Mala said.

'He wants to marry in the old way,' Susi said, and smiled. 'I hear your parents are looking for a bridegroom.'

Mala laughed but looked down shyly.

'I can't even think of it,' she said. 'My people are proud. They are known for their correctness in this town. I can't leave the house except with the man my father finds for me.'

'My brother isn't in a hurry,' Susi said. 'Think about it. He can give you a good life.'

There was a certain breeziness about Sanker that she liked. She had only seen him briefly, but his confidence and sense of responsibility were evident. She put her thoughts away as she approached her house. Her mother stood talking with the neighbour woman and barely gave her a glance.

Then, Vasu, a relative of Mala's father, arrived accompanied by a group of people crammed into two cars. It was an impressive show and even the neighbour woman was silenced. Perhaps she had met her match in Vasu. He had a reputation for lying, scrounging off on liquor, a habit of exaggerating, and possessed as well a sense of drama. He also had a son, of marriageable age, born out of wedlock. He got down from the car, smiling, and waited for the others to bring up the rear of the procession to Mala's house.

Several women carried trays of fruits, sweets and clothes. Vasu inquired for Mala's father in a formal manner.

'We've come with the plenty of the season,' he announced when Mala's father appeared and gestured them in.

The usual questions were asked and then Vasu jumped up as if possessed by a strange spirit.

'Don't you really know me?' he asked. 'I'm the man you spat at. At that old man's funeral. What did I know about drumming?'

'I've forgotten all that,' Mala's father said.

'Correctness!' the man hissed. 'Each man lives differently. He has his feelings. You threw water on that fire. What's happening to your correctness? This!'

The man spat on the trays he had brought as gifts. The sweat, the various perfumes the women wore and the man's raucous breath filled the close air in the living room with some kind of rottenness.

Mala appeared in the silence that fell over the gathering. She held a travelling bag and her eyes were red.

'I'm taking the shame out of this house!' she said and pushed past them.

She walked quickly towards the bridge.

The marriage, without any fanfare, was performed at the registry office. Mala's father gave his unwilling approval. No one else was present at the official occasion. As they travelled down to Kuala Lumpur in a second-hand car Sanker had recently acquired, Mala looked at the country flashing past her. All her mornings, after those baths, she thought, had not been useless. She was coming into her own at last. She couldn't suppress a sense of triumph.

They came to a busy row of shops, above which were flats. Sanker rented part of a flat. He had slept until then in his one-room office as a requirement of the businessman making his first million. The dust, the noise and the traffic assailed Mala even as she mounted the steps, behind Sanker, to the rooms upstairs. They had to share the hall and the kitchen with a woman and her child. Only the bedroom provided some space for a marriage to breathe, grow and acquire some purpose.

'Lucy,' the Chinese woman said, coming out of the kitchen to meet them. 'My son. No husband.'

But, looking out of the dirty window, Mala saw what had once been jungled hill and remoteness had been cut level and made a home. She smiled at Lucy and the boy, about three, whose face was still covered with the remnants of his breakfast.

'Sankah, good man,' Lucy said. 'Make a lot of money. Like Chinese himself.'

It might have been the car journey or the windless hall, but Mala felt giddy and looked for a place to sit.

'Better go to the room,' Sanker said. 'Rest.'

He opened the door to the bedroom, to an unmade, stained mattress and the barest of furniture. He ran down the steps and returned with some packages of food and hot tea in a plastic bag.

Sanker was at his office most of the day or out on assignments. Mala didn't know exactly what he was doing. He thrust some money into her hands at night, after they had made love, and told her to buy the things necessary for a home.

'All this will change,' he said, 'when we've more money. Just do some simple cooking. Make use of whatever we've now. Lucy manages even without a husband.'

Mala had adjusted a little to the situation. A meal was there if Sanker wanted it. The days he followed his business out of his office, she ate alone. Lucy had made it clear from the first day that she didn't want her son fed by any stranger. She was, however, pleasant about other matters. Mala derived fascination just watching Lucy's transformation in the evenings. She ceased to be the sloppy, flabby woman she was in the mornings. A smart dress emphasized her suddenly ample, firm breasts, the make-up gave her a new-found vitality. The boy had an old woman to look after him on some days. When there was no one he cried and tired himself and lay curled on the cold terrazzo floor of the hall. It was from there that Lucy picked him up, grumbling, in the early hours of the morning.

'Children, they give us no time,' Lucy said around noon, when she got out of bed. 'Bawl! Bawl! All day. Prevent them.'

The advice was unnecessary. Sanker had taken Mala to a doctor who put some metal inside her. After that Sanker ceased to be gentle in bed with her. She was reminded of the way her mother had punished her with water. The slapping, the bending down and the humiliation had followed her into marriage. There was the lethargy too, the following morning.

'We'll have children when we're better off,' Sanker said to mollify her.

She cleaned the pots and pans, saucers and cups, sometimes more than once in the course of the day. She gave Sanker his tea when he ran up the stairs and burst into the hall. Dinner was soon prepared and then the waiting for her husband began. He swayed in some nights, reeking of liquor, mumbled something about 'contacts' and fumbled for her in the dark.

'I'm working hard for all of us,' he said the next morning, rushing through breakfast. 'The ones who come later will benefit.'

He got a colour TV for her, raking up the money from somewhere. Once she went down to the office to clean it. It was so bare that she wondered how business could be conducted in it at all. Lucy surprised her as well. There was something common between her and Sanker. Lucy never mentioned the work she was doing but when she stayed home she displayed her fatigue as someone proud of having slogged away. She fed her boy something that made him sleep for hours. Lucy then sat on the floor, in a thin, loose dress, flipping through a pile of glossy magazines.

'Ask your man buy furniture,' she told Mala. 'Share half half. This looks like pig cage.'

Mala passed on the word. Sanker and Lucy came to an agreement and the sofa, armchair and coffee tables arrived. Lucy spent whole mornings on the sofa, under the dust-blackened fan that was never switched off. One afternoon a man delivered a sound system Lucy had ordered. It was an expensive, complex set. From it came all kinds of music, but mainly Chinese songs that filled the flat with militant resonance. Lucy never allowed the boy near it. Once she smacked his fingers for touching it and she wiped off the mark with a velvety, thick cloth. Mala had to distract him from his howling.

Sanker took her to an English film one night, sitting beside her with restless absorption. While he sighed in wonder, she watched with embarrassment the couple on the screen, half naked, embrace then dance in a nightclub led on by a bare-breasted woman who wriggled sensuously, and finally make love with unashamed hunger.

'See, see,' Sanker muttered. 'One day we could be like that.'

He was full of his dreams on the way back to the flat. They would buy a better, new car, move out to a house in a prestigious area, fly to a holiday in a foreign country.

'They showed all those things in the film,' she said.

'What's there to be ashamed about?' he said, drawn out of his preoccupations.

Susi visited them for a week, dragging Mala out to the various shopping complexes. She bought a dress, make-up and shoes.

'Have you anything to tell me?' she asked Mala confidentially.

'What do you mean?'

Susi giggled, rubbing her belly.

'He says when we've more money,' Mala said.

'You should enjoy yourself,' Susi said, accompanying Lucy out that night.

She left for home reluctantly. Sanker had changed during her stay. He made Mala discard her saris and wear dresses.

'Don't rub tumeric on your face,' he said.

'It won't be smooth and clean,' she said.

'I bought a lotion and other things,' he said. 'Lucy can teach you how to use them.'

She submitted. Lucy worked like a magician on her face. When she showed Mala a glass, she gasped. Her face resembled that of the women she had seen at the shopping complexes.

'My! My!' Lucy said, slapping her thighs, pleased.

As Lucy removed the make-up, Mala's face felt cool and then shrunken. She cried on returning to the flat, after Sanker had her hair cut. The hairdresser had handed her the snipped hair in a bag that carried the salon's name and logo. She laid out the truncated length, once a part of her, which had reached down to her waist.

Lucy became attached to her. She described the places in the city she frequented and the food she ate, with guests, at large crowded restaurants.

'Why you like this?' she said. 'All time in here. No children. Good time taste many things. I show you.'

Mala shook her head, only accepting to look after the boy when Lucy went out. Lucy was not easily put off. Sanker was angry with Mala for refusing Lucy's services.

'She only wants to show you the city,' he said. 'You must learn about people and their ways.'

'You take me out,' Mala said.

'I don't have the time,' he said, sensing that she accused him of not wanting to be seen with her during the day.

'He have woman work for him,' Lucy told Mala one evening. 'Plenty customers. That why he marry.'

Lucy did not elaborate. Sanker grumbled at dinner, 'Too

much work.'

'Did anyone help you before?' Mala asked.

'A secretary,' Sankar said. 'She was too expensive. You could do some work for me. But you're afraid of leaving this flat.'

Lucy's boy was proving to be too wild for Mala. He had been left so much to himself that he turned aggressive if she fed or dressed him. Mala thought about Sanker's suggestion. It was time she shed some of her fears. Lucy encouraged her.

'Go, help your man,' she said. 'He go mad, if not.'

'I can read and write,' Mala told Sanker. 'Enough?'

'You must know typing, how to answer the phone,' he said.

'I can learn,' Mala said.

'Practise here first,' Sanker told her, smiling.

He bought her a second-hand typewriter and a manual on typing. Mala spent her mornings getting in practice. The process was trying. Her fingers flew all over the keys. She aimed for speed, but only achieved mistakes. A frustrating garble met her gaze during the first weeks.

Sanker sighed. He put down the copies abruptly.

'What's the matter with you?' he asked. 'Have you got sticks for fingers?'

'I haven't done this kind of work before,' Mala said.

'That doesn't mean you've to spoil good, expensive paper,' he said.

Mala did not cook meals that day. Sanker had to buy dinner from the shop around the corner.

Though Mala was tired, her typing gradually showed some improvement. Sanker gruffly acknowledged her progress. She kept at it. The traffic roared past her flat. Lucy's boy bawled for attention. Lucy herself would prattle away from the sofa, but Mala heard none of this. She was glad that she didn't have the long hair that would fall over the machine. She had learned to write formal, pleasant letters and correct simple mistakes when Sanker announced that she could go down to the office.

'Ask Lucy how to dress for work,' he told her.

Lucy bustled about Mala. She made Mala put on a dress, then take it off. She tried various tones of lipstick, eyebrow pencils and make-up. Mala saw in the dresser mirror a girl stiff and frightened. Lucy had done good work—Mala hardly recognized herself. And she wanted to be that way. For a moment she recalled the dawns she had stood under the mango tree, up north. She had changed, she realized, but into someone not of her making.

Sanker ran a packaging business. He had the rates drawn up neatly on a card. The firm that provided the boxes had its phone number underlined in red and pinned on the wall facing the typewriter. Lorry owners' phone numbers were listed on a separate card. A little black book, indexed, contained clients' names. When Sanker sat at his table on the other side of the small office, he was a different man.

'We aren't husband and wife here,' he said on showing her into the office one morning. 'Don't bring unnecessary problems to me. Do whatever is necessary.'

He briefed her on the work at the end of which he relapsed for a moment into the Sanker she knew. In bed that night he was affectionate to her.

'It's all for our own good,' he said. 'Once I get my big contracts we can start a new life.'

Mala lay, consoled, on his heaving chest. When he talked about business a certain thickness entered his voice and he moved restlessly on the bed. She had to talk to him then, guessing at his ambitions, agreeing and sympathetically massaging him into sleep.

In the morning he inspected her clothes, make-up and the way she carried herself.

'You slouch too much,' he said one morning.

'Make-up mustn't be that thick,' he said on another. 'They might think you're a country cow.'

'Clothes should follow the body, not hide it,' he commented on a third.

Mala had learned to adjust herself according to his criticisms.

Always, he gave her an encouraging hug, just before they descended the steps to the office. Mala was careful to earn that affection. Though most of the time she could not understand his ferocity or that distant expression on his face, she treasured these moments of nearness. They compensated for the silence of the family she had left behind and the scorn of that gossip, the neighbour woman.

Mala began to enjoy the activities of the day. Whenever she answered the phone she sensed the pleased pause at the other end. She gave the rates, the kind of services available and took down times and dates if the client wanted to hear from the 'boss'. It was strange hearing Sanker referred to as 'boss'; he became someone important and unreachable in her life.

The office changed its atmosphere in the few months that Mala attended to its secretarial demands. Sanker was out most of the time, hunting down that first major contract. He spoke to her over the phone from various parts of the city. He described an individual in detail and asked if the man had shown up at the office.

'No,' Mala said.

'Be nice to him when he comes,' Sanker said.

In Sanker's absence, a few men called at the office. These were lorry drivers or packaging subagents. They sat on the oblong, backless settee Sanker had installed against the wall. They flicked cigarette ash in the potted plants on either side of the settee.

'The boss isn't in,' she said. 'He will be back at eleven.'

'We can wait,' the young men said.

Mala typed or answered the phone. The men sat on, crossing and uncrossing their legs.

'How's business, Miss?' one of the young men asked.

'Only the boss knows,' she said, too shy to refer to her husband by name.

'Secretaries know better than their bosses,' another said.

Mala went on with her work, glad if a phone call came through to break the tension.

'This one won't even talk lah!' one of the young men said as they got up to leave.

Mala complained to Sanker when he returned from one of his fruitless excursions.

'Too many men come in here,' she said.

'This is a place of business,' he said, looking at the list of people who had rung up while he was gone.

'Lorry drivers and those other men!' Mala said.

'They may bring some orders,' Sanker said. 'Get on with your work.'

At night he persuaded her that she must learn to take care of herself when he was absent. He emphasized how important it was for her to be courteous to them. He ended by saying, 'A customer is always right.'

Sanker had stacked the folded-up cartons behind his desk. An almost empty filing cabinet stood behind Mala's desk. Labels of his company were pinned on the walls along with posters of various foreign scenic landscapes. Sometimes there were busy mornings. Men came and went. Mala typed invoices, rang up lorry drivers and made entries into the office ledger. Sanker stayed in the office on those days.

'A special client is coming today,' he announced one morning as they went down to the office.

He paid more attention to her clothes and appearance during that daily inspection. She wore a tight dress he recommended. Even Lucy came out of her room on hearing Sanker talk excitedly. She whistled on seeing Mala.

'You smart girl now!' she said. 'Can even do my work.'

'Any woman can do your work,' Sanker said.

'What does she do?' Mala asked before they reached the office.

'Nothing you can't do,' he said carelessly.

Mala watched Sanker seat himself upright at his desk.

'Order some flowers,' he told her, giving her the florist's number.

The flowers, arranged in a boat-shaped container, gave the office a cold, formal colour. Whenever the phone rang Sanker leaned forward quickly. At last, a nasal stream of broken English came over the line. Mala handed the phone to Sanker.

'Yes, yes,' Sanker said. 'Any time. Come over. Everything will be ready for you.'

He put down the phone and rushed out of the office.

By the time the client arrived, Sanker had brought a smaller table from the adjoining room. A caterer delivered some savoury, covered dishes, three glasses, a bottle of whisky and a jug of cold water. The man himself came soon after, a confident smile greeting them.

'My secretary,' Sanker said, introducing her.

The man shook hands with Mala, quickly, easily, in a burst of pleasure.

'Nice, nice,' he said, surveying everything.

Sanker nodded at her. Mala sat at her desk, confused by the signal.

'She will serve us,' Sanker said.

Mala understood and went with suppressed anger to the cloth-covered smaller table.

'No need to trouble her,' the man said, his pallid face crinkling into a smile again.

Mala got used to refilling their glasses unobtrusively while they talked endlessly and the man swallowed the balls of meat or bits of steamed fish. He drank more than Sanker, but he didn't stumble on a single word. At last he rose, smiled at Mala and moved toward the door, which Sanker held open for him. Sanker took some time returning from seeing the man off.

'We've something big here,' he said.

Then he noticed Mala's expression and, breaking the office rule, came to her.

'I should have showed you how to serve the food and drink,'

he said. 'These are things we've to do until we're well off.'

They had a quarrel that night, but Sanker was adamant.

'I saved you from that black hole up there!' he said. 'Is this how you show your gratitude?'

'All I want is a child,' Mala said, sobbing. 'Not to wait on any man who comes to that office.'

Mala didn't go down to the office the following morning. Sanker pleaded with her, but she only put a pillow over her head.

'Yes, bury yourself like an insect!' Sanker shouted and stormed out of the room.

'Why make unhappiness, ah?' Lucy said, later in the morning. 'Just do what he want. How I feed that boy? Obey men, that's all. Want go out? Change place, change feeling.'

They wandered through the crowded, softly lighted cubicles of the shopping arcade. Mala followed Lucy wherever she was led.

Lucy stopped at a boutique and looked at the dresses draped over the mannequins. The dummies had blue, vaguely staring eyes. As the two women peered through the pane of glass, a man entered the case and stripped a mannequin with brutish efficiency. There she stood, bare, imperturbable, while the man arranged the latest dress over her shoulders and between her cleftless thighs. When the man had finished, he twisted her arms into a new posture. The dummy had acquired a fashionableness which Lucy praised.

Mala was tired, but she dragged on after Lucy. They sat, at last, in a low-ceilinged snack stall. The tables were small, neat pieces resting on a thick, stained carpet. Lucy picked a dirty well-thumbed menu and taught Mala how to choose her food. Mala went through the motions suffused by the steady, dull light and the cold that poured in via the air-conditioning vents. Mala recognized in the gestures of Lucy and in the pale smile of the special customer the day before the silent pressure of a force from which there was no escape.

Neighbours

Karim Raslan

Datin Sarina prided herself on being well-informed. She was always the first to call her friends, sometimes even her enemies, with the latest bit of news. News, mind you, not gossip. There was a difference. The first was confirmed and therefore true whilst the second was unconfirmed and possibly untrue. Untrue at least until it was confirmed and to be quite honest it couldn't be confirmed unless it was repeated a few times.

She was also very proud of her ability to ferret out the truth, however unpleasant. Ignorance and stupidity were insults to Allah: the truth was always worth fighting for. For example, she had been the first to alert the world to Tengku Mizan's second wife, an achievement she regarded as equal to her husband's 'hole-in-one' the year before at the Golf Club. She had seen the girl, Aida, at Habib Jewels. The face was, of course, familiar to her: Sarina was an avid reader of *URTV* and *FAMILY*—she knew her artistes: her Wanns, her Zielas and her Jees. She'd sidled over to where the girl was sitting and watched her pick over the expensive trinkets, opening her ears wider as the girl lisped her husband's name.

When she saw the gold supplementary credit card she knew her research was done. She dashed home and called all the ladies in her circle. She spared none of the details, regaling them with the size of the diamond, 'don't play the fool: two carat, you know?', her scent, 'Giorgio satu botol—smelly!', the thickness of her make-up, 'like elephant skin lah' and the shortness of her skirt, 'no shame, can see her buttock!' Proud of her sleuthing abilities, she relished her nickname, *Radio Sarina*.

Sarina was forty-five years old, romantic by disposition, shortish and a little too plump to be good looking. As if to compensate for her stoutness, she liked to think she was voluptuous. She wore the loudest colours possible, shocking reds, turquoises and vermilions and tottered around on four-inch heels. She wore make-up at all times, serious jewellery for at least eight hours a day and exercised sparingly. Married to Dato' Mus, a civil servant ten years her senior, the couple had three children, all of whom were now studying abroad. Her husband's busy schedule and the children's absence had forced her to find other sources of entertainment, if only to stave off boredom.

Which was why it came as such a pleasant surprise when she heard that the house next door had finally found a new owner. It had been deserted for the past three years and she relished having neighbours once again—if only to have someone new to talk to and about. According to the estate agent the people were called the Kassims and they were from Penang.

Patient as always, she waited for the newcomers' arrival. And what a move. Lorry-loads of furniture and fittings arrived, followed by contractors and their workmen. The next few days were a riot of comings and goings as lorries, vans, cars and motorbikes unloaded all manner of people and goods. It was only when she was making an inventory of the furniture, totting it all up in her mind that she realized how much time she had spent looking at her neighbours. She was suddenly conscious of how wrapped up she had become in the Kassims.

It was all very well to be nosy about people like Tengku Mizan: they deserved all that was coming to them. Besides, everyone knew Mizan—his inability to keep his hands off big-breasted women was legendary. However, interest in the Kassims and people like that was a different matter; it was a bit embarrassing really. They were nobodies. It served no purpose—she couldn't talk about them to her friends. After a great deal of thought she decided that her interest in the Kassims had been a little extreme. However, it was educational—she had to learn about everybody. She shouldn't limit her interests.

Hastily then, she decided she should be a little more disciplined about these things. So she ignored the house next door, exercising a noble restraint when the servant girl came running to her one evening to tell her that the family had arrived, in not looking at the house. Instead of rushing off to have a look at her new neighbours, she retired to her bedroom, drew the curtains and went to sleep. Self-control was very important in these matters.

She continued to treat the arrivals, then, as a temporary distraction, one that would be absorbed and made familiar in good time. This she considered was the correct way for a lady in her position to behave. Of course, the occupants of both houses soon made their own introductions. Her broken-tailed pariah cat, Chomel, impregnated one of her neighbour's silvery Persians very noisily late one night. And her own servant girl, Amina, who was, it must be said, irrepressibly flirtatious, had done her utmost to get herself impregnated by the neighbour's surly chauffeur.

It was some time, however, before the heads of the respective households actually met. Sarina well understood the trials of house-moving and chose, she thought, once again with great restraint not to impose herself. One particularly hot afternoon she did, in breach of her own personal sanction, send cold drinks over to the house when she heard—through Amina—that the electricity had yet to be connected. Towards the end of the fourth week, and just after the Isyak prayers, Encik Kassim called at the gate, introduced himself and was invited in to have some coffee.

He was almost six feet tall. Somehow she had known he'd be tall. He was ramrod straight, smooth shaven, golf-tanned and smiling. Such a smile, she was quite disarmed. He couldn't have been more than thirty-five years old and was well-dressed—he was wearing a well-tailored pair of pants and a pink polo shirt that set off his healthy colour. Sarina felt a tremor of excitement as well as irritation with herself for not seeing him earlier: her new neighbour was so very good looking. She was a little lost for words at first. But Kassim smiled again and, as if aware of his effect on her, made himself quite comfortable without troubling her. He was just so athletic, so attractive. She couldn't wait to tell her sisters; they'd die of jealousy.

Mus and Kassim soon dispensed with introductions and started talking about business. He said he was a lawyer and she was even more impressed. She slipped away into the kitchen as they started discussing market capitalizations, PEs, flotations and hot tips—subjects that always bored her. Once in the kitchen she prepared coffee for her husband and her new neighbour.

Arranging the coffee service on a silver tray, she marvelled at the splendour of this, her 'everyday' coffee service. She felt sure that the charming Encik Kassim would notice the fine quality of the porcelain. She could imagine the expression on his wife's face when he, as she felt sure he was bound to, described the thick gold inlay of the saucers and the delicate transparency of the cups. His wife would be jealous, envious and not a little flattered to be living next door to people of such distinction and quality. There were times when she felt that she was one of a dying breed: a Scarlett O'Hara in a land of pygmies.

Placing the tray down on the small side table between her husband and the visitor, she glanced at Encik Kassim, expecting him to exclaim aloud, 'Allah, what exquisite porcelain you have, Datin. Could it . . . could it be Noritake?' But he didn't, at least not initially. She was unsure that the men noticed her departure. As it was, the two men had progressed from business to religion.

'. . . Datuk, these people they say that it's our duty to intervene and direct those who are transgressing the Koran. Well, I think that's wrong. Islam brings all men together under the guidance of Allah. We are beholden to Him to live as closely as we can within the dictates of the Koran. That doesn't mean that we should force the unwilling . . . Oh, two sugars please, Datin, thank you very much. What nice coffee cups, Datin.'

Sarina looked on admiringly as he drank his coffee; she was going to like this young man. He was so observant and such a gentleman. Didn't even slurp as he drank his coffee. Even Mus was beaming: Mus enjoyed a good theological debate and he was pleased to have a similarly inclined neighbour.

'Encik Kassim, you are so right. These preachers would have us living in the desert sands. The spirit of observance is of most importance, not mere outward display. There are many ways of serving Allah and it is important to allow each individual his right to choose his own way, and his own time within the dictates, as you say, of the Koran and the Hadiths.'

She watched Encik Kassim closely. He had a handsome sculpted head, a large forehead—he was a lawyer, after all—and brown eyes. Oh, if only she was young again, she thought, only to be shocked by the impropriety of her thought. Kassim nodded politely as Mus made his points. Such nice manners. Observing him so closely, she felt sure she knew him or at least his family. It didn't seem possible that she didn't know him. He was obviously far too polished to be just anybody. She couldn't help liking the way he deferred to her husband and smiled so pleasantly—there just weren't enough nice young men around like this Encik Kassim. If he hadn't been married she would have rushed out and called all her unmarried nieces there and then.

'. . . it is not of interest to me that you or anyone else might drink alcohol, gamble or commit adultery. There is, of course, only one figure to whom we all owe obeisance and that is Allah. I might possess views about your behaviour which I could voice, were I inclined to do so, just as you would be free to reject whatever I have to say. Similarly I am free not to have to act according to your interpretations of the Koran and the Hadiths—because interpretations are all that they are, neither wrong nor right, merely differing views pertaining to the same subject...' Once Mus started it was often difficult to stop him.

'We are no longer living in small Bedouin communities in the desert. Neither are we personally equipped to act as judges against our fellow man. To be a judge of men's morals, personal or public, is something quite different.'

'Datuk, I cannot agree with you more. It may be every Muslim's solemn duty to seek to attain the purest state before the Will of Allah. But that doesn't empower us to be moral arbiters and judges ourselves.'

'I'll leave the highest state of grace to those who know better,' Mus replied cheekily. He was enjoying the discussion. 'I always say,' he continued, 'that Allah has endowed me with a brain that allows me the liberty of making my own decisions as to how I should lead my life. And I have chosen rightly or wrongly to seek the humblest place in heaven and no more. In short, Encik Kassim, I am an ordinary mortal using the blessings Allah has given me, to ask the questions that Allah must have expected us to raise.

'Come, come, don't let me bore you with my talk. Drink your coffee and I will show you the garden wall that I was telling you about earlier.' And with a broad sweep of the hand, Mus drew the conversation away from religion to the commonplace.

Having been silent earlier, Sarina spoke up. She was very keen to meet Mrs Kassim now. If the husband was this good looking and well-brought-up, the wife had to be exquisite.

'Encik Kassim, I do hope that your wife will do me the pleasure of calling on me when the family has settled in. Please don't be afraid to ask for any help. I understand how very tiring it is to be moving house.'

'I will tell her,' he replied warmly and then added, 'actually my mother says she is related to you, Datin; her mother is Datin's mother's cousin.'

Sarina couldn't contain her excitement.

'Oh, really, I should have known—you seemed so familiar. How interesting. Mus we're related! You must be Tok Su's *cucu* then? I remember now!' Mus smiled as well. She knew he was as pleased as her.

'I can assure you that my wife will call around as soon as she can. She would have come with me tonight, but her mother was not feeling well, so she had to go to Damansara Heights.'

'Come, Encik Kassim, I'll walk you out. We can have a look at this troublesome wall.' The two men stood up and walked out into the garden, where the shadows cast from the street lights drew patterns across the damp lawn. Sarina watched as the two figures, both so tall and poised, passed through the streaks of light, disappearing and reappearing. And as she watched them growing shadowy and dim in the dark she realized that from a distance it was hard to tell the difference between the two men. 'What a pleasant surprise,' she thought to herself as she cleared away the coffee things in preparation for bed. 'Such a nice young man, and a relative, too.'

The next morning, after her prayers, Sarina chose to watch the sunrise—a special luxury that she allowed herself now that her children had left home. As she sat, quiet and composed on the veranda outside her bedroom, she tried to think about the household. But try as she might she couldn't help but think of Encik Kassim. Visions of him flashed through her mind. And, if she was honest, it was because of Encik Kassim that she was now sitting on her veranda. Her veranda afforded her a view of her neighbour's master bedroom and whilst she tried to pretend to herself that she was enjoying the cool morning air, she couldn't banish entirely the real motive for her early morning vigil. Thoughts of the young man had swirled through her dreams all night long and as soon as it was possible she had arisen and taken her place on the balcony.

Just then, she noticed a light being turned on in the room opposite her veranda. The previous owners, a nice Chinese family called Teh, had known that anyone who had a mind to, could see into their main bedroom if the light was left on. As a consequence they had been scrupulous in their use of curtains when getting changed. Of course, the new occupants were not to know and Sarina, realizing this, had waited patiently on the veranda. She knew that she ought not to sit on the veranda now, but the prospect of seeing Encik Kassim again enthralled her too much.

The first streaks of sunlight began to tell upon the lawn, airily slicing the dawn mists. Even without Encik Kassim, this was still her favourite time of day, and her reluctance to sit on the veranda drifted away much like the mists hanging over the garden. A delightful bluish tinge clung to the lawns now damp with the morning dew and swallows from the neighbouring trees swooped down to drink from the swimming pool. She had planted her garden with care, tending it lovingly over the years; the beds of heliconias had flourished and flowered, showering the garden with their crimson brilliance and dragon-like intensity. She never lost her wonder at their startling voluptuousness and the way they cascaded pod after pod. Alongside them she had planted pale silvery hibiscuses, ferns and more ferns. The garden was looking lovely and she let herself be lost in the play of colours and scents that surrounded her, forgetting for a moment her new neighbours.

Changing her mind once again she made a mental note not to glance over at the house opposite. She would enjoy the morning air and then return inside, deferring to the Kassims' modesty. She felt sure that nice Encik Kassim would understand. It was not uncommon for her to make such fine resolutions: not to talk about Raja Karina and not to spend too much of her husband's bonus. Inevitably, over tea at the Hilton or in her sister's house she would find the excitement of the occasion loosening her tongue and then, before she could stop herself, she had imparted to all assembled the truth about Raja Karina's little operation in Geneva or agreed to buy yet another set of diamonds.

Thus it was that she pledged to herself not to look at the bedroom window of her neighbour's house whilst sitting directly opposite it. As was always the case with such situations, Sarina felt defeated by surrounding circumstances. Here she was, trying not to be nosy, minding her own business as she enjoyed the early morning coolness, only to be thwarted by the Kassims next door, who insisted on leaving the lights on in their bedroom for all to see. She began to feel annoyed with the Kassims. After all, she thought, they must know that people could look in.

Maybe it was a deliberate act, some kind of deliberate oversight; maybe they were exhibitionists? Perhaps the young man wasn't as wholesome as he appeared? She laughed to herself: he was as wholesome as ketupat, just a million times better looking, that was all!

Maybe he was shameless? And she laughed again. Much relieved to discover that the fault, if indeed there was any, lay with her neighbours, she let her eyes settle on the room.

The room was entirely unadorned, spare and empty. There was a bed and a bedside table, no more. The wife, this Puan Kassim, was obviously not the sort of woman who cherished the small, poignant tokens of love—a family photo or bottle of scent. Having met Encik Kassim only the night before, she tried to create in her mind what she thought the wife would be like. Yes, she thought to herself, the wife must be exquisite but cold and hard.

Then, in the house opposite, the door opened from the bathroom and a woman entered the room. Her sarong was tied casually around her waist, her breasts exposed. Sarina was taken aback and with a jolt she turned her head away to face the garden, now mockingly enrobed in the gathering sunlight. Surprised by the sight, she determined to forget ever having seen it. She wanted to tear herself away from her vantage point, now shorn of the gentle, innocent pleasure it had once given her.

But she was unable to do so. Her curiosity had taken hold of her entirely and she felt impelled to look again: if Mrs Kassim was half-undressed, then maybe her husband would be too? Sarina was embarrassed by what she had seen, more angered by the invidious position that it had put her in. She wasn't a voyeur or a pervert. But look she did, and with a terrible avidity.

The woman was tall and slim with small breasts. Sarina felt a pang of jealousy at the woman's slimness—if only she had persevered with her diets. The woman had surprisingly powerful shoulders—shoulders that wouldn't have needed shoulder pads—and bedraggled hair that kept falling into her eyes though she tried to push it back. Because of the distance Sarina was unable to make out the woman's face clearly. But she thought her good looking enough, with striking features and, like her husband, she was tall and erect—she had such bearing. There was a firmness and masculinity about her, emphasized in part by her lack of curves. She, this Mrs Kassim who wandered around her house bare-breasted, had no hips and thighs to speak of. The bearing of the woman, her pencil-slim shape and demeanour served to remind Sarina of the vast gap that separated the two of them. She was a woman of softer, older ways whilst Puan Kassim was stronger and more dynamic.

Mrs Kassim seemed unhappy. Her hands rifled through the bed clothes for some jewellery or underclothes. Sarina smiled to herself as she remembered similar fleeting encounters with Mus, and the men before Mus, meetings that had been snatched in between dances and dinners, baby-sitting and badminton. Those were in the days when sex had been something exciting for her and Mus. Now it was a chore as tiresome as dusting the furniture or washing the car, a chore that one underwent unwillingly with less frequency as the years progressed.

By now the light had reached its most perfect moment, lending a bronzed glow to all that it touched and she turned to her garden once again. The ranks of bougainvillea in her garden seemed to strain to receive the welcome warmth of the sun, so different from the harsher glare of midday. She had almost forgotten about Mrs Kassim as she watched, charmed and warmed by the steady illumination of her garden. Suddenly she felt the soft delicious cool of the breeze that curled its way through the suburbs, kissing her face as it passed by.

Mrs Kassim was sitting on the edge of her bed, applying cream between her legs. Sarina winced, both from the sight and from the memory of having had to do the same in the past. Then the woman started rubbing herself with greater rigour, arching her back and cupping her breasts with her free hand. Though Sarina had never herself masturbated, she knew that this was what Mrs Kassim was doing. She had been a little disturbed initially. She knew that she should have been shocked by what she saw but she wasn't and she carried on watching. She wanted to know as much as possible about this woman whose body shuddered with each stroke.

Just then another door opened and Encik Kassim came into the room. Sarina felt her own breathing quicken and she placed her hand on her chest, squeezing her own breast inadvertently. This was what she had been waiting for and she moaned silently. The wife did not notice him as she continued to stroke herself. Her strokes quickened and she shuddered violently. Encik Kassim walked around the bed until he was standing directly in front of her. Undoing his trousers he nursed his penis into her mouth. Sarina pressed her breast again and shivered.

She couldn't believe it! They were making love; this was far more than she had expected, though she couldn't say that she hadn't hoped for it. Even so she wasn't sure if she should be shocked or thrilled. Encik Kassim pulled off his trousers and underwear, throwing them across the room in his hurry. He leapt on to the bed and straddled it on all fours like a dog. She gasped and her hand dropped from her breast: what was he doing? He had a strong muscular back with just a hint of a paunch. His penis was monstrously enlarged.

The wife turned around and grabbed Encik Kassim firmly by the waist. Sarina could almost feel the bruises on his body. They were so violent and animal-like with one another! So, she thought, this was what it was like to make love passionately. She imagined herself for a moment in the place of Mrs Kassim, touching that young man and being touched by him. It was like one of those blue movies she had watched years before, only more real and more fervent. Her head was spinning with the possibilities.

Seductively and slowly the wife let her sarong fall to the floor. It slipped off her slim thighs and gathered in a pile at her ankles. Sarina swallowed hard; her mouth went dry. The woman's belly didn't taper off into a mound as her own did. The woman, or at least what she thought was a woman, had a penis of her own, a penis that was also erect. It was a pondan. She mouthed the word silently, a pondan.

'This can't be the wife!' she thought. 'No, surely not! How *could* he! He was so nice!' She didn't know what to think. He'd been such a polite and charming young man and a relative of hers as well—how could he do *this* . . . to her? It couldn't be! Her head spun painfully. She felt deflated and angry as if she had been let down. Encik Kassim had disappointed her, cheated her with his charming smile and his brown eyes.

The woman positioned herself behind Encik Kassim . . . her handsome Encik Kassim. Now she really was shocked, horrified in fact but still she watched, engrossed by the ugliness of it all. She was unable to pull herself away. But as she watched she became aware of the unnaturalness of what she was doing. Why was *she* watching? Why did she feel compelled to watch? Was there something wrong with her? Why couldn't she be like other people and mind her own affairs? Somehow she felt that it was her nosiness, her selfish persistence that had brought Encik Kassim to this.

Had she been more respectful of his privacy, none of this

would have happened. She would have thought him charming and good looking. Now he appalled her. It was all her fault, her responsibility. She had pushed him. Just as the thoughts rushed through her head the woman eased herself into him, shaking her head with pleasure.

She pulled herself out suddenly and slapped Encik Kassim hard across the buttocks as if he were a fat kerbau and sneered. And as she did, Sarina saw that he, *her* despicable Encik Kassim, moaned like a woman. He was no longer the man she had met the night before—sprawled across the bed like an animal, he seemed grotesquely subservient and feminine. The woman—she just couldn't call him a man, it was too monstrous—stood up. Encik Kassim moaned again and thrashed his buttocks in the air like a bitch on heat. Sarina wanted to retch. What was going on? She saw that the woman's features were hard and prominent like a man's. Did she have an Adam's apple? How had she missed it earlier? The woman turned the overhead light off.

With the light now off, Sarina realized that it would be possible for the couple to see her on the veranda. So, the blood draining from her face and terrified lest she be seen, she went back to her bedroom. It was a rare moment, a moment of shocking clarity. She could see herself as she was—the pretence and the falsity of how she lived her life had slipped away. Everything around her was sheared of its innocence. It was all a sham. She was a fat, overweight woman, neglected by her husband, whose emotional life was so thin and insubstantial that she could only find satisfaction in the private lives of others, a parasite who fed off the secret lives of others. She had nothing herself: she was nothing herself.

A Sense of Home

Kee Thuan Chye

I don't know how I got the idea of how my mother came to be kept by a rich businessman and had two children by him, but the story goes something like this. The first time he ever saw her, she was coming off the ferry that had brought her to Penang from Butterworth. He was in his car with a friend, and he told his friend that he liked her and wanted to get to know her. Then he persuaded his friend to approach her and ask if she would like a lift to wherever she was going. His friend obliged and that was how the whole mess began.

On thinking back, I realized it couldn't have happened that way but the idea stayed with me until only two years ago, when I was already forty and finally found the courage to ask my mother how it actually happened. Her version was more plausible but disappointingly ordinary. I'm not sure now which version I prefer.

Up till before I turned ten, I refused to believe that this rich businessman, Heng, was my father. I called him Papa only because my mother insisted. He wasn't listed in my birth certificate as my father. The man who took that honour, if you could call it that, was Quek Siew Thim, my mother's husband. I assumed the family name of Quek, not Heng. Besides, I preferred Quek Siew Thim to be my father because I liked him. He seldom spoke beyond a few syllables, never raised his voice to me, never acted like a father, partly because he didn't live with us and only came some weekends from his home on the mainland during which he would often take me to see movies. I looked forward to his visits. On days I expected him to arrive, I would wait by the window to watch the bus stop outside our house. It could take a few hours and several buses before I saw him alighting from one. Then I ran to open the door to admit this diffident-looking man, his eyes always to the ground, 'looking for gold', my mother often said, carrying a small case like the ones primary school kids took with them to school, 'looking like a medicine seller', my mother said.

I noticed that she didn't welcome his presence, never showed him tenderness or affection, and the rare times when she spoke to him, she was either affecting a harsh tone or actually scolding him, sometimes throwing in the most unthinkable swear words. He also slept in the back room, alone. And although this seemed odd to me, I was discreet enough not to ask anyone why. There were big things that I could sense even though I was a child. In the absence of clarification, I tried to figure out the situation myself. I guessed that my mother was having a secret thing with Mr Heng and Mr Quek didn't know, so I should keep my mouth shut about it. But I wondered why, since Mr Quek was her husband, she didn't behave like a wife towards him. And why my elder brother called him Papa whereas he called Mr Heng 'Uncle'. I began to sense that Mr Heng must have some claim to me that he didn't have over my brother. And some claim over my sister as well because she, too, called him Papa, which she seemed to have no problem with. In fact, whenever he was around, she clung to him quite a bit, encouraged by our mother, who sought to have greater hold on him through his affection for the girl.

I don't know if it was instinct on her part but my sister bonded pretty well with him, exactly the opposite of me. I actually hated him. He could seem very stern to me, largely because of the way he looked. His strong eyebrows met at the centre, forming a formidable 'T' with his straight, unyielding nose. At the base of that stretched a pair of thin, taut lips that always appeared clenched against his jutting square jaw. The puffy flesh above his upper lip weighed down on his mouth causing its corners to sag, accentuating its hardness. On rare occasions when he gave me a smile, it looked more like a grimace. I couldn't be inspired to smile in return. His features conspired against him even more by refusing to be elastic so that he seemed to be always wearing a set expression. I could never tell if he was ever happy. In all my growing-up years, we never shared a laugh.

I dreaded the times he pulled out my loose milk teeth with just his thumb and forefinger. I often think that because of his crude method of extraction I ended up with bad teeth. He tried to discipline me but I resisted. Once, he was going to slap me for throwing a tantrum at my mother, because she forgot to buy me a comic book she had promised. I pulled away and showed him a clenched fist. To his Chinese-educated mindset, it was the ultimate sign of disrespect. I trembled when I realized the brashness of my gesture. He of course was compelled to come at me, to reclaim his standing and teach me what every Chinese child should know. But my mother held him back. She pleaded with him that I was too young to mean anything by it. He was silent in his anger as he glared at me, and that frightened me even more. I ran up the stairs to a safer distance, but I couldn't escape his face. More than anger, it showed profound disappointment, as if this fist that I brandished had shattered the stone of his sternness and challenged a belief that he held in his heart. And he did have a heart. It was probably then that I realized, to my horror, that he could have had a hand in my making, that the thing my mother was having with him did extend to his having contributed to producing me.

You see, despite my age, I had an inkling of how children were made even if I didn't know the technology. It came from watching movies, from seeing the hero and, usually, the heroine slumping on to a bed locked in embrace, their hands struggling with buttons, and in the next shot their garments being dropped down the side of the bed; from seeing the aftermath of the struggle, with the man and the woman now lying side by side, a blanket up to their armpits, both looking pleased and uttering guttural dialogue, then she resting her cheek on his chest, and he wrapping his arm round her shoulder causing her to turn to her side and the blanket to slip down and expose the flesh around the curve of her breast.

I naturally wondered why men and women did these things as I saw more movies with such scenes, and when I began creating my own movies on paper, drawing the pictures and inserting the dialogue in word bubbles, it was not solely out of innocence that I always included a scene that had a man and a woman connected at the hip. I, however, made sure that they were completely naked, because I could never understand why in the movies the couple was always covered with a blanket even while they were in the act of getting each other excited. Did they need to reach for the blanket, pull it over themselves and right up to their shoulders in order to proceed to do their business?

When I was five, my mother brought me to Kuala Lumpur for a rendezvous with Mr Heng. It was one of the rare times when she could be with him for a whole weekend, and it had to be away from Penang on the pretext that he had business to attend to in another town. We stayed in a majestic hotel suite. On the first evening, while it was still bright, I wondered what they were up to and peeped into their room. They were asleep beside each other with the sheets up to their waist. It was like in the movies but this was the aftermath. It was however unlike in the movies because my mother's breasts lay exposed, resting comfortably beside his hairless chest. I stood there gazing for a minute, my five-year-old mind wondering what to make of it. Then I realized I had seen something I shouldn't have. I tiptoed away, but the impression stayed.

By the time I got to Form One, seven years later, I was already wise about the fundamentals of reproduction. One day, in

English class, the teacher took us through A.J. Cronin's *Hatter's Castle*, which we read in its abridged version. At the end of one chapter, the young man and his girlfriend walked along a canal, holding hands, and enjoyed the night and the twinkling stars; then at the beginning of the very next chapter, it was revealed that she had become pregnant. I felt cheated and complained to my classmate Siang, 'I doan believe it! How can she get pregnan? The book diden say they did anyting waat!'

Siang, in all his innocence, replied, 'What do you mean? The book said they were holding hands.'

'You can't get pregnan just holding hands!' I cried.

'Can lah!' he asserted with the confidence of his ignorance. 'Jus hold hands only can get pregnan.'

'No laaah! You got to do more dan dat,' I said.

'Like wat?' he asked.

'You go and ask your parents lah!' I said, and laughed a superior laugh.

Monologue II

Kirpal Singh

And so now as he sat alone he thought of the ceiling fan, of that woman round that well and, of course, of himself. He was weary. It was not a sign of becoming sick and tired but of just knowing that there were too many, too many battles to fight. He had been fighting for far too long. For as long as he could remember. From the time he realized the meaning of that little knot on his head. Oh yes. Now that he sat alone and thought he realized that this knot of hair had made all the difference. He had travelled many roads but this one had made the biggest difference. The knot of hair on his head. Hair. Samson. Strength. The pillars of wisdom. The pillars of the community which he was himself sometimes aping. Sometimes quoting. Sometimes creating. How does an old man create a pillar of the community? Which community? Whose community? There was talk of a non-community sense which had worried many pillars of the community. Which? He dared not think. He sat alone. He thought of the fan. And sometimes he also thought of extensions. Fanny. Funny. Not a good alliteration. Funny fanny. People did not like his sense of humour. Not always. Many a time he knew they joked about his jokes. Most did so behind his back. Some did it openly. He liked those. Courage, man, he thought, courage. Was there courage when she had opened her blouse on his insistence and he had seen that deep scar left by the nasty accident she had had some years ago. He wanted her so bad he made her remove her blouse. Even in the dim glow of that warm light, the scar stood out. His stood down. What a blow. A blow. His manhood. So was this all that manhood amounted to? Standing down in the face of a scar on the body of the woman he had wanted to make love to so badly? The main problem with Mandarin was that it was very hard to make love in it. Better to make love in Hokkien or in Cantonese or in any dialect. The mandarins always stood down in the face of any possible scar. They were scarred. They were scared. Mandarin had layers. He sat alone and thought. The ceiling fan went round and round and round. Sometimes his head went round and round too. He was weary. Sick and tired. Too many battles to fight. Language was just one. His mind went funny. Fanny. Layers. Delicious layers. Mandarins were delicious, he realized. You peeled them and ate them. You could not peel scars off. She must have tried to get rid of that ugly scar. She had told him he was not the first to be frightened. Not the first. Nor would he be the last. Perhaps. There were too many battles to fight. He had fought so many he forgot when, where, how, why. The many pillars of the community had frequently asked him to join them. One had even joked he could do that beautifully in dialect. His poor wife had said no and she had been adamant. She had her own battles. Her own scars. But she knew Mandarin. That made the difference. Their roads had diverged a long long time ago. Only the realizations came late. Other realizations came later. Like how the mandarin was a delicious fruit with many layers which could be peeled. Like love. Like making love. How does one make love in Mandarin? Was courage to be found in fortitude? Commitment? Responsibility? Do unto others as others do unto you. A scar for a scar. A fanny for a fanny and a funny for a funny. Pillars of the community didn't like that. Many didn't like his sense of humour. Many didn't even know he was being funny. Others did unto him. Oh yes, they all did. Big things. Small things. Just things. Sometimes he sat alone and thought and became weary and sick and tired and wondered about the pillars of the community he had helped in this way and that. Where were they now? These pillars? What is manhood if it crumbles in the face of a scar? One night in Bangkok can make a strong man crumble. But he liked crumbles. Apple crumbles. Pear crumbles. Peach crumbles. Crumbles. Nice word that. He thought as he sat alone. His mind went round and round like that ceiling fan and like that woman around that old well. Do unto others. Had he done unto others. If she frightens me I should frighten her too. Basic survival kit. So if she kisses me I must kiss her too. Simplicity leads to simplicity. Courtesy begets courtesy best courtesy begets best. Begin at home, always. Like charity. That little knot of hair on his head had started it all. His strength. His fighting those many battles. His marriage. Mandarin. Delicious layers waiting to be peeled. Scars waiting to be healed. Championships waiting to be run and won. Did he enjoy this? Did he realize what he was doing sitting alone and weary? Alone alone on a wide wide sea. He recalled. Yes. That man had suffered. That ancient mariner. Where had courage been then on that wide wide sea alone? He had grandeurs of illusion. Most didn't enjoy his sense of humour. Mistah Kurtz he dead. What if that had been mastah Kurtz he lives. Now that would have brought many battles into the story. So many layers to peel. So many delicious layers which no one wanted to peel because in the peeling lay the crucial truth. Where did the good fanny lie? Should he be jealous if the fanny could never be reached because of that scar? Because he was scared and she was too? Pillars of the community. Pillars. Fallen pillars. Made of clay. Round shining mandarins. There was a time when he would have fought and fought. Now he just sat there. Alone. Alone alone on an empty bench. Around him the birds flew and the children walked. Tomorrow's pillars. Samson's hair. That little knot on his head. Samson breaking down those huge pillars. Round and round the mill he went. Just like that woman going round that well. Pillars made of clay. She had been scared to undo her blouse. He had wanted her to. He had yearned for that special moment of knowledge. When she did and he saw that scar he just could not understand what this knowledge was all about. After such knowledge what pillars? Courage, man, courage. Never say die. Strive on. He did. Carry on. He did. Just do it, they said. Do your duty like a man. He did. I must also bear it like a man. Sometimes he wondered whether they knew that the pun was just too much. Bear with me. I must bear it like a man. What did that little blighter Malcolm future king of England know when MacDuff had said those terrible words? She, his wife was dead. He, his little child was dead. Butchered. Murdered. Just too many fights and battles and no real winner. He sat alone and thought. He was weary. All lose when they fight battles without knowing Mandarin. He was starting to meander. Life was a meandering. Some did it much better than others. Meander leander. These days no one was too tender. There had been a time when even those who meandered tendered. Time was, he thought, as he sat alone, time was when those he fought with meandered and knew what real knowledge was all about. After such reflection what knowledge? Was he going forward? Was he starting to slide? Was he starting to ebb and flow like that tide which had washed thousands off their feet because it came so suddenly and no one had been prepared? Turning and turning in this huge and senseless mire of wealth and wealthmaking he had forgotten that making love was difficult in Mandarin. There were too many layers to peel. Knowledge is power. It is. He smiled. Even as he sat alone he smiled. That fan would always remain in his mind. Just like that funny fanny. Always. Always. There is one story and one story only. The very teacher who had taught him that had forgotten it herself. But who would know that one day these demons of the past would come and visit him? Visit her? Visit everyone? But it was promised! Here we go round the mulberry bush, the mulberry bush. But there were layers to peel and they were delicious and so people got soaked in that deliciousness and they forgot the demons and as they ate from their own loins they forgot that Samson had long hair. That little knot had grown. From strength to strength. And the pillars came rumbling down. Crumbling down. Rumble, crumble, oh what a shumble. No such word existed. Language was too small for all that was going on in his head as he now sat there alone and weary. The time was drawing near. He felt it in his bones. He felt it in his head. He felt it. Felt. Had that teacher known that the one story was his story? Possession was such a peeling thing. Possession peeled layers off. After the peeling people forgot. Origins. Humble beginnings. Terrible sufferings. Scars. Scars and more scars. Was that another story? Another story for another time? This was the new millennium. The new millennium. The third. He was the first. The first to have broken through that one story and given it a different significance. Given it a different scar. And they all suffered. Mostly alone. Like him. Sitting there weary and alone and suffering and not knowing if this was night or day. How can we know what we know? Knowledge was power. If we cannot know we cannot have power. There were simply too many battles to fight. And there were these scars. And mandarins. The many pillars of the community around him expressed concern that he was not always listening to good advice. His, they said, was a stubborn nature. He did not fully understand affairs of the state. The nation. Top priority. A priori. Quid pro quo. Status quo. That woman still went round that well. That ceiling fan was still turning. This time he was sitting alone. Do unto others. Blessed are those who do not forsake themselves. A new realization. How often had he forsaken himself? How often had he wanted her fanny. How often had he wanted to fight those many battles and how often had he received frightening knowledge of scars? Don't go that way, he thought. That way madness lies. To ask for mercy from the merciless was to exact a sentence of silence. The quality of mercy is never strained. And so mercy is never pure. He thought hard as he sat alone and weary. Did he write that? In another life? In another life he had always known there was one story and one story only. The longest night. The longest day. Quid pro quo. Status quo. Blessed are those who shall inherit the earth and nothing but the earth. Knowledge was not good. It poked fun and the fanny. And it was not always very funny. Oh my wife, my wife, my wife—she farts. Why was it that people did not want to know that which lived below their waists? Were they scared of the scars they would find? In my kingdom are so many mansions everyone will have not one but two or three. And so they all fought many battles to gain their mansions. Those who delivereth, getteth. How could he come if his pillar had fallen? Would they forgive him after all this knowledge? Round and round the birds flew knowing some great moment was at hand. The darkness gathered. The light had been dimmed to hide the scar. He had wanted this so badly he did not know how to handle himself. She was there. She was ready. She was his. She was. As he sat alone thinking and wondering his mind meandered. He had known a leander in his time. He had tendered. There had been public tenders, private tenders, tenders and just privates. Parts he knew existed below the waist which he was not to speak of. The pillars would crumble if he did. He did. And his pillar crumbled. There was knowledge in the air. But the power had gone. Adios amigo, adios my friend. The road we have travelled has come to an end. How could the mind take possession of this? This meandering, this leandering, this fanny? To leer is not the same as to peer. Even when words rhyme their rhythms don't. He had known glorious rhythms in his life. The rhythm of that ceiling fan going round and round. The rhythm of the pain as his own pillar crumbled. The rhythm of the rain as he sat there alone and weary and wondering if the people knew that something was at hand. The unique moon orbit cycle and a moveable feast. Were all feasts moveable? Were all moon orbits unique? Did everyone come at the same time. Let my people come. Yes, let my people come and see what folly it is to fight so many battles and lose the mandarins. Those delicious layers waiting to be properly peeled by proper hands whose proper lips will savour those delicious peels. Was this true? Had that travelled road come to an end? Mistah Kurtz he dead or alive? Had he dared to look at this abyss of his own making and realize that Mandarin was not a language he could make love in? His wife had warned him not to make too much of those pillars of the community whose community he had sought for through thick and thin. Thick and thin. Thick equals blood and thin equals water. Yes. That was right. He had been taught that. There was one story and one story only. He knew that story. It was his story. The story of an old man sitting alone and weary waiting for the scars to go away. And the lights to come on. And the people to know that through suffering Samson knew himself and made a whole world collapse. Samson's folly. He did not speak the right language. He did not know the right code. Or if he did, his right code did not come on cue at the right time. Redundant. Cue on right time. Redundancy. It takes a long long time before most find out the meaning of this strange word. To be redundant is to be funny. Jacks and Jennies of all trades knew what the word meant. They had lived through it, some many times. Was he now learning this word? He knew it always came back to language. Reality was language personified. In my beginning is my end. And in my end? What? What exactly was his end? Was there such a thing? Was that that one story which was his? Everyone had stories to tell. We all begin with stories. Do we end with stories too? Or do we just end? You cannot make an omelet without breaking an egg. Why did he think of this line sitting alone on that strange night when knowledge possessed him but power was not there? There came a strange smile to his eyes. Eggs were there for making omelets. He was there for that story to be told and retold and then for it to end. Was his own end near? Was this why he thought of that fan and of that woman going round the well and Samson going round the mill at Gaza? His little knot of hair. Those delicious layers had been peeled. There was comfort in this. He could rest now. Rest. And dream of that wonderful life below the waist. Into that haven of freedom, my father, let me awake. As he sat there alone and weary a smile came upon his gentle lips and he started to dream his glorious dream. Alone.

Surja Singh

Lloyd Fernando

Surja Singh was twenty-eight when he died. When I heard of his death, I was not surprised. We were in the same army, and he knew which country he was fighting for. I didn't. He was a patriot in the old style, and that kind isn't around these days. I'm not saying this to excuse what I did.

He was strong and healthy, considering that this was during the Japanese occupation of Malaya in the early 1940s, when food was scarce. His entire life was a preparation for the battle to free India from the clutches of the British. The way Naidu spoke, I took it that it was at Imphal in Burma that he died, where the great thrust forward of the Japanese and Indian forces into India during World War II was first blunted and then thrown into disarray by the torrential monsoon rains.

'Heroes die young,' I muttered lamely.

'He couldn't escape,' Naidu said. 'He didn't have a chance.'

We were talking at cross-purposes. Naidu and I were no particular friends. But together with Maran, who sat opposite us at a table in a Batu Road coffee shop, we had been in the same platoon under Surja Singh in the INA, the Indian National Army, which had been formed with Japanese support, and we hadn't seen each other since the British reoccupied Malaya. Jaafar, my schoolmate, sat with me and listened to us reminisce.

I said, 'Surja Singh's name should be added to the INA Memorial. You know—the one next to the cenotaph. Near the padang in Singapore. The sports ground.'

Naidu said, 'Cannot. No more. The mat sallehs—the white men—blew it up. Two days only they were back, they did it. Taap. Gone.'

Maran spoke. 'I say. What about the INA? Maybe they'll charge us as collaborators.'

Naidu said, 'Cannot. Too many of us. Now we're wearing ordinary clothes also. No uniforms, how can they find?'

Maran said, 'Jaafar also got uniform, what. Uh, Jaafar? You also joined something, right? The Heiho? The Japanese organized only for the—Malays. And they sent you all to Japan. What for they train you?'

Jaafar said, 'No, lah, didn't go to Japan. That only for rajas and ungkus. We got basic military drill. But not to fight.'

'Ay, I'm still using the uniform trousers, you know.'

Naidu said, 'Anyway, now the mat sallehs got other problems. They want to change the country and call it the Malayan Union. But the Malays don't want it.'

'Why? Everyone will be equal, what.'

'Ay, Jaafar, why uh?'

Jaafar sipped his coffee, a smile playing on his face. He said, 'Did they ask the Malays? Anyway, you all not interested, what. The Chinese don't want. Want to go back to China. The Indians don't want. Want to go back to India. All want to go back, what for to give you anything.'

'Hah, like Thivy,' I said. 'He was president of the IIL, the Indian Independence League, which formed the INA. He went back to India the fastest. Now he's back as the Indian representative in Malaya. If they want to charge collaborators, he's a collaborator, too. No, they won't dare.'

'Hope so,' Maran said. 'Ay, kopi satu! One coffee!' I know this was a lousy way for former INA soldiers to talk. Only a few months back, we had been going through rigorous military training in the INA Officers Training School at Batu Pahat. Every night we sang rousing soldiers' songs in Hindi about marching forward together and fighting the British and driving them out of India.

Us lal kila Delhi ko
Barbad karo, tum!
(Destroy that Red Fort in Delhi!)

We meant the words as we sang. At least I did. I relearnt from Surja Singh the pride of being true to oneself, of belonging to one's place, to one's time. I could never forget him for that.

Yet here we were, only months after the reoccupation, not even protesting that the whites had begun ordering our lives once again, and we were packing up to go 'home'. Jaafar was right: so much for our patriotism. Maran was happy as a storekeeper in a British military camp. Naidu, to judge from his flashiness, had merely continued his black-market activities from INA times into the period of the British reoccupation. I, like Jaafar, was studying for the Cambridge University certificate examinations. So none of us had taken the INA seriously after all. We were just time-servers; nothing very criminal—we were too goddamn venal for that.

But where was the treason? To whom did we owe loyalty? Surely not to the whites—that much, at least, I learnt from the INA. Then again, was this our country? We never thought of it like that. It was just a place to make a living. It didn't occur to us to look at each other in any other way. Time-servers, all of us. Except Surja Singh.

'And he is dead,' I said aloud.

'Who?' Naidu looked over a saucerful of hot coffee, which he held at his lips.

'Surja Singh.'

'Ahh, him. I never liked him.'

'Poor bugger,' Maran said, without any real sentiment. Actually he didn't care much about Surja Singh one way or the other. 'I never understood why he wanted to be so—so *different* from the other officers. Even on the first night we arrived in Batu Pahat, remember?'

I did. A hundred or so of us, specially chosen for the officers' training course, had made the journey from Singapore packed like cattle—first on a goods train, then in lorries. At three o'clock in the morning, we were finally in the barracks in Batu Pahat.

The officers who were to be in charge of our training moved among us casually. The Commandant, Captain Kishur, and his deputy, Captain Varma, were the only Gurkhas I knew who had joined the British-recruited Indian regiments that transferred to the INA after the Japanese came in. And there was Surja Singh. Even physically he was impressive: over six feet tall, broad shouldered, muscled, not perfectly proportioned—on the whole he looked angular—but giving a general impression of strength and possessing a confidence that stemmed from his love for his country.

He came and sat on the floor with Maran, Naidu and me, as we were eating a limited ration of sweet rice. Compared to the regular starvation style gruel cooked in our house, such a meal was heaven for me.

'Cadet Sena, sah'b,' I said, when he asked my name. All of us spoke only in Hindi.

'Ap baccha hai. You're just a boy,' he said, commenting on my youthfulness. I could see from the start that he was not going to take me seriously, and he was right not to. I wasn't taking the INA seriously either. I was in it for food: because I could get three square meals a day, and my family would have one mouth less to feed. For that I was willing to square-bash, have my life ruled twenty-four hours a day and risk being killed in a war between parties I cared little about except for the contrasting ways in which they subjugated us.

He asked Naidu, 'Why did you join the INA?'

Naidu answered, 'To fight for India and free our Motherland.'

There were many others, including myself, who spoke that way. The times made us speak like that. We partly believed what we said.

Surja Singh looked at the three of us without speaking.

Maran said, 'I hope we'll be sent to the front after training.' He wanted the adventure of war. The Japs and the INA had advanced on the Burma front and were approaching the Indian border. This caused great excitement. Wars were being fought all over the world, around us and about us, but not by us. Now, for the first time, we were to be personally involved in our own war, and it was a new experience we craved.

Jaafar said, 'The war's not over yet. Even now. If the mat sallehs don't stop the Malayan Union, they will be sorry. Then they will know.'

I was troubled because I didn't know what to say.

Surja Singh said. 'You want to fight in the war? You will get your chance. But first you must train and make yourself strong. We must all be fit and ready for the struggle. Now that Gandhiji and Nehruji are in jail, India will never be free unless we help her from outside.'

His face showed a quiet intensity. It was light brown, verging on Caucasian fairness. Though he was a Sikh, he was beardless and wore no turban and his hair was cropped short. Even the kangan—the plain metal bangle—was missing from his wrist. In a patriotic gesture, a lot of Sikhs in those years gave up the five marks of Sikhism to reduce the external differences among us Indians.

'But if—I mean, when—we win, it will be a victory for the Japanese. They'll become our masters in place of the British.'

The silence that followed made it clear that I had said something disloyal. Many of us had doubts about just how we related to the Japanese, but few expressed them aloud. We didn't talk because in our minds we were still the drones created by a foreign empire to serve it, and our thinking faculties had atrophied.

Surja Singh broke the silence. 'That can never happen. Or we will fight them, too. You have not heard Netaji speak. You don't know him. Netaji will never allow it.' Netaji was Subhas

Chandra Bose, who had broken with Gandhi and Nehru because he thought them too soft. He thought World War II an opportune time to rid India of the British. Willing to join with anyone who would help him do this, he joined the Japs when they swept down Malaya and Singapore. It was under his leadership that the INA was formed.

The bugle sounded, and we all assembled for roll call before dismissal. 'I didn't like the bugger,' Naidu was saying. 'He was too strict.'

One thing Surja Singh detested was inefficiency. Another was time-servers. Like Naidu and me.

He took us for physical training every morning; later he lectured us on tactics. After each morning's three-mile run and numerous leaps and bounds on the way, he would still be fit and fresh while we staggered and panted to the end of the session. He was a born leader, combining cheerfulness with firmness. The inability to stand up to strain displeased him because he interpreted it as a lack of discipline and consequently a threat to the attempt under Netaji to free India from the outside.

The other officers did not think I was a time-server. In fact, within a few months, they were regarding me as a *sword-wala*: a candidate for the sword of honour, which was awarded to the best officer cadet at the end of the course. Surja Singh was sceptical. Though he didn't show it, I knew it. I tried to win his goodwill but never succeeded. There was a barrier: perhaps because of my youthfulness, perhaps because I asked too many questions.

Then he was posted to the Burma front, and I never saw him again. I heard that within six months he had been decorated twice for gallantry. When he was wounded, he was posted back to the School as being too valuable a soldier to lose.

Maran said, 'Ya man, he was brave. Even after he came back, the same. You remember Nadeson? Sure nobody would have done what he did that night.'

I asked, 'What happened?'

Naidu said, 'I remember. You went to Singapore. What for uh? You were sick or something?'

I said, 'For an operation. Appendicitis. I heard something about Surja Singh there, but not sure. What happened?' Actually, even the little I heard made me certain he was the kind of man who could not live long.

I knew that morale was low because Captain Kishur and Captain Varma frequently went hunting in the forest nearby, leaving Surja Singh in charge of the camp. Then, corruption at the branch headquarters of the INA in Batu Pahat became more rampant, and rumors spread that Kishur and Varma were on the take for foodstuffs stolen from the INA and sold in the black market. That and the heavy INA and Japanese losses at the Burma front broke our spirit with surprising ease. When the prospect of our transfer to the front receded, we no longer saw the point of intensive training.

That was about the time I went for my operation. In the end, I didn't get it because the doctors said I didn't have appendicitis but simply groin strain. By that time the war was nearly over, so I just went home.

Naidu said that one night at roll call, Deputy Commandant Varma was making one of his insincere speeches about how we must be ready to give up our lives for India, how we must train hard and shirkers must be thrown out. The men couldn't take it.

A voice from the ranks shouted, 'OK, first we throw you out, Captain Varma!'

Darkness had fallen, and Varma could not identify the voice. He jerked his head back and said, 'Who said that?'

Dead silence. The tension was broken by the ludicrous sound of a grunt.

The soldiers laughed.

Varma picked on the company joker. 'Nadeson! Step forward.'

Nadeson marched up close to Varma. 'Ji, sah'b,' he said innocently and saluted. The company laughed again.

'What did you say just now?'

Nadeson was a fool. He carried his joke too far. He cowered in mock fear at Varma's question, and the company laughed again. When Varma struck him across the face with his baton, Nadeson winced slightly and then stood still. After the fifth blow, the entire company stood up in a body, shouting protests.

Maran said, 'You should have seen us. Anything could have happened the way we were crowding up on Varma. He was scared. He couldn't move, his eyes were wild.'

Naidu said, 'That bloody Varma—I could have killed him that night.'

Jaafar asked, 'Were you in front?'

Naidu said, 'I should have given it to the bastard.'

I said, 'Why didn't you?'

Just before they got near to Varma, Surja Singh had leapt out of nowhere on to a table nearby. With what seemed like a single movement, he flung off his cap and shirt and shouted, 'If you want to kill anybody, kill me!'

Maran said, 'Real hero, lah. Just like Indian film star. He was crouching, ready to fight. His eyes were shining, like what I don't know. He shouted, "Come on!" But we were all so surprised; we didn't know what to do. We just stood there. And then he talked to us a long time.'

I said, 'What did he say?'

Naidu said, 'Ahh, usual stuff. About discipline, duty and so on.'

Maran said, 'At first I didn't listen because I was thinking, sure we all get court-martial or something. But the way he was talking, he really got me, you know.'

Jaafar said, 'Got you?'

Maran said, 'Like make you feel shame, you know? He told us we had no discipline, so how could the men under us have discipline. Sure we would make the Japs distrust us in the front lines. He said our INA is a small army, but it would be a famous one, how can we spoil its name. Like that, man. In the end most of us felt bad. He was speaking so powerful, his voice so full of feeling.'

Naidu waved a hand dismissively. 'Ahh, act only. He thought he was too great. Why he want to be so special? Always giving us lectures, always so strict. Serve him right he got it in the end.'

I got angry. Here we were: we had got out of the INA easily, no fighting at the front, full bellies and everything. I said, 'What do you mean, "serve him right"? Have you ever met anyone like him anywhere? Have you?!'

Naidu shouted back, 'Don't shout at me, you! Who do you think you are to talk like that, putting yourself up so high.' We glared at each other.

Maran pushed my coffee towards me. 'Come on, drink your coffee.' I sipped, still staring at Naidu.

Maran looked at his watch and said, 'At eleven o'clock I have to be in Gurney Road. I'm meeting a British major. A bloody crook, if ever I saw one.'

Naidu turned away and said, 'You got a deal?'

'Tyres. Six hundred of them. All I have to do is drive into his camp, load them on to my truck and drive out.'

'How much does he want?'

'Three thousand.'

Jaafar whistled. 'Five dollars a tyre. Lucky fellow.' He looked at me. 'Ay, Sena. Still thinking of Surja Singh?'

I said, 'I was just thinking of him lying dead there in Imphal.'

Naidu said, 'Imphal? Who said Imphal?'

'He died in the INA advance on Imphal, didn't he? He knew he would die, and he was going to die for India gloriously. Do you know anyone else who believed in the INA like he did? He died like a hero like he always wanted. How can we talk of him like that?'

Naidu laughed. 'He didn't die at Imphal.'

Maran said, 'Sena doesn't know.'

Naidu waved a hand. 'I don't want to talk about him. You tell him.'

News of the Nadeson incident, Maran said, reached the INA headquarters in Singapore. After an inquiry lasting a week, the entire company of officer cadets was confined to the barracks for a month. They were given fatigue drills in addition to their daily regime. Kishur and Varma were removed from their posts and ordered to return to Singapore. Surja Singh was appointed temporary Commandant, effective immediately, and given special powers to clamp down on black marketing.

Maran said, 'Can you imagine? Commandant and Deputy Commandant of the School—no power. Their junior now in charge, showing them how to run it.'

Jaafar said, 'Was he trying to put back the discipline?'

Naidu spat. 'Discipline! Imphal was nearly over. The monsoons had come. The Japs had lost, we had lost and our forces were pushed back from Imphal. We lost our chance for India for good. But do you think Surja Singh admitted that? Not that bugger.'

Maran said, 'He pushed us so hard in our training day after day. Everything he did made Kishur and Varma feel small. Didn't know where to show their face.'

Naidu said, 'I tell you, huh, they hated him worse than we did.'

Jaafar said, 'You hated him?'

'Yes, what. Most of us. Ask him.'

Maran said, 'Maybe a few.'

Naidu said, 'You do two route marches every week, twenty-eight miles each time, full kit, you know. Then tell me whether you won't hate him or not.'

Maran stood up. 'I have to go. Don't want to lose three thousand dollars.'

I said, 'Wait.' But I didn't know what I wanted him to wait for. Except that it seemed like we had no heart—talking of Surja

Singh one moment, and the next moment one of us getting up and going off to chase three thousand dollars. 'You haven't told me where he died.'

Maran said, 'Ay, Naidu, tell him, lah. I haven't time. OK, see you.'

'No, wait a minute. Five minutes. Tell me a little more—don't just stop like that.'

'Surja Singh, Surja Singh! You want to make me lose money, uh? I don't want to talk about him anymore.'

'How did he die—how did he die? Just tell me that before you go.' It was important for me to know how he died. This wasn't just curiosity; I was also afraid of what I would be told.

Maran sat down again impatiently.

Tension had been building up owing to Surja Singh's methods. His strict inspection routines reduced the black marketing of INA supplies. The fatigue drills he imposed on the habitual shirkers caused smoldering resentment. Kishur and Varma were humiliated by their junior's efficiency. While awaiting transport to Singapore, they further stoked discontent, conducting whispered conversations with little groups during the break after evening meals. There was an air of something about to explode.

One morning when the cadets assembled as usual for physical training, Surja Singh did not appear.

Maran said, 'Funny thing, you know, nobody was surprised. All of us lined up on the parade ground, looked at each other and waited. There was no leader. Somebody went and called Kishur and Varma. They came with mocking smiles on their faces, not saying one word about Surja Singh, and led us on our usual three-mile morning run. As we neared the town boundary, somebody shouted, and we all broke ranks and rushed to one side of the road. There he was lying in the drain. Surja Singh. Stabbed to death.'

My brain was in a whirl. His death was like a personal accusation hanging over me. Intently I watched a man at the table next to ours draw up his phlegm and spit it into the spittoon under his table.

Maran got up. 'That's all I know. You can ask Naidu about anything else.'

I said, 'Who did it? Stabbed to death. By whom?'

'Black-market people, maybe. Who knows? We suspected some people, but we never found out. He had about thirty stab wounds on his face and body.'

'Thirty!'

'He was tied up, feet tied to neck, blood all over, bundled in a gunnysack and thrown, do you know where? In the drain right in front of the ILL branch at Batu Pahat.'

'So he prepared all his life just to die like that,' I said. 'Stabbed and put in a gunnysack. Who did it? Did they get them?'

Maran said, 'I was like you, I wanted to find out. But it was dangerous. He was a good guy, lah, he really wanted to fight for India. But there were people who did not like him.'

I was still in shock. 'Was it Kishur and Varma? Someone else? Who?'

Maran said, 'Ay, Naidu, why they took us past the ILL headquarters that day? They never did that before. Why, uh? Why they did that? They were not even surprised when they saw his body. Now I remember, you also not surprised. I think you knew who did it, am I right? Who, uh? Those guys, uh?'

Naidu said, 'Ahhh, no use talking. He was no use. All those punishment duties he gave me.'

Maran said, 'Many got punishment fatigues. Could be one of those fellows did it. But how to prove anything.'

Naidu said, 'You're wrong. People in the camp, yes, but not those fellows.' He took out a cigarette from a slim gold-plated cigarette case, tapped the end on the case smartly and lit the cigarette, exhaling the smoke with a swishing sound. 'I know who did it.'

I said, 'You know? Did you report them?'

'You think I'm crazy, uh? Get myself killed for nothing. I

knew about it a week before. Those guys came to see me.'

'Who were they?'

'Never mind. They knew I hated him. They asked me to join them. I said no.'

No point asking Naidu why he didn't warn Surja Singh in advance, but I asked him anyway.

'Why should I? You know all the things he did to me? What's the use of talking. Anyway, maybe those guys were only joking. Then what would happen to them? Not fair, is it? Better to keep my mouth shut.'

I persisted. 'At least you could have warned him. Why didn't you?'

Naidu pushed his chair back and stood up. 'Wait a minute, are you trying to accuse me? You were not even there. All this while I have listened to you and been patient. Something in your attitude: you want to make out like Maran and me are crooks or something.'

I said, 'No, I don't mean that.' But the fact was I was thinking that country to Surja Singh was everything: he loved his country with a concentrated passion; he lived and fought for it with complete integrity. Why wasn't there any weeping for the passing of such a one?

Naidu was saying, 'If we are crooks, what are you? You just got a medical certificate and disappeared.'

'It wasn't my fault I wasn't there.'

'You're a quitter. You didn't stick with the INA. We did. We were there until the end, slowly starving while the Americans did their island-hopping across the Pacific, wondering what was going to happen to us, now that there was no Burma to fight through to get to India. We stuck it out. And where were you, uh, tell me that.'

Maran said, 'Ay, cannot wait anymore. See you again.' He went off. Naidu picked up his gold-plated cigarette case and, laughing, began walking away, too. Turning, he pushed his thumb through his fist at me.

'That to you. Easy for you to talk after it's all over. Surja Singh was nothing.' He paid for his coffee and went out.

That left Jaafar and me alone. We didn't speak for a long time. At last I said, 'You are thinking—what are you thinking? I told you we didn't know who we were fighting for.'

Jaafar didn't look at me. He said, 'No, man, I was thinking what a pity about Surja Singh.'

'Naidu knew his killers. He was probably one of them. Yet there he is, walking like a free man. Is that what you're thinking?'

After some time Jaafar said, 'Yes.'

'You're still thinking some more. What else?'

Again Jaafar was silent for a while. At last he said, 'I was only just "wondering" which country will you fight for now?'

Victoria and Her Kimono

M. Shanmughalingam

Queen Victoria gazed at the Lion of the Victoria Institution. Albert Ramanan was however so busy slapping Mohamed Ali, he did not realize that his Queen's portrait had begun to tilt left on its own in mid-1941. It had never happened in the school's history from 1893. Right-ward it might be a good omen, but was this sinister?

Ramanan, the Form One English master, was tall, dark and 'hands on!' Hands for slapping my misbehaving students' cheeks and shaping their characters rather than for 'hail and well met, shaking'. He strode into the school in his topi, closed coat, silver buttons, white long sleeves shirt and long trousers, starched till they seemed brittle. In his coat pocket were red, black and blue fountain pens and sharp pencils. Sharper than these was his temper, hot and deadlier than chili padi. His temper was hotter than the tropics when there had been no rain for weeks. He never loosened his collar even while perspiring under the overworked, creaking ceiling fans. As an old boy his students considered his conversion from student to teacher as a case worse than a smuggler turned customs officer.

He was a son of the enterprising offspring of Jaffna Tamils in Ceylon who crossed the seas in the late nineteenth century on the strength of a telegram 'Work Arranged. Come.' Armed with an English education, these work horses came and helped to develop this land of coconut milk, rubber-tree-milk, tin and tinned milk, buffaloes' and cows' milk. They manned the junior ranks of the Education Service and Public Works, Railways and Telecomunications departments, for the honey of a regular salary, government housing, a pension that nourished pride more than the family.

Amongst colleagues in the staff room, Mr Ramanan was a man among men, a chap among chaps. He swapped stories with his headmaster, Dr Jones.

Ramanan told Dr Jones and his collegues in the staff room about the colourful messages his father sent to his bosses in Kuala Lumpur. One cable:

'Rain so heavy stop! Whole district flooded stop! Bridge absconded full stop!'

A second:

'Wife died stop. Request emergency leave to go to the crematorium to "fire her" full stop.'

He requested boots for his department's Malaria Eradication Programme. A British expatriate officer from the Federal Treasury sent the routine rejection:

'Does your department propose to stamp out malaria literally?'

Father then counter proposed:

'An eradication programme for sarcastic Treasury officials. They should be stamped out literally.'

He told them also about his father's system for grading leaders. Well above average ones were ranked:

'Able men.'

These Able Men were differentiated by the length the first vowel was stretched.

An Aable Man ranked higher than a mere Mr Able, thus starting the double AA rating above the A. An even more Able Man rated triple AAA as the first vowel was stretched to an 'Aaable Man'. You lent emphasis by raising your eyebrows and head higher the more able the leader was. Among the triple AAAs there had to be one supreme one. Since there were no stop-watch recordings of which of the triple AAA Aaable Men this was, there was a unique title for him. The most of all aaable men was crowned:

A 'cape—aaable man'.

On hearing this Jones told Ramanan:

'I hereby dub you a capeaaable man. You are the best teacher in the school. Since I'm returning to England shortly you should have the privilege of buying my Jaguar at a discount.'

Jones knew it was an offer the anglophile could not refuse. Ramanan's entire savings sailed away in his principal's steamer. Apart from the headmaster's, his were the only hands that held its steering wheel. Driving the Jaguar made him feel he was 'headmaster on the road' even though his purse leaked badly down to his toes on the accelerator. Although Mrs Ramanan could drive she had been allowed in the car only as a passenger.

The Victoria Institution sat on its throne at the top of Petaling Hill in Kuala Lumpur. Its headmasters were Oxford and Cambridge graduates. The melody of the school song was based entirely on *Gaudeamus Igitur* from Oxford. The VI's crest however displayed both its origins and its ambitions for its pupils with the tasteful light and dark blues of both universities.

On the first day of school the whole class classified Ramanan as 'fierce, to be approached with great caution, if at all'. He introduced his class to Charles Dickens' *Oliver Twist* (*Tales Retold for Easy Reading*). So grateful were the students that they nicknamed him Bill Sykes. Ramanan got wind of this but had no confirmation of it.

Among the normal run of essay topics designed to occupy, if not excite, the eager pupil, 'My Holiday' and 'My Family', Mr Ramanan one day offered 'My Pet'.

Mohamed Ali, a Muslim, to whom dogs were anathema was nonetheless inspired.

'My pet is a dog named Bill Sykes,' he began.

That first sentence confirmed Ramanan's suspicions about his nickname. The class sat fascinated, betting out of the sides of their mouths on whether Mr Ramanan's collar button would burst before Mohamed Ali's collar parted company with its shirt.

Mr Ramanan charged up to Mohamed Ali, as he lifted him bodily from his seat.

'Oohh your dog's name is Bill Sykes! I'm going to your house straight after school today. I shall call out for Bill Sykes just once. If your dog does not dash out answering to that name, God help you. I shall give you a good flogging. We shall see whether you survive it. No criminal can survive my rattan cane.'

'No, Sir. The dog won't come out, Sir.'

'Why not?'

'He died last night, Sir.'

'Then show me where you buried him.'

'Cannot, Sir.'

'And why not?'

'He is missing presumed dead, Sir.'

'A bit of a rogue you are.'

Ramanan twisted his ruler around the flesh on Mohamed Ali's buttocks as Ali winced, veering away from him.

'How old are you?'

'Thirteen years, Sir.'

'Thirteen years of what?'

'Thirteen years of wasted life, Sir.'

The Lion was satisfied.

The nickname Bill Sykes died as promptly as the dog did, never to be heard again.

Queen Victoria contemplated her lion's victory with pride, if somewhat askew. The British empire marched on as Ramanan sat marking exam scripts in the classroom in the humid morning air, nodding approvingly at the neatly knotted string holding each script together, top left. But even the best regulated of empires was not without its insurrections. Index number 67 had knotted his answer script on the right so that Ramanan could not turn the page over. He asked his class monitor to locate the culprit. Several minutes later, index number 67 turned up from another class.

'Careless wretch, what's your name?'

'Liew Fook Yew, Sir.'

Ramanan jumped up, kicking his own chair to amplify his rage. It was an act he had picked up from his wife.

'Are you scolding me or telling me your name?'

'No, Sir! Yes, Sir!'

'Make up your mind. Is it Yes or No?'

'No, Sir, I'm not scolding you, Sir. Yes, Sir, that's my name, Sir.'

'Cross your arms, hold your ears and recite "tie knot on left hand" while doing twenty squats and sit ups.

'You can have the honour of bringing my chair back and then get lost.'

'Sorry, Sir. Thank you, Sir.'

Ramanan knew better than to ask Liew to clarify his second double-barrel answer. Liew would have been a nightmare witness in court with his 'No' and 'Yes' answers. The Lion was content to send No. 67 packing while he continued with the lesson. Fook Yew, a VI teacher's son, told his classmates later about his uncle with the same name.

'My uncle had brought out his own chopsticks when served spaghetti in a New York restaurant.

'"Wanna fork Sir?"

'"Me Malayan. Eat first. Then fork."'

Ramanan told his students never to ask anyone which school they came from. If they were from VI, they would tell them on their own. If they were not, then they should not embarrass them. As a student he was told 'you can tell a VI boy but you can't tell him anything'. He improved on it now. 'You can tell a VI teacher but you can't tell him anything.'

The annual athletic sports meet was exceptional. The headmaster expected every boy except those with wooden legs or medical certificates to run in the qualifying rounds starting with the cross-country run.

'Your MC must come from a medical doctor. A certificate from our Dr Lim who has a Ph.D like mine won't do.'

During the qualifying rounds a student collapsed and died on the athletic track. The next day Ramanan read out the regular circular about the athletic events for the day. The whole class responded in unison.

'Sure die lah.'

They paraphrased in chorus Tennyson's *The Charge of the Light Brigade* which they had rehearsed the previous afternoon.

Theirs not to reason why
Theirs but to do and die
Mr Ramanan to right of them
Sports Master to left of them
Headmaster in front of them
Volley'd and thunder'd.

Ramanan was unimpressed.

'You have heard of people dying in their sleep. So don't go to bed tonight.'

All of them turned up for the athletic rounds that day and thereafter.

While the Victorians had many victories in sport there was one major defeat by the Methodists Boys' School (MBS) attributed to an American teacher who introduced cheering Yankee-style.

The VI boys, brought up in the English tradition of understatement, cheered their team:

'Jolly good, good show, come on boys, well played.'

They were taken aback by the thundering yells that echoed round the football stadium:

'MBS! MBS!
Rah! Rah! Rah!
MBS! MBS!
Rah! Rah! Rah!

Zim! Boom! Bah!
Raaa—aah!'

The cheering went on relentlessly throughout the entire match. The MBS team was inspired. The gentlemanly VI team and its supporters were startled and demoralized. This even spilled over into the boys' attitude to away matches. A small still voice in the assembly hall was heard to ask:

'Why did we travel third class? Because there was no fourth!'

The wit evoked a deserved laughter, but no upgrade in class of travel.

Ramanan grumbled to his wife about the VI's defeat due to aggressive ungentlemanly behaviour and the students whining about travelling third class.

'Could it be a sign of worse things to come, Ayah?'

Mrs Vickneswari Ramanan was as fair as Ramanan was dark. They were called the kopi-susu couple. They had contrasting personalities. She applied talcum powder to her face as soon as she woke up. Since she woke up before the children did and went to bed after them, they wondered what she looked like without talcum powder. Fragrant white jasmine flowers ringed and perfumed the bun on her black hair. Ramanan whose grey hair was attributed to his wisdom called hers 'Indian-ink hair with white border'. Vertically below the talcum powder were sarees or sarongs in riotous colour contrasting with Ramanan's perpetual white-washed wear. She had such exquisitely beautiful hand writing that she become the calligraphic gladiator of the whole community. Relatives and neighbours sought her out to narrate their messages through her. She added her own garnishing, provoking laughter in the reader not intended by the narrator. However they avoided her at funerals. She kept a solemn face while whispering jokes about the participants including the mourners, making those near her guffaw.

'Look at those tears from our Sungei Klang crocodiles. They were fighting like roosters only last week.'

Some avoided direct eye contact with her because even then she could make them laugh from a distance with her mimicry.

When they left the house Ramanan walked briskly, Vickneswari followed six paces behind with the eldest child following six paces after her. In sixes the family Indian-filed following him on his outings.

His children were terrified of his temper. Vickneswari reassured them:

'Don't worry if he loses his temper. I will find it for him. Then I'll remind him not to be so careless the next time.'

Her passion was the Tamil film. She would grab any one of her children nearest to her by the wrist after their lunch with her announcement:

'I am taking you for a treat at the cinema. Hurry, the film is starting.'

She could walk right into the middle of a Tamil film and tell instantly who her hero was as he would be dressed wholly in traditional Indian attire and spoke in Tamil only. He was the one most polite to his parents, particularly his mother. The paragon of human virtue, he was the first to offer his blood for transfusion, even for the chief villain. The latter, in contrast always sported Western suits even in the hottest midday sun, peppering his conversation with English words.

He smoked, he drank, he swore, he womanized, he smuggled, he robbed, he gambled and, of course, he cheated. One feature about him told you that he was the crook. He spoke to his Tamil-speaking parents in alien and rude English. The first time his parents said anything to him his reply would be:

'Shadaaap!'

The next time his parents had the audacity to address him while he was busy plotting several crimes to be executed simultaneously with his henchmen, his second reply would be:

'Yeee diat!'

If his parents dared address him a third time he would dismiss their remarks with a:

'Naarn sense!'

Should his parents feel compelled to communicate with him again he would point to the main door of the house with his gun and bark at them:

'Gettout yeeediat!'

'He was so Westernized, Ayah,' Vickneswari rubbed it in.

Ramanan teased her yet again. 'Victoria if you are not reading world history or doing pooja, you're at the cinema or you're telling me the entire plot. Are you rehearsing to be a Tamil film actress?'

She grabbed at the opportunity:

'You have never seen a Tamil film. You Westernized rice Christians cannot appreciate our own culture. Your grandparents in Jaffna converted to fill their rice bowls and to get scholarships in Methodist mission schools in Ceylon. Although my parents named me Vickneswari and most people call me that or Vicki for short, you insist on calling me Victoria. You even speak Tamil with a nasal British accent. Do you want to be a karupu sutu vellai kaaran, Ayah?'

Queen Victoria's portrait lurched further left in late 1941 as the clouds of war gathered over the Pacific. Japanese armed forces moved through Siam. As their air force bombed strategic towns, their troops commandeered bicycles from Malayans and rode south, one of the few military invasions anywhere propelled by bicycles. The British had assumed that any external attack must come by sea in the south. Using lateral thinking the Japanese came by land from the north on 8 December 1941. By 12 January 1942 they had occupied Kuala Lumpur and by 15 February 'impregnable' Singapore.

School buildings in the towns were used by the Japanese military as barracks, stores, training centres and, in many cases, as the HQ for the kempeitai. With its attractive site on Petaling Hill above the commercial centre, the VI was an obvious choice. Queen Victoria's portrait lurched left down to horizontal as Emperor Hirohito advanced right up to have his picture taken.

Her spirit was not amused.

Mr Ramanan told his Victoria how Col. Watanabe Wataru had demanded that Malayans who had long submitted to British rule and 'indulged in the hedonistic and materialistic way of Western life' be taught seishin and be trained to endure hardship to get rid of this. Watanabe introduced Nippongo to replace English and Chinese which were abolished in schools. Every morning, every student and teacher had to stand at attention while facing east towards Tokyo and sing *Kimigayo*.

'May the Emperor's reign last ten thousand years . . .'

At the kunrenjo from 6 a.m. to 9 p.m. they breathed and lived seishin. Col. Watanabe had reminded the trainees that if they don't have seishin they count for nothing in the world. They must never give up anything, no matter how difficult.

Mr Ramanan observed that 'this period of subsistence on tapioca, cow herding and petty trading was the good news. The death railway in the north, the reign of terror with the kempeitai informers, spies, physical abuse, brutality, torture or imprisonment for a wide range of misdeeds (including the lesser ones of listening to the BBC or failure to bow low enough at Japanese sentry points), shortages of food and the hyper-inflation of their "banana" currency which featured bananas on their notes, that was the bad news.'

'You thought the British would be here forever. They have retreated. One day the Japanese will also have to retreat. Until then, let us be flexible. Pretend to play along with them, until we are a free people. Don't take them too seriously. We should outsmart them without their realizing it. Don't be trapped in the past, my dinosaur Ayah.'

'Play along? For you it's all play acting or a scene from a Tamil film. Why should I give in to these brutes?'

'I will fool the Japanese into thinking what I want them to think. I'm as miserable about the Japanese military occupation as you are. But instead of knocking my head on the wall, I'm concentrating on climbing over it.'

Ramanan continued giving private tuition classes in English secretly in his house.

'Be warned Ayah. Our neighbours say the Japanese are hunting down those who persist in teaching English. I am learning Japanese already. I even wear my home-made kimono every morning to create the right atmosphere.'

'Teaching English is what I do best and that's the only thing I can do. Will you give up your saree and sarong for a kimono permanently?'

'The kimono is temporary like everything else in life. It is just maya. The British colonial period was maya as is the Japanese now. Life itself is an illusion but within it I create mini-illusions with my acting. You don't have to be so rigid. That's why I keep the old photographs and you hold the negatives. Those negatives are typical of the way you think. I have started making tapioca cakes for sale. The military certainly won't mind. I might sell them some cakes or barter them for rice and sugar while wearing my kimono. The Asian bamboo bends with the wind and does not break. The trees that refuse to bend may crack in heavy storm. Like you refusing to learn Japanese and over-practising your British English.

'When we eat rice and curry on banana leaves, everyone else including the Chinese, Malay and European customers eat with their fingers but you stand out like a British stick-in-the-mud insisting on your fork and spoon. Your cousin Kuppusamy after spending a year in London calls himself Sam Cooper, BTE (Been to England). Could it be your influence Ayah? You expect me to walk at least six paces behind you to show the world that you are my superior, risking your life as you may step on a landmine first. While I carry the family photograph in my purse your wallet contains Queen Victoria's photo. If you are consistent in your male chauvinism you should be carrying Prince Albert's instead, Albert Ayah.

'I hope you don't become a white elephant like your Jaguar camouflaged and hidden in our backyard. There's no petrol available for us civilians but you don't need petrol to change your fixed way of thinking.'

'You know, I have always been hard on myself. I believe that discipline like charity begins at home and I practise it daily. I start my day at 4 a.m. and I go on till I fall apart at night barely able to finish my dinner notwithstanding your great cooking skills. In spite of coming from a very poor family, I refused any form of dowry from your wealthy parents. I learnt to love the English language from all the story books I read as a child. I suppose in those formative days I could not escape identifying the English language with everything British. I still remember how you guffawed and teased me when my students tried to grow daffodils in their little gardens after I recited Wordsworth several times to them. You said I was destined to "wander lonely as a cloud". This language has enabled my mind to travel freely from my very humble childhood home throughout the world and through time.

'The teachers in my English school not only taught me to read or write in English but to think in English. The language became my "window on the world" as my teachers promised me it would. I not only think in English, I even see in English. It is too late for me to switch and think in another language. I have gone too far into the language and into English literature to even think of retreating or making U-turns. If it is a sin to teach English, I would rather remove my false teeth and start being speechless than pretend to be what I am not. I have more doubts than you have. One of the few things in my life that I do not have doubts about is how useful, even powerful, the English language can be to anyone who masters it. Not just for the British or those in their colonies but for every man or woman on this planet including both of us. You say it is the language of our colonial past. My father introduced English to me in his own quaint way. Your Tamil films make it the language of villains. Use it, abuse it or adapt it for our part of the world but you cannot ignore it. King Canute could not turn back the tide in the eleventh century. The tide of English will continue regardless of Japanese military might today or any other force tomorrow. The assertive Americans speak and cheer in English even though their spelling is funny. I see it as the tongue of the future for the whole world.

'You are fortunate in being a bit of a linguist. You are at home in Tamil, English, Malay and Cantonese and now you are expanding your skills to elementary spoken Japanese.

'Many people try to be good at many things. Some become jacks of all trades and masters of none. I tried to specialize and excel in one thing. That one thing was literature in English. You think of many things at the same time. You say I am one-track-minded. I like to think that I am being focussed. Why can't we live and let live? Not only you and me but all of us, English-speaking, Japanese-speaking, Malay-, Tamil- and Chinese-speaking without the use of force on others.'

Ramanan cursed the darkness of the Japanese military period. Vickneswari struck a light for her pooja to Lord Ganesha as she spread thirunur across her forehead.

'If not for the Japanese we would not have realized what Asians can achieve. That's what some nationalists in India are saying. During the British times we Asians were employed only in junior posts. The British colonialists kept us down in subtle ways. Now we have to bow physically to the Japanese but we can be promoted to senior positions. Look at what Hitler is doing to the Jews in Europe. War can turn armies into barbarians and savages. It is the war and the military you should curse, not the Japanese. The Japanese have opened the eyes of all Asians in spite of their brutal methods. Of course it is most risky to go out. You have to remember to pay respects to every sentry on duty, since they represent the Japanese Emperor.'

'I should know. If we are cycling anywhere and see a Japanese sentry post we have to leap off our bicycles and bow very low. Then we have to seek the sentry's permission. If he grants it we have to bow very low to thank him. At any occasion if we did not bow low enough we would be punished. We would be required to stand in the blazing sun and hold a heavy stone over our heads for hours. If we slackened at this, our heads would be chopped off and stuck on top of a long pole for the entire local population to see. On seeing this skull, other cyclists and motorists would stop their bicycles or cars even further before reaching the sentry post. They would start bowing earlier and much lower, taking the maximum precautions to ensure they did not offend the prickly sentries.'

Vickneswari travelled by rickshaw to the market. The rickshaw pullers would jostle around her. She was their patron saint from the heavens of Court Hill, the only one in Kuala Lumpur who did not bargain over the fare. The rickshaw pullers wore rubber soles tied on one end to their ankles and the other end to their big toes. Fleet of foot, they whizzed through the streets of Kuala Lumpur in an era which knew nothing of traffic lights, speed limits and parking tickets. They roamed freely. They were there before the tramcar, the taxi and the bus. Their filling stations and petrol stations were the coffee shops and the itinerant hawkers. They were the major transport system of Kuala Lumpur during the Japanese occupation.

Late at night, when Ramanan and Vickneswari listened to the news over the radio, their children were posted in the drains along the boundary fences of their houses on look-out duty. They learnt to distinguish between the various sounds. These ranged from the clicks of the long swords on the tarmac to the distant sound of the soldiers' boots.

Sometimes the soldiers came and rounded up the men to work on the 'death' railway in Burma. Some young men came back with no arms or no legs, scarred, psychologically and physically, with festering sores. Were they the lucky ones? The others never came back.

Arbitrary brutality was part of everyday life, often occasioned by no more than an accident or a misunderstanding. A dog barked at some Japanese soldiers. 'The dog should have read

Sherlock Holmes,' remarked Fook Yew, 'then we'd all have been better off.' Fook Yew's father made the mistake of politeness.

He shooed the dog away so that it would no longer disturb the serenity of the conqueror. The soldiers slapped and kicked him furiously. It was not his dog and he was just being a good Samaritan. They did not ask whose dog it was; they slapped first and never asked afterwards. Vickneswari who knew more Japanese than the rest of the neighbourhood clarified matters to them. It was not good enough. They barged into Fook Yew's house and insisted that the dog be killed immediately before their eyes. Every man and boy (but not their dogs) went scouring throughout the entire neighbourhood for an hour in vain. Meanwhile, Vickneswari continued trying to pacify them in her best Japanese. They left only after warning them that they would be back to see personally that the dog was killed. All because a single dog which did not belong to Fook Yew did what dogs normally do, namely bark. Unlike Oliver Twist, no one asked for more.

Ramanan was walking once, when he saw a military truck filled with coconuts overtake him. It then stopped at the roundabout nearby. He froze and watched as a number of Japanese soldiers jumped out. The soldiers carried wooden stakes which they drove into the roundabout. Then they nailed planks on them to shape them into a 'T'. Finally, they arranged the coconuts on the stakes. Flies were swarming round them. It was then that he realized that they were not coconuts.

They were decapitated heads.

He took a long time to recover from that trauma. It explained something else as well. Much later teachers in the VI would chide their students in exasperation on how they had tried to repeat their lessons to them.

'We have been trying to drill this into your coconuts for days,' they would exclaim as they threw their chalks and dusters at them. Yet the VI Lion was conspicuous in never referring to the students' heads as 'coconuts'.

As the years of the occupation passed, Ramanan continued to irritate his Victoria with his whining about Japanese military misdeeds.

'Victoria, did you know that trainees at these kunrenjos had to march in the hot sun with their entire military gear on their backs for almost forty miles? Of course there was no mercy shown. Even those who were down to their knees, exhausted, were forced to crawl the last few miles. At first we thought that the Japanese invaded our country to grab our rubber, tin and palm oil. Now I hear that they were dogs in the manger. They just wanted to make sure that they could prevent the Allies from having access to our economic wealth. The Japanese do not have enough ships to transport these raw materials to their industries at home.

'They thought they were very smart and tried to make petrol and oil from our rubber but the rubber particles choked up the engines. These barbarians cannibalized the dredges from our world-famous tin industry to grab machinery for their industries.

'The British eat bread and wheat products whereas the Japanese are rice eaters like us. Yet, under the Japanese, we have to import even more rice than ever before. We also have to import medicines, soap, all our cloth and clothings. They force our farmers to surrender their own crops. Now they have no choice but to look the other way when rice is smuggled from Siam or Burma. They have literally broken the very rice bowl of almost everyone in Malaya. As a matter of survival we are forced to grow our own root crops and to be grateful for tapioca, sweet potatoes and your rasa velli kelangu.

'During the British regime even the humble office boy in the VI had all the basic necessities from being able to eat rice at least for two meals a day to being able to brush his teeth everyday with toothbrush and toothpaste. Now all of us have to chew the ends of twigs which have fibre for our primitive toothbrushes. For toothpaste we are reduced to ground charcoal or salt. Look at the concoctions people are experimenting with, mixing ash, cinnamon bark, flowers, leaves, lime, palm oil and what not, just to produce a bar of soap.

'The price of a miserable sarong has rocketed from less than $2 to $1000. An entire household has to share one sarong. If the wife has to go out, the poor husband has to stay home. Imagine that!

'I have heard that bodies were floating in the Sungei Gombak, tied with ropes; some were only heads, others were only legs.'

'But Ayah you have to admit that the reign of terror in the early days that you complained about has been replaced with black markets and boredom. No doubt there is still danger and deprivation but the terror is much less now and at worst only sporadic.'

Meanwhile, the Japanese military were on the lookout for coconuts, chickens, Chinese and English language teachers.

'Now we are hunting for *two*-legged dogs.'

Early one morning a Japanese military truck loaded with teachers en route to their death sentence stopped at Ramanan's gate. He was on the Japanese military's wanted list as an over-zealous English language teacher to be silenced permanently. A soldier approached the front door of his house while calling out for him. When Japanese soldiers approached Malayans they were accustomed to the latter retreating or at best freezing on the spot. Instead Vickneswari who was practising her Japanese wearing her kimono at that time ran out of the house towards him:

'Ohayoh gozaimasu,' she began with a low bow before her pre-emptive strike:

'I'd like to know where that useless man is too! He has abandoned me and all my children. If I find him I'll peel his skin off just for a start. Then I'll . . .'

She went on on the top of her voice and made several angry and melodramatic gestures about what she was going to do to her husband that a stepmother or mother-in-law in a Tamil film would be proud of.

'Let me go with you in your truck and we'll search for him together. But I get to assault him first . . .'

The Japanese soldier had never seen a non-Japanese woman in a kimono in Malaya. Seeing Vickneswari in her unusual outfit charging towards him made him quite disoriented. For the first time since the Japanese invasion of Malaya, a Japanese soldier did something quite out of character. He retreated. Not merely that. He went so far with his truck he never came back again. He reckoned that the punishment that she planned to mete out to her husband was more severe than the mere death sentence he had on offer.

The Japanese military truck disappeared from view and from earshot completely. Long after that Ramanan who had been crouching in the garden behind the house emerged. Vickneswari felt he moved in even slower motion than the stars staging a fight or a romantic sequence in a Tamil film. He had removed his false teeth to make himself look much older. He had practised saying to the soldiers if he was caught:

'I've rethireth anth am thoo olth tho theeth Englith.'

Ramanan began to say and to do things he had never ever done before. For the first time in his life he called his wife 'My Queen'.

'You . . . literally saved my life. Forgive me . . . for underestimating you and not listening to you all these years.'

Yet again he did something else for the first time in his life. The Lion of the VI staff handed over the keys of his dearly beloved Jaguar to the just-discovered Tigress of Asia.

His newly crowned 'Queen' gazed at the keys jangling in his erstwhile fearsome palm still shaking with fear. She turned to his pale and gaunt face without his false teeth for the first time, too.

'The British King nearly died . . . Long live the Asian Queen . . . eh?'

'Queen' **Vickneswari R** tilted her face upwards to the right. She was amused.

Kimmy

Ovidia Yu

Frankie Ong was one of the junior counsellors at the YMCA camp that year. Junior counsellors did all the things that counsellors couldn't be bothered with—like counting kids before swimming, counting kids after swimming, keeping kids quiet during rest hours and rummaging in the storeroom for extra bedding.

Another of their duties was waiting, after the camp was over, for the last kids to be picked up by their parents. Which was why Frankie Ong was waiting with Kitty and me in the nearly closed-up hall at 7 p.m., with all the fans off and all the chairs folded up and stacked against the walls.

Frankie Ong was looking terribly irritated. All the other kids had left by 5 p.m. and all the other counsellors had gone too. I kept very quiet. It's better to be quiet when people are in a Mood. Mom was very often in a Mood. Right at that moment, however, she was in Indonesia with Uncle Wang, so it wasn't any good Frankie Ong calling our apartment every ten minutes like he was doing. Mom had sacked Ali Lan and Geok Min like she did every now and then, and there was no one about to answer the phone.

I told Frankie that Mom wouldn't be back in Singapore for another week, at least, but Kitty said, 'Don't listen to Kimmy, she's an awful liar.'

Since Kitty was twelve and two years older than me, Frankie

Ong believed her. I didn't mind. I wouldn't tell him that Mom had said for the fortune she forked out for the camp and everything they could damn well keep us a week more. He probably wouldn't have believed that either.

Frankie strode over to the telephone. (Again.)

'I'm hungry,' I whined to Kitty, because I was.

'Oh, shut up,' Kitty said impatiently. She was trying to hear what Frankie Ong was saying over the phone, but she dug into her bag and gave me a stick of Wrigley's Juicy Fruit Gum. I put it into my mouth, but it didn't help much. I decided to listen to Frankie too. He was just saying . . .

'—just the two of them. Kitty and Kimmy Seow. Twelve and nine—'

'I'm ten,' I said, but he didn't listen. Nobody listens to me, but that doesn't bother me.

'—no, they aren't crying or anything. No, not upset at all . . . I've been trying but no one answers . . . but it's already seven-something, I can't stay here all night . . .'

Then he made a lot of listening noises like 'Yeah, I see,' 'Uh-huh' and finally, 'OK—OK—OK' in a frustrated sort of tone. Then he came back to us.

'You're sure there's no one else I can call to come and pick you up?'

'You could call our grandparents,' I said, 'except—'

'Except what?' Frankie Ong demanded.

'Except they live in Hong Kong,' Kitty snapped. 'Stop that, Kimmy!'

I was staggering around, pretending I had been shot in the stomach. I staggered a bit more and fell down on the floor. Kitty nudged me with her foot.

'You'll have to excuse her,' she said, 'Kimmy's very young for her age.'

'Which is ten, not nine,' I put in.

'The floor's dirty, Kimmy.' Frankie Ong hauled me to a sitting position then sat down beside me on the dirty floor.

'Look, you two, suppose I call a taxi and send you back first.'

'The apartment's all locked up,' I said.

'Always is when Mom's out,' Kitty added. 'Look, Frankie, why don't you just go on home. Mom will turn up sooner or later and we'll be just fine till she does. I can handle Kimmy till then.'

'I don't need to be handled,' I said.

'I think you should just go on home first,' Kitty said again. I knew what she was planning. She had the key to the backdoor of Mom's Lucky Plaza boutique. We could slip in once it closed and spend the night there.

'I can't just leave you here alone like that,' Frankie Ong said wearily. 'I just spoke to Mr Tan on the phone. He said to just wait and see what happens.'

I was counting 'justs' on my fingers, having noted that Frankie used them a lot.

'What we could do is go back to my place first. I live quite near here. We can leave a note with the Jaga with my address and you kids come back with me first. Could your parents have had an accident?'

'It'll be in the papers tomorrow,' Kitty shrugged.

'Is there any dinner at your place?' I asked.

'Yes.' Frankie Ong said. That seemed to settle things. He went off to find the Jaga.

'But what if Mom comes here?' I asked Kitty.

'She won't, dummy,' Kitty said.

'But you said, wasn't it, that she was turning up?'

'Oh, shut up, Kimmy,' Kitty said.

I shut up and followed them out. Kitty carried my bag for me.

What Mr Tan knew about Kathryn Seow was that she owned a modelling agency, two boutiques and shares in a restaurant. She was a very rich lady. Very rich ladies often donated large sums of money to institutions that were nice to their little girls. Very rich ladies were also often absent-minded. No reason at all, Mr Tan told Frankie Ong, to make a fuss or call the police just because she hadn't picked up her daughters after the camp. Frankie Ong would simply have to keep an eye on them for a few days, just until their mother turned up. She would be very apologetic, very grateful.

What Mr Tan didn't know about Kathryn Seow was a great deal more interesting. When, as a teenager, she'd arrived in Singapore (from Hong Kong) she'd had a brief affair with an American businessman.

The American businessman started her off on her modelling career and still sent her money for Kitty and tips on high fashion. (He was in that line too.) That was why Kathryn Seow rather liked Kitty, even though Kitty had a square jaw, a flat nose and showed great potential as a wrestler. Once she had broken Kimmy's arm across her knee, rather like one might break a ruler. Kitty had been much nicer to Kimmy after that. Kathryn hadn't really minded. She didn't like Kimmy much.

Kimmy was small and some people said she was pretty. She looked like her father, who had looked a lot like Malcom MacDowell. Kathryn Seow had meant to marry him, but after a few months together in London (she had been at a designer's course, he studying dentistry), he had gone back to Australia and promptly married a childhood sweetheart. When Kimmy was born (back in Singapore) Kathryn sent her off to him care of Qantas. Ron sent the baby right back, without even a note, but plus a bad cold. Kathryn put the baby in the oven and turned on the gas, but the servant took her out before she suffocated. After that, Kathryn kept Kimmy around, though she sacked the servant. She still didn't like Kimmy very much, though. Kimmy was beginning to look a lot like Malcolm MacDowell.

Mr Tan didn't know all this, so he couldn't have told Frankie Ong, who consequently didn't believe Kimmy when she said that her father was in Australia and Kitty's father in America. Kitty said that Kimmy would never accept it, but their father had been American and had P-A-S-S-E-D A-W-A-Y in '76.

Frankie Ong deduced that Kimmy was a sensitive kid with a vivid imagination.

We stayed at Frankie Ong's house for five days altogether. Frankie Ong's father was really dead. They had a picture of him in the living room and they had tins of joss sticks in front of it. Frankie Ong's mother put a plate of fruit in front of it too. Because she only spoke Malay and Hokkien, we had a hard time communicating. Our servants had only spoken Cantonese and that was all I could speak.

Frankie had three brothers at home—Danny, Bobby and Kenny. There were two sisters too, Mei Lin and Met Hwa. Another sister was studying in Australia. I told him that that was where my father was, but he didn't believe me.

I really liked it in Frankie Ong's house. It was huge and on stilts even though it wasn't any place near the sea. I thought it was on stilts so that when the sea came up it wouldn't get wet, but Mrs Ong told me it was for when it flooded during rainstorms. I hoped and hoped that it would rainstorm while we were there so I could see the water come right up the drive and under the house but it didn't rain a drop. I'm not a very lucky person.

Frankie Ong grew resigned to having us there. He still made frantic phone calls to Mr Tan but they were sounding less frantic after Mr Tan had got in touch with Emmelina, the manageress of Mom's boutique in Specialist Centre, and Mr Anderson, Mom's lawyer, and been told by both of them that Mom was on a working holiday, she was often absent-minded and to please keep an eye on the girls while they tried to get in touch with her.

Once Frankie knew for sure we wouldn't be stuck with him for good, he became better-tempered. In fact, he was pretty nice and Mrs Ong, his mother, was simply wonderful. She was a great cook and never slapped anybody. She asked about the scar that ran down my back from my ear. She saw it when she was plaiting up my hair. I told her that I'd fallen on to a glass coffee table and smashed it and Mom just sliced down my back with a sliver of glass to teach me a lesson for not taking care of her things. Mrs Ong's other son Danny looked and said, 'How many stitches?' Danny was studying to be a doctor.

'Oh rubbish,' Kitty said when asked. 'Kimmy's always making up stories like that. She broke the table and cut herself, that's all. Don't listen to her—she's an awful liar.'

Frankie pulled me on to his lap. He often did that after he got to like us better. I liked it too. It felt cosy. I started pulling the pens out of his pocket. He always had coloured felt pens that I liked to draw with.

'Did your mother—no, put that down, Kimmy, and listen to me—Kimmy, sit still; tell me honestly: did your mother really do that to you?'

I tried to wriggle off his lap, but he wouldn't let me.

'No,' I said. Then I giggled and sang in Kitty's voice, 'I'm an awful liar!'

'Stop that!' Kitty said, but she wasn't really mad at me. Later on she slipped out and bought me a packet of dried coconut strips from the Indian shop down the road. Kitty was very good to me.

Finally, we heard from Mom herself. She called one night and talked to Frankie and Mrs Ong. She charmed them completely. She's a very charming person and she smells very good too. She said she would arrive in Singapore on Thursday night and come over to pick us up on Friday.

'I don't want to go home,' I told Frankie. 'Can't you keep me?'

'So sweet, she is,' Bobby Ong said. He patted my cheek. I stuck out my tongue at him, rudely.

'Kimmy!' said Frankie sternly, meaning it wasn't right. I wound my arms around him and stuck out my tongue at him too, but not nastily.

'Who wants to keep you? You're so naughty!' Frankie said. He stroked my hair. 'Your mother doesn't want you. I don't want you, what is Kimmy going to do? . . . No, Kimmy, I was just joking, Kimmy; come, don't cry, of course your mother wants you . . .'

Mrs Ong put her arms around me and scolded her son for talking about my mother in front of me. Of course I missed my mother, but never mind, tomorrow she would be back and I would be able to go home and everything would be all right.

Mrs Ong let me do the washing up with her, which I liked very much. They washed all their plates and things by hand, one by one, with just a mop thing and soap water out of an old ice-cream tub.

Frankie taught Kitty and Kimmy to play checkers. He played three games with Kimmy, then it was Kitty's turn. Kitty played to win, biting her lower lip in determination, and he was finding it harder and harder to beat her. Concentrating, they forgot all about Kimmy, who wandered into Frankie and Bobby's room to look at Frankie's old Marvel comics, at the bottom of the cupboard.

Suddenly, Kimmy screamed, and again and again. Kitty was on her feet and away before Frankie knew what was happening. By the time he reached the bedroom, Kitty was on her knees beside the sobbing Kimmy, rocking her gently. Bobby, still wet from his shower, was standing uncomfortably against the wall, holding his towel in front of him.

'I don't know.' He said in response to Frankie's queries, 'I didn't see her . . . I just came in and started dressing—and then she saw me and just screamed and screamed. I didn't do anything—I didn't. I think she hit her head on the shelf. I don't know what happened to her.'

Kimmy was clinging to her sister, just clinging to her and crying and trembling. She had wet herself. Frankie had never seen anyone so terrified before. She reminded him of the white rabbit he had once had to chloroform for a biology practical.

'It's all right,' Kitty was soothing her. Obviously this was nothing new to her. 'No one's going to hurt you. See? I've made him go away; there's no one going to hurt you. Kitty's going to make it all right. Don't cry. It's all right.'

Kimmy began to calm down. She cried more naturally, instead of in the harsh sobs that were half-screams. Kitty went on rocking her gently, but it was clear that the worst was over.

'What was that?' Frankie asked, very subdued. He wondered if it could have been a fit. He had never seen anyone in a fit but had heard it was frightening, and what he had just seen was frightening.

'Uncle Wang—he's our Mom's husband—sometimes he hurts Kimmy. She's always like this when—I think she's just a bit scared. She must have thought Bobby—I mean, if she just saw him there without his clothes on, she must have thought—'

Bobby was frightened nearly to tears himself. 'I didn't see her,' he protested. 'I mean, she was sitting on the floor behind your bed, how was I to . . .'

Mrs Ong and her daughters had arrived by then, demanding in excited Hokkien to be told exactly what had happened.

Kitty, who had already picked up quite a bit of Hokkien, told them that Kimmy had slipped and knocked her head on the shelf. She showed them the bruise. Kimmy always made a great fuss about nothing, she said. She looked sharply at Frankie and Bobby, who remained silent: Bobby in relief, Frankie in growing bewilderment.

Kitty put Kimmy to bed and stroked her till she went to sleep. Frankie went in to see her later. The bruise was swollen and angry red on her left temple. Danny had offered to put something on it, but his attempts to look at the damage only brought fresh tears from Kimmy. Danny gave up, with dirty looks at Bobby, muttering that no one got hysterics over a little knock on the head.

Frankie asked Kitty what it was that their stepfather had done to Kimmy that frightened her so much. Kitty couldn't remember what she had said—she had been too worried about Kimmy—and didn't know what he was talking about.

In their room, Bobby was still miserably insisting, 'I didn't do anything to frighten her, you know. I wouldn't.'

'Yeah, yeah.' Frankie was vaguely sorry for his brother, but had other things on his mind. It was Kitty that most worried him. What Kitty had told Bobby and himself when her guard was down, what she had fabricated for his mother and sisters. Her denying the original story later. Kitty lied.

Lying in bed, his mind went over and over Kimmy's stories, but Kimmy was a liar. But they only had that on Kitty's word, and Kitty was a liar. He had just seen for himself. What if Kimmy hadn't been lying? Then their mother was a monster. But he had spoken to their mother himself and she had been a sweet, charming woman.

When he finally fell asleep, Frankie dreamt of an enormous woman holding a crying Kimmy between thumb and forefinger and slashing her back with a glass shard. There was blood all over, and the little Kimmy was struggling to get to him, 'I don't want to go home,' it whimpered. 'Can't you keep me?' Frankie woke in a cold sweat. In the hot, dark room he could hear Bobby muttering in his sleep, 'I didn't, I didn't, I didn't.' Frankie did not dare go back to sleep.

The next day, he asked Kimmy what it was her Uncle Wang had done that scared her so much. A very subdued, red-eyed Kimmy shrugged. She was all dressed up, ready to be picked up by her mother. She scuffed one small foot against the other.

'Oh nothing,' she said carelessly. 'I guess I lied about that.'

'It was Kitty that told me about that. Does Kitty lie too?'

'No. Only me.'

'Then tell me what happened.'

Kimmy looked confused, 'I thought it was a lie. Did it really happen then? But Kitty told me it was a lie. I don't know. It's so hard to tell. Will you play checkers with me? Will you let me win? Just one more time? Please? Please? Before Mom comes, just one more time, please?'

They played checkers and he let her win. Winning made

her so happy because Kimmy didn't get to win very often.

It was nice to see Mom again. She had bought a new car and had a new boyfriend with her. When Kitty asked, she said Uncle Wang had had to stay in Indonesia on a business thing. I wasn't sorry.

'Silly little goosey,' Mom said, 'what have you done to your face?' She touched her fingers lightly on my forehead. It hurt and I pushed her hand away.

'It was because of that horrible man without any clothes on,' I started to explain.

'What horrible—' Mom began. Kitty stepped in as usual.

'Oh Mom, you know how Kimmy makes up stories. She was clumsy and knocked her head looking for comics, that's all. Don't listen to her.'

'Was it true?' Mom asked me. 'Kimmy, tell me the truth now.'

I wasn't sure what I was supposed to say. I edged away from Mom. Kitty shook her head sharply and I was relieved.

'No, it was just a lie; I'm sorry, Mom, please don't hit me—' The last came out as a half-scream as she raised her hand, but it was only to brush back a wisp of hair. I felt really stupid and giggled nervously.

'Kimmy—' both Mom and Frankie said at the same time. But they both stopped there and did not go on. Just stood there staring at each other with horrible looks on their faces. Kitty shut her eyes like she was praying. I fidgeted. Still they did not move, but it was like they had a lot to say, only it wouldn't come out. I wondered if it was really happening or whether it would turn out to be another lie, but I couldn't ask Kitty. She wasn't moving either, and her eyes were still closed. Mom's new boyfriend cleared his throat. He was dark like a Malay, but had a Chinese face.

'Children have such vivid imaginations, don't they?' he said. 'If you'll let us know how much—I mean, we'll give you something for keeping an eye on the girls. They had a good time, I'm sure. When I was young it was quite an adventure.'

But no one was listening to him. Mom and Frankie could have been stone, but their eyes were alive, and how they hated each other. I thought they could just be standing there forever.

Mr Tang's Girls

Shirley Geok-Lin Lim

Kim Mee caught her sister smoking in the garden. It was a dry, hot day with sunshine bouncing off the Straits. The mix of blue waves and light cast an unpleasant glare in the garden, whose sandy soil seemed to burn and melt under her feet. Everyone stayed indoors on such Saturday afternoons: Ah Kong and Mother sleeping in the darkened sunroom and the girls reading magazines or doing homework throughout the house. Kim Mee had painted her toenails a new dark-red colour; she was going to a picnic in Tanjong Bederah on Sunday and wanted to see the effect of the fresh colour on her feet bare on sand. The garden behind the house sloped down to the sea in a jungle of sea-almond trees and pandanus; a rusted barbed-wire fence and a broken gate were the only signs that marked where the garden stopped being a garden and became sea-wilderness. A large ciku tree grew by the fence, its branches half within the garden and half flung over the stretch of pebbles, driftwood, ground-down shells and rotting organisms which led shallowly down to the muddy tidal water. It was under the branches hidden by the trunk that Kim Li was smoking. She was taken by surprise, eyes half-shut, smoke gently trailing from her nostrils, and gazing almost tenderly at the horizon gleaming like a high-tension wire in the great distance.

'Ah ha! Since when did you start smoking?' Kim Mee said softly, coming suddenly around the tree trunk.

Unperturbed, without a start, Kim Li took another puff, elegantly holding the cigarette to the side of her mouth. Her fingers curled exaggeratedly as she slowly moved the cigarette away. She said with a drawl, 'Why should I tell you?'

'Ah Kong will slap you.'

She snapped her head around and frowned furiously. 'You sneak! Are you going to tell him?'

'No, of course not!' Kim Mee cried, half-afraid. There was only two years' difference in age between them, but Kim Li was a strange one. She suffered from unpredictable moods which had recently grown more savage. 'You're mean. Why do you think I'll tell?' Kim Mee was angry now at having been frightened. In the last year, she had felt herself at an advantage over her eldest sister whose scenes, rages, tears and silences were less and less credited. The youngest girl, Kim Yee, at twelve years old, already seemed more mature than Kim Li. And she, at fifteen, was clearly superior. She didn't want to leave Kim Li smoking under the cool shade with eyes sophisticatedly glazed and looking advanced and remote. Moving closer, she asked, 'Where did you get the cigarette?'

'Mind your own business,' Kim Li replied calmly.

'Is it Ah Kong's cigarette? Yes, I can see it's a Lucky Strike.' Kim Li dropped the stub and kicked sand over it. Smoke still drifted from the burning end, all but buried under the mound. 'What do you know of life?' she asked loftily and walked up the white glaring path past the bathhouse and up the wooden sidestairs.

Kim Mee felt herself abandoned as she watched her sister's back vanish through the door. 'Ugly witch!' She glanced at her feet where the blood-red toenails twinkled darkly.

Saturdays were, as long as she could remember, quiet days, heavy and slow with the grey masculine presence of their father who spent most of the day, with Mother beside him, resting, gathering strength in his green leather chaise in the sunroom. Only his bushy eyebrows, growing in a straight line like a scar across his forehead, seemed awake. The hair there was turning white, bristling in wisps that grew even more luxuriant as the hair on his head receded and left the tight high skin mottled with discoloured specks. Now and again he would speak in sonorous tones, but, chiefly, he dozed or gazed silently out of the windows which surrounded the room to the low flowering trees which Ah Chee, the family servant, tended and through the crisp green leaves to his private thoughts.

They were his second family. Every Friday he drove down from Kuala Lumpur, where his first wife and children lived, in time for dinner. On Saturdays, the girls stayed home. No school activity, no friend, no party, no shopping trip took them out of the house. Their suppressed giggles, lazy talk, muted movements and uncertain sighs constituted his sense of home. And every Saturday, the four girls played their part: they became daughters whose voices were to be heard like cheerful music in the background, but never loudly or intrusively.

Every Saturday they made high tea at five. The girls peeled hard-boiled eggs, the shells carefully cracked and coming clean off the firm whites, and mashed them with butter into a spread. They cut fresh loaves of bread into thick yellow slices and poured mugs of tea into which they stirred puddles of condensed milk and rounded teaspoons of sugar. Ah Kong would eat only fresh bread, thickly buttered and grained with sprinkles of sugar, but he enjoyed watching his daughters eat like European mems. He brought supplies from Kuala Lumpur: tomatoes, tins of devilled ham and Kraft cheese, and packages of Bird's Blancmange. Saturday tea was when he considered himself a successful father and fed on the vision of his four daughters eating toast and tomato slices while his quiet wife poured tea by his side.

'I say, Kim Bee,' Kim Yee said, swallowing a cracker, 'are you going to give me your blouse?'

The two younger girls were almost identical in build and height. Kim Yee, in the last year shooting up like a vine, in fact being slightly stockier and more long-waisted than Kim Bee. Teatime with Ah Kong was the occasion to ask for dresses, presents, money and other favours, and Kim Yee, being the youngest, was the least abashed in her approach.

'Yah! You're always taking my clothes. Why don't you ask for the blouse I'm wearing?'

'May I? It's pretty, and I can wear it to Sunday School.'

Breathing indignation, Kim Bee shot a look of terrible fury and imploration at her mother, 'She's impossible. . .' But she swallowed the rest of her speech, for she also had a request to make to Ah Kong, who was finally paying attention to the squabble.

'Don't you girls have enough to wear? Why must you take clothes from each other?'

Like a child who knows her part, Mother shifted in her chair and said good-naturedly, 'Girls grow so fast, Peng. Their clothes are too small for them in six months. My goodness, Kim Yee's dresses are so short she doesn't look decent in them.'

'Me too, Ah Kong!' Kim Mee added. 'I haven't had a new dress since Chinese New Year.'

'Chinese New Year was only three months ago,' Ah Kong replied, shooting up his eyebrows, whether in surprise or annoyance no one knew.

'But I've grown an inch since then!'

'And I've grown three inches in one year,' Kim Bee said.

'Ah Kong, your daughters are becoming women,' Kim Li said in an aggressive voice. She was sitting to one side of her father, away from the table, not eating or drinking, kicking her long legs rhythmically throughout the meal. She wore her blue school shorts which fitted tightly above the thighs and stretched across the bottom, flattening the weight which ballooned curiously around her tall, skinny frame. Her legs, like her chest, were skinny, almost fleshless. They were long and her ankles rose to meet the backs of her knees with hardly a suggestion of a calf. In the tight shorts she didn't appear feminine or provocative, merely unbalanced, as if the fat around the hips and bottom were a growth, a goitre draped on the lean trunk.

Everyone suddenly stopped talking. Mother opened her mouth and brought out a gasp, the sisters stopped chewing and looked away into different directions. Kim Mee was furious because Ah Kong's face was reddening. There would be no money for new clothes if he lost his temper.

'And you, you are not dressed like a woman,' he replied without looking at her. 'How dare you come to the table like a half-naked slut!' He had always been careful to avoid such language in his house, but her aggressive interruption aroused him.

'At least I don't beg you for clothes. And what I wear is what you give me. It's not . . .'

'Shut up!' he roared. 'You . . .'

'Go to your room,' Mother said to Kim Li before he could finish. Her voice was placid as if such quarrels were an everyday occurrence. If Ah Kong's bunched-up brows and protruding veins all balled up like a fist above his bony beak put her off, she didn't show it. 'Peng,' she continued, sweet-natured as ever, 'maybe tomorrow we can go over the cost of some new clothes. The girls can shop for some cheap materials, and Ah Chee and I will sew a few simple skirts and blouses. We won't have to pay a tailor. They'll be very simple clothes, of course, because it's been so long since I've stitched anything . . .' So she chatted on, rolling a cosy domestic mat before him. Soon, they were spreading more butter and drinking fresh cups of tea.

Kim Li did not leave the table till Ah Kong's attention was unravelled; then she stretched herself out of the chair, hummed, and sauntered to her room, casual as a cat and grinning from ear to ear. Her humming wasn't grating, but it was loud enough to reach the dining room. What could Ah Kong do about it? He had again slipped into silence drowsing along with the buzz of feminine discussion acknowledging that, Sunday, he would once again open his purse and drive off in the warm evening to their grateful goodbyes.

But there was Saturday night and the evening meal late at nine and the soft hours till eleven when his girls would sit in the living room with long, washed hair reading *Her World* and *Seventeen*, selecting patterns for their new frocks. And by midnight, everyone would be asleep.

There was Ah Chee snoring in her back room among empty cracker tins and washed Ovaltine jars. He had acquired her when his second wife had finally given in to his determined courting and, contrary to her Methodist upbringing, married him in a small Chinese ceremony. The three of them had moved in immediately after the ceremony to this large wooden house on Old Beach Road, and, gradually, as the rooms filled up with beds and daughters, so also had Ah Chee's room filled up with the remains of meals. She never threw out a tin, bottle or jar. The banged-up tins and tall bottles she sold to the junkman; those biscuit tins stamped with gaudy roses or toffee tins painted with ladies in crinoline gowns or Royal Guardsmen in fat fur hats she hoarded and produced each New Year to fill with love letters, bean cakes, and kueh bulu.

Ah Kong approved of her as much as, perhaps even more than, he approved of his wife. Her parsimonious craggy face, those strong bulging forearms, the loose folds of her black trousers flapping as she padded barefoot and cracked sole from kitchen to garden, from one tidied room to another waiting to be swept, these were elements he looked forward to each Friday as much as he looked forward to his wife's vague smile and soft shape in bed. Ah Chee had lived in the house for seventeen years, yet her influence was perceivable only in a few rooms.

Ah Kong seldom looked into Ah Chee's room which, he knew, was a junk heap gathered around a narrow board bed with a chicken wire strung across the bare window. But, at midnight, when he rose to check the fastenings at the back door and the bolts on the front, he looked into every room where his daughters slept. Here was Bee's, connected to her parents' through a bathroom. A Bible lay on her bed. She slept, passionately hugging a bolster to her face, half-suffocated, the pyjama-top riding high and showing a midriff concave and yellow in the dimness.

Across the central corridor Kim Yee stretched corpse-like and rigid, as if she had willed herself to sleep or were still awake under the sleeping mask, the stuffed bear and rabbit exhibited at the foot of her bed like nursery props, unnecessary now that the play was over. He sniffed in Kim Mee's room; it smelt of talcum and hairspray. The memory of other rooms came to mind, rooms which disgusted him as he wrestled to victory with their occupants. But no pink satin pillows or red paper flowers were here; a centrefold of the British singers, the Beatles, was taped to one wall and blue checked curtains swayed in the night breeze.

Kim Mee slept curled against her bolster. In a frilly babydoll, her haunches curved and enveloped the pillow like a woman with her lover. He hated the sight but didn't cover her in case she should wake. There was a time when he would walk through the house looking into every room, and each silent form would fill him with pleasure, that they should belong to him, depend on his homecoming and fall asleep in his presence, innocent and pure. Now the harsh scent of hairspray stagnated in the air; its metallic fragrance was clammy and chilled, a cheap and thin cover over the daughter whose delicate limbs were crowned with an idol's head aureoled and agonized by bristling rollers. Again the recollection of disgust tinged his thoughts, and he hesitated before Kim Li's room. He didn't know what to expect any more of his daughters, one spending her allowance on lipstick, nail polish, Blue Grass Cologne, and this other somehow not seeming quite right.

Kim Li was not yet asleep. With knees raised up, she sat in bed reading by the minute diagonal light of the bed lamp. He stopped at the door but could not retreat quickly enough. She turned a baleful look. 'What do you want?'

'It's twelve o'clock. Go to asleep,' he said curtly, feeling that that was not exactly what he should say. However, he seldom had to think about what to say in this house, and his self-consciousness was extreme. Suddenly he noticed her. She had cut her hair short, when, he couldn't tell. He remembered once noticing that her hair was long and that she had put it up in a ponytail, which made her unpretty face as small as his palm. Tonight, her hair was cropped short carelessly in the front and sides so that what might have been curls shot away from her head like bits of string. 'She's ugly!' he thought and turned away, not staying to see if she would obey him.

He stayed awake most of the night. This had been the case every Saturday night for many years. Sleeping through the mornings, drowsing in the lounge chair through the afternoons, and sitting somnolent through tea and dinner hours, his life, all expended in the noise, heat and rackety shuttle of the mines during the week, would gradually flow back to being. The weakness that overcame him as soon as he arrived at the front door each Friday night would ebb away; slowly, the movements of women through the rooms returned to him a masculine vitality. Their gaiety aroused him to strength, and his mind began turning again, although at first numb and weary.

He was supine and passive all through Saturday, but by nightfall he was filled with nervous energy. After his shower he would enter his bedroom with head and shoulders erect. His round, soft wife in her faded nightgown was exactly what he wanted then; he was firm next to her slack hips, lean against her plump rolling breasts; he could meet her submissive form like a bull sinking into a mudbank, groaning with pleasure. Later after she was asleep, his mind kept churning. Plans for the week ahead were meticulously laid: the lawyer to visit on Monday; the old klong to be shut and the machinery moved to the new site; Jason, his eldest son, to be talked to about his absences from the office; the monthly remittance to be sent to Wanda, his second daughter, in Melbourne; old Chong to be retired.

His mind worked thus, energetically and unhesitatingly, while he listened to his daughters settle for the night, the bathrooms eventually quiet, Ah Chee dragging across the corridor to bolt the doors and soft clicks as one light and then another was switched off. Then, after the clock struck its twelve slow chimes, he walked through the house, looking into each room while his mind and body ran in electrical fusion, each female form in bed renewing his pleasure with his life, leaving each room with a fresh vibrance to his body. So he would lie awake till the early hours of Sunday, calm yet vibrating strongly, breathing deeply, for he believed in the medicinal value of fresh night air, while his mind struggled with problems and resolved them for the next week.

Tonight, however, his sleeplessness was not pleasurable. Old, he thought, old and wasted his daughters had made him. He couldn't lie relaxed and immobile: the bodies of women surrounded him in an irritating swarm. He heard Kim Li slapping a book shut, footsteps moving towards the dining room, a refrigerator door opening and its motor running. 'Stupid girl!' he muttered, thinking of the cold flooding out of the machine, ice melting in trays, the tropical heat corrupting the rectangles of butter still hard and satiny in their paper wrappers. But he didn't get up to reprimand her.

All day Ah Kong would not speak to Kim Li; this would not have appeared out of the ordinary except that she sat in the sunroom with him most of the morning. Kim Bee and Kim Yee escaped to church at nine. In white and pink, wearing their grown-up heels and hair parted in braids, they looked like bridesmaids, ceremoniously stiff with a sparkle of excitement softening their faces. The Methodist Church was ten minutes' walk away. Mother no longer went to church, but her younger daughters went every Sunday, since it was still their mother's faith, and were greeted by women their mother's age, who sent regards but never visited themselves. The pastor was especially nice to them, having participated in the drama eighteen years ago.

She's a stray lamb. Those were barbaric times after the Japanese occupation; otherwise, she would probably not have consented to live in sinful relationship as a second wife. And, although I suppose it doesn't matter who the sin is committed with, Mr Tang is a well-known, respectable man. Her situation is more understandable when you know how careful and correct Mr Tang is with everything concerning himself and his family. It's a pity he is so Chinese, although, of course, divorces weren't as acceptable until a few years ago, and, even now, one shouldn't encourage it. Yet, if only he would divorce his first wife, she could return to the Church and the children . . . They're lovely girls, all of them, although the eldest hasn't been to service in a while, and the second seems excitable. The two young ones are so good, volunteering for the Sunday School Drive, singing in the choir (they have such sweet tones!) and so cheerful. A little anxious about the Scriptures. They want to know especially what has been written about the Day of Judgement, which isn't surprising seeing . . . Now, if Mr Tang weren't a pagan, he couldn't maintain this terrible life, keeping two households in separate towns, but, of course, he's old-fashioned and believes in the propriety of polygamy. Pagans have their own faith, I have no doubt, and Christ will consider this when the Day comes, but for the mother . . .

For Kim Bee and Kim Yee, Sunday service was one of the more enjoyable events in a dull weekend. Fresh as frangipani wreaths, they walked companionably to church, for once in full charge of themselves. They radiated health and cheerfulness from the hours of imposed rest, from their gladness at meeting the friends their parents never met but still approved of and from the simple encouraging emotions of welcome, love and forgiveness which welled up in hymns and which were the open subjects of the pastor's sermon.

'Love, love, love,' sang the choir. 'Our Father, Our Father,' they murmured and flooded their hearts with gratitude, with desire. Radiant, they returned from church at noon, in time for lunch and, later, to say goodbye to Ah Kong who drove back to

Kuala Lumpur every Sunday at two.

All morning Kim Li sat cross-legged on the floor next to Ah Kong's chair. Now and again she attempted to clip a toenail but her toes seemed to have been awkwardly placed, or, perhaps, she had grown too ungainly; she could not grip the foot securely. It wasn't unusual for the girls to sit on the floor by Ah Kong's feet. As children they had read the Sunday comics sprawled on the sunroom floor. Or Mother would bake scones, and they would eat them hot from the oven around their father. It was a scene he particularly savoured, a floury, milling hour when he was quiescent, feeling himself almost a baby held in the arms of his womanly family. This morning, however, Kim Li's struggles to clip her toenails forced his attention. Her silent contortions, exaggerated by the shorts she was wearing, bemused him. Was she already a woman as she had claimed last evening? Ah Kong felt a curious pity for her mixed with anger. Yes, he would have to marry her off. She moved her skinny legs and shot a look at him slyly as if to catch him staring. If she weren't his daughter, he thought, he could almost believe she was trying to arouse him. But he couldn't send her out of the room without admitting that she disturbed him. Once he had watched a bitch in heat lick itself and had kicked it in disgust. He watched her now and was nauseous at the prospect of his future: all his good little girls turning to bitches and licking themselves.

Leaving promptly at two, Mr Tang told his wife that he might not be coming next Friday: he had unexpected business and would call. He didn't tell her he was planning to find a husband for Kim Li. Complaisant as his wife was, he suspected she might not like the idea of an arranged marriage. Nor would the girls. By mid-week, he had found a man for Kim Li, the assistant to his general manager, a capable, China-born, Chinese-educated worker who had left his wife and family in Fukien eleven years ago and now couldn't get them out; he'd been without a woman since and had recently advised his clan association that he was looking for a second wife. Chan Kow had worked well for Mr Tang for eight years. What greater compliment to his employees than to marry one of them, albeit one in a supervisory position, to his daughter? Chan Kow was overwhelmed by the proposal. He wasn't worthy of the match; besides, he was thirty-three and Mr Tang's young daughter may not want him. But he would be honoured, deeply honoured.

Ah Kong called Mother with the match sealed. Would she inform Kim Li and have her agreeable for a wedding in July, the next month, which was the date the fortuneteller had selected as propitious for the couple? When he arrived on Friday night, he was surprised and relieved to find the family unchanged by his precipitous decision. 'You did the right thing,' his wife said late at night after the girls had gone to their own rooms. 'My goodness, I was afraid Kim Li would yell and scream. You don't know the tantrums she can throw. Well, she took it so calmly. Wanted to know his name, his age, what he looks like. The girls were quite upset. Kim Mee is so sensitive. She was crying because she was afraid you will arrange a marriage for her also, and I couldn't say a thing to her. But you should have seen Kim Li. She was so excited about it. Started boasting that soon she was going to be a married woman and so on.'

Ah Kong grunted.

'I told her a married woman has all kinds of responsibilities. She's lucky she'll have a husband who'll take care of her but she will have to learn to get along with him. Well, she didn't like that. She wants to let her hair grow long now, and she needs some new dresses and nightclothes, of course. And we have to shop for towels and sheets for when she goes to her own house . . .'

'Spend whatever you like,' Ah Kong said, and his wife fell silent. He had never said that before. She began calculating all she would buy for the other girls and for the house as well as long as he was in a generous mood.

'When am I going to meet the lucky man, ha, ha!' Kim Li

asked the next morning appearing suddenly in the sunroom. Startled, he opened his eyes with a groan. He thought he might have been asleep and had wakened on a snore. 'When am I going to meet this Chan Kow?' she repeated loudly. His wife came hurrying in from their bedroom next door. He said nothing and closed his eyes again. 'Ah Kong, I want to meet my husband-to-be. Maybe I can go to Kuala Lumpur with you and have a date with him, ha, ha!' Behind his shut eyes, he sensed her looming figure; her voice had grown strident.

Without opening his eyes, he said, 'In an arranged marriage, the woman doesn't see the man till the day of the wedding. You can have a photograph of Chan Kow if you like.'

'No, I want to go out with him first.'

'Kim Li, you're having a traditional wedding. The man cannot go out with the woman until after they're married,' her mother said in a mild tone. 'You mustn't spoil the match by acting in a Western manner.'

The other three girls huddled by the door listening to the argument. Kim Mee felt a great sympathy for her sister. It wasn't fair of Ah Kong to rush off and pick a husband for Kim Li. What about love? It was true that Kim Li was stupid and had been rude to Ah Kong, but this wasn't China. She wouldn't accept such an arranged marriage even if it meant that she had to leave home and support herself. She looked at her sister curiously. Imagine, she would be married next month! In bed with a stranger, an old man who only speaks Chinese! Kim Mee couldn't think of a worse fate.

Kim Li left the sunroom scowling; her mother couldn't persuade her that she didn't have a right to a few dates with Chan Kow. She didn't appear for tea, and all through Sunday she was languid. She walked slowly through the rooms as if she were swimming underwater, lazily moving one leg and then the other, falling into every chair on her way and staring blankly at the walls. Ah Kong ignored her; she was as good as out of the house.

When he came back next Friday, Kim Li had gone through a total change. 'I'm a woman now,' she had said to her sisters and began using Kim Mee's make-up every day. She pencilled her eyebrows crudely, rubbed two large red patches on her cheeks and drew in wide lips with the brightest crimson lipstick in Kim Mee's collection. After every meal, she went to her room and added more colour. Blue shadow circled her eyes, and her clumsy application of the mascara stick left blotches below her lids like black tear stains. She teased her short hair into a bush of knots and sprayed cologne till it dripped down her neck. Kim Mee didn't complain. Her sister who roamed up and down the house peering into every mirror and rubbing the uneven patches on her face had all her sympathy. To be married off just like that! No wonder Kim Li was acting crazy.

Ah Kong stood at the door afraid. No, he could not possibly allow Chan Kow to meet his daughter before the wedding, this painted woman who was smiling at him provocatively from her bedroom door. He could not understand from where Kim Li had picked up her behaviour; in her blue shorts with her wide hips tilted, she presented a picture he was familiar with and had never associated with his home. No, his wife was always submissive, a good woman who could never suggest an immodest action. Was there something innate about a woman's evil that no amount of proper education or home life could suppress! It was good she was marrying soon, for her stance, her glances, her whole appearance indicated a lewd desire. He turned his eyes away from her and stayed in his room all night.

Lying in bed on Saturday morning, he asked the mother to take the girls to town. 'I've work to do, and they are too noisy,' he said. He was very tired. That he had to lie to his wife, with whom he'd always had his way! He felt this other half of his life falling apart. The shelter he had built for eighteen years was splintered by the very girls he supported, by their wagging hips and breasts.

'I don't wanna go,' Kim Li was yelling. 'I'm setting my hair.'
'You must come along.' Mother was patient. 'We're shopping

for your trousseau. You have to pick your clothes. Then we're going to the tailor shop and you have to be measured.'

'All right, all right. I'm going to be a married woman, ha, ha! Do you wanna know about my wedding night, Kim Mee? You have to be nice to me. I'll have all kinds of secrets then.'

Only after the front door shut behind their chatter did Mr Tang go to the sunroom where Ah Chee had pulled down and closed the louvres. Next to his chair she had placed a plate of freshly ripened cikus. Because it grew so close to salty water, the tree usually bore small bitter fruit, but this season it was loaded with large brown fruit which needed only a few days in the rice bin to soften to a sweet pulp. Stubbornly refusing to throw any out, Ah Chee was serving ciku to everyone every day. Mr Tang slowly lowered himself on to his green leather chaise. Using the fruit knife carefully, he peeled a fruit. It was many years since he had last tasted one. Juice splattered on to his pyjamas. He spat out the long shiny black seeds on the plate. His hands were sticky with pulp, but he kept them carelessly on the arms of his chair and let his head drop back. Gradually the cool dark room merged into his vision. Ah Chee's banging in the kitchen faded, and the silence flowed around his shallow breathing, flowed and overcame it until he felt himself almost asleep.

A body pressed against him softly. It was his wife's rolling on him in their sleep. He sighed and shifted his weight to accommodate her. The body was thin and sharp; it pressed against him in a clumsy embrace. He opened his eyes and saw Kim Li's black and blue eyes tightly shut, her white and red face screwed up in a smile. His heart was hammering urgently; he could feel his jaws tighten as if at the taste of something sour. 'Bitch!' he shouted and slapped her hard. Kim Li's eyes blazed open. He saw her turn, pick something and turn to him again with her arms open as if in a gesture of love or hope. Then he felt the knife between his ribs. Just before he fell into the black water, he saw the gleaming fisheyes of the fish-woman rise from the klong to greet him.

My Cousin Tim

Simon Tay

I

I remember Tim as I wait here and sweat under the green tent, the backs of my thighs soaking under my black pants, the base of my spine marked out on my black shirt, sitting on the red vinyl chair, picking at groundnuts and kua-chi from the unsteady tables. I don't play cards and haven't much to say to the other relatives.

My part of the family went down to Singapore when my father did his university and never came back. We've lost touch with almost all of them since and even my father has trouble recognizing Uncle Keong Tim's brother-in-law and some of his cousins. 'Keong Tat's son', that's how I'm introduced and then I shake hands, nod, ask whether they want a packet drink, get it for them if they do and go back to my seat and sweat some more.

Tim's family was the only one we really kept in touch with. First, because Uncle Keong Tim used to have business in Singapore and then because Tim, or Ek Tim as everyone called him then, couldn't pass Malay and was sent down to study at my school and stayed with us.

We were fourteen then. I had just got my own room because Ee Lin, my eldest sister, was in England studying. The room wasn't really given to me; I just moved in. First, I only slept there but then, slowly, my clothes, portable cassette player and tennis rackets followed. I was a squatter in a strangely pink room with frilly curtains.

Ee Lan complained, 'Mum, I'm older, even Ee Cheng is older than him. One of us should get Ee Lin's room, not him.' My mother had learnt by then to control the four of us by the skill of caprice. Her decisions were never consistent or ruled by any discernible principle. That made us think twice before bothering her with one of our squabbles and leaving it to her to adjudicate who was right; we learnt in this way to resolve things between ourselves by bargaining, trading or, most of the time, fighting and shouting. We were more unruly than my father might have liked, but none of us could ever be accused of being a tattletale or mother's favourite. Ee Lan tried her luck that day and failed. I was a boy, my mother said, and it was best that I have my own room until Ee Lin came back for holidays. Ee Lan, sixteen, raged against the sexual discrimination of the entire world, about jobs and the right to vote and how hunting animals was no longer important and we were all equal now. My mother, unmoved, kept cutting cucumbers for dinner. To keep the peace as we grew, she persuaded my father to renovate and build three extra rooms in the garden where his favourite papaya trees grew, but that was much later.

I enjoyed my room for six months before Tim came to stay and share it. My mother broke the news to me. She was sure we would get on: my cousin was a very nice, quiet boy, very polite. He played the piano—Grade Eight—and Auntie June often asked him to play classical pieces after dinner. This sort of news was less than impressive to me at an age when my favourite singer was David Bowie. Tim had to do a lot to convince me that his presence was anything but an intrusion. When he arrived he first made friends with my sisters. He played piano while they tried to sing and dreamt of taking part in Talentime. Then he won my father over, listening to him talk about gardening and fruit trees, helping him and the gardener on Saturdays.

He was a dark-eyed, fair boy with bak-pau cheeks, well-groomed, short hair and a powerful frame which seemed too big and mature for the short pants we wore to school. He was good at all subjects and even his Malay, which had ruined him for Malaysian schools, was fine by our standards. His best subject was maths. It was something he had an instinct for; he was solving problems before the teacher could and practising from a Sec Four book. He was also a good runner and tennis player and played songs during recess on the school piano in the hall, any number which our classmates requested. He was always nice, cheerful and helpful to everyone. In a month he made more friends in the class than I, a bit of a loner, had during the whole of Sec One.

I should have been jealous, I guess, and I think I would have been if not for Tim. He quietly spoke up for me with my family so my parents and even my sisters occasionally saw my point of view, and our house became more peaceful. Every friend he made in school he insisted get along with me and be my friend too. He helped me with maths and my other weak subjects when we studied together in that room, without ever acting too smart. He always asked and deferred to me in geography and history, which were my strong subjects up to then; I was doing well in them but came close to failing the rest.

We played a lot of tennis together too, both at school team practices and on our own. All day on Saturdays and Sundays. And, on Thursdays and Fridays, we'd wake up early—Tim leaning over to nudge me after the alarm went—pack our uniforms into sports bags, change, pick up our rackets and basket of tennis balls and go. We'd play at the club until it was eleven and the sun was hot, almost overhead—my rocket serve and forehand pitted against Tim's steadiness and ability to exploit my awkward backhand—then shower or swim instead of showering and rush off to school.

I improved, learnt to hit less wildly and played singles for the school team. One Saturday afternoon, we took on my father and another doctor who had up to then confounded the directness of our youthful game with lobs and drop shots, and we beat them for the first time.

The next year, when we were in morning session, we continued the routine by simply reversing it and playing after school. We won the under-16 Doubles Championships and Tim was the runner-up in Singles. Our school was champion that year and sometimes the girls at the club would ask us to join them for a game and a swim after. We both played for Combined Schools and wore our badges and track tops around at every opportunity.

But if there was any one thing that really won me over, it was his sense of humour. Beneath that quiet, polite, eager, agreeable exterior, Tim had a vein of wicked humour. He breathed cutting asides to me in the very presence of the person he was making fun of: our teachers, my father, his father, our tennis coach, the giggly girls we'd meet. These were too many to remember. What I remember more clearly were the occasional pranks.

Tim was a great mimic. Each Sunday night, in our room, he'd imitate my father giving his latest lecture on gardening. He telephoned Ee Lan and pretended he was the RTS newscaster she had a crush on. He called up our class monitor, a crew-cut boy named Yew Huat, and, mimicking our teacher, told him to go to the staff room early the next morning for a meeting. When Yew Huat later told us about the practical joke and confidentially asked for our help to find out which of our classmates had done it, I almost gagged trying not to laugh.

We had started out so different, but Tim grew darker and, with exercise and our eating contests, I got taller and bigger. By the end of that first year, people who just met us thought we were brothers. By the end of the third year, our discipline master, Mr Tan, caught Tim for long hair and thought he was me.

To sit here on this occasion and think of these things saddens me. I feel old when I touch these memories, not thirty-three but sixty-three: my father's age. But I can't help myself. I only visited this town, this house, to see Tim in the holidays when he came home. I see the market and hawker stalls where we temporarily escaped the constant hunger of adolescence, the courts near the old tin quarries where we'd play all afternoon, the river at the edge of town which made a natural water slide from the rocks it had smoothed, where we'd swim in the hot afternoons, and the street of narrow houses, stylish brothels during the tin boom but run down even in our youth, where fat, dark women sat in the doorway under the red light and called us as we each, laughing, tried to push the other towards them.

I see the bungalow with its roof tiles still green and shiny, the lions of prosperity by the gate, the garden and patio at its centre, where Auntie June would trim her rose bushes at four-thirty and have tea, and the room Tim and I would share. I see them all as they were. Nothing of the slow erosion of time and prosperity the town and the house have suffered registers in my mind. My memories are fuelled by guilt: I lost touch with Tim some years ago. It was my work, first at university and then in the firm—a manager in an accounting firm just has too many partners to answer to and too many juniors to lead. It was my marriage.

These things must, I know, weigh more in the balance of things than the friendship of a cousin, but when I sit here I cannot excuse myself. I should have kept in touch with him.

We were seventeen when he left. One weekend, Uncle Keong Tim visited and told him and my parents the plan after Sunday dinner. Ek Tim was going to England. There he would do his A-levels in a special school and finish them in one year. He would be in university by eighteen and, because he was Malaysian and didn't have to do army, would be finished with his first degree by twenty-one. After all, Tim had gotten six P1s and two P2s in the exams.

My father said he thought it was an excellent idea and that

he would have done it too but for the fact that I had to do NS. I would go to university in England after that. I had, my father recalled perfectly, five P1s (not mentioning the three P4s with which I had marred my certificate). Maybe, my uncle finished, Ek Tim would still be there, doing his Ph.D. Then the two brothers talked about the possibility of pooling their resources to buy a flat in London so they wouldn't have to pay rent for us; a place to stay when they visited on holiday and hold as an investment. I was at the table still finishing my second helping.

I looked closely at my uncle as they spoke. He was my father's younger brother, the second son of my grandfather, but he had more white hair and wrinkles, looser skin and a buttery paunch which he wore under a sports T-shirt. These things might have made him look older than my father who kept himself fairly slim, but he overcame them with joviality, a sense of liveliness. He was always willing to share a beer with us, to jokingly offer us a cigarette before pointing to my father and saying that the doctor did not approve.

Uncle Keong Tim was a businessman, a trader, and often said part of his business was getting on with people. He had other plans for Tim, though. Something professional like an engineer or lawyer. As I looked at him and my father, I remembered an old family photograph, taken when they were eighteen and seventeen respectively. There, posed formally in the studio on either side of my grandparents, dressed in dark suits which my father kept the habit of wearing, they looked so similar. Now they were unmistakably different.

I wanted to say something about their plans for us, although it was clear it was not my place to. It was just dazzling. Not just that our fathers knew our exact results but that Tim was leaving and the days of tennis and school work were going to dissolve. It seemed like we'd just been allowed to wear long pants to school and go to parties where there were girls and, suddenly, our parents were talking about us getting degrees and Ph.Ds. Perhaps that was the first occasion I seriously thought about the passage of time. I finished my food and kept quiet. Tim went in May, two months later, and things were never the same again.

This is the fourth day of the nightwatch. Auntie June calls out Tim's name every now and then and cries out for Uncle Keong Tim, wishing father and son had made up in time. Then Seok, Tim's sister, calms her. Auntie has insisted that someone keep watch around the clock. She'll only let Seok put her to sleep after the volunteers for the midnight shift have been shown to her. My father and his brothers tried it the first night, but they are a little old for it and the second night it was only me, my sisters, Seok and Ek Lam, Tim's younger brother. We joked about how we used to meet at family dinners and share the kids' table. None of us mentioned how Tim used to mimic his father and all the uncles when none of them was looking.

My sisters left for Singapore yesterday, after the weekend, promising to apply for urgent leave and return in time for the funeral. That left just three of us last night. I can hardly believe the nightwatch is planned for three more days. I'm getting quite tired and have had my fill of kua-chi, groundnuts and packet drinks, of the routine of counting up the number of people still around at midnight and going out to buy tah-pau. Even the town's famous poh-piah has lost its magic for me. Ek Lam usually goes with me on the midnight run but we aren't much company for each other. I hardly know him and have seen him on perhaps three occasions in the last ten years. I know he is twenty-nine now and has basically taken over the responsibility for the family business since his father went into semi-retirement. I know he's trying to turn it around, but I can't think of him as anything but Tim's pesky younger brother, twelve, still playing with marbles when we were sixteen and trying to meet girls at the club.

As for Seok, she's the one holding things together, looking after Auntie June, the distant relatives and friends who keep turning up, and there is hardly time to talk to her about anything else other than the logistics of keeping us going. Last night though, she said tiredly that she couldn't believe the trouble of it all, the exhaustion of patience and goodwill involved.

Both her father and Tim had once remarked they wanted it just for three or five nights but her mother had insisted. It was so funny, she said, that Tim and her father would at last have agreed on something.

We laughed. It was a tense, tired laughter that arises only when a joke touches the most sensitive of issues and you are surprised that nothing has broken, that the world still stands even after you have spoken, even joked, about what was unspeakable.

I thought of Tim and laughed in a way I haven't for many years. Even in absence, my cousin Tim makes me laugh.

II

The first time I saw Tim after he left, some ten months or so later, he had his arm insinuated around a blonde who showed off ample cleavage each time she dipped to pick up her pint. Well, not quite. But I once said that to him, years later, when we were talking about changes in life, when he called me to say he couldn't come to my wedding. Mention that one day when you give my eulogy, he said. Actually, he was alone when he picked me up at the airport. It was a whole hour later, after I'd put down my bag in his flat, washed up and changed, that we met up with the girl at the pub on the corner. As this thought arose, I wanted to share it with Seok, like her marrow-funny joke of the previous night, but there hasn't been time.

The blonde's name was Maggie. It was April in my last year at school, before NS. I'd persuaded my father to allow me to visit Tim during the Easter holidays, to let me travel alone since I wouldn't be able to do so until after the army.

'Give him a proper welcome to London, Maggie. It's his first time and he is my cousin you know?' Tim said and the girl got up with a laugh, came over to my side of the table and hugged me. I think I might have gasped at the soft pillowy surprise of that embrace. Tim barked out a laugh. After that pint and two others, we left her, taking our farewell hugs in turn.

In that crush, my—how do I put this?—my excitement was obvious. She called out to Tim, 'Your cousin catches on quick. What's his name again?'

'Ek Teng,' I began but Tim had already answered, 'Call him Eddie.'

For those twenty days I was Eddie. Tim called me Ek Teng when we were alone but to everyone else, even his Chinese friends from Malaysia: Eddie. It was easier for the people he introduced me to at the university library, a broken down old building in the middle of the city where we'd meet after his lectures, at the shows and dinners we went out to and the disco parties. For the same reason, he was now Tim, rather than Ek Tim. Funnily enough, when I came home and became Ek Teng again, he always called me Eddie and addressed his letters to Eddie Sng.

His letters. I remember them well. The first came quite quickly after my visit. 'Dear Eddie,' he began, 'I hold you to your solemn promise made during your farewell party after one bottle of champagne to write to me regularly and never destroy my letters because one day we'll both be famous and our correspondence will be studied by professors. Now I will catalogue all the sins you committed in London so that you will ensure this letter never falls into the wrong hands (i.e. your father's or mother's).'

The list followed: the Soho sex shops we visited on that first day after leaving Maggie, the apparatus and magazines we poured over, the single-seater booths we sat in at the back of the shops, putting in 50p coins to watch clips of Triple-X movies, the strip show the next night after drinks at the pub, the live sex show on the first Friday, the next night's drunken party where Tim played jazz on the piano and introduced me to a tall, skinny blonde named Babs, who, as he promised, wanted to learn about the East and French-kissed me for every pantun or sentence I recited in Malay, the night Babs and Maggie came for dinner and we watched *Emmanuelle* on video. And that was just the first week.

'Don't be angry with me, Eddie,' Tim wrote, 'don't be shy either. It's all part of a well-rounded (pun intended) education. Our fathers would be proud of having raised such, shall we say, upright sons who seek to learn things in London which they cannot in Singapore or Malaysia. To show you how I am progressing in this education, I enclose proof that Maggie is a real blonde.'

I remember staring at the curly hairs which fell out of the envelope for a while, then bursting out in laughter. It still makes me laugh now when I think of the clean-cut young boy who came on that first day to share my room.

But, on second thought, I don't think this is a story I should tell Seok on this occasion.

My father says he will keep the midnight watch with us tonight. I've been trying to dissuade him. He's busy the whole day with relatives and friends only he and his brothers or Auntie June can recognize and have anything to say to: that's the excuse I give.

Really, I'm a little worried about his ulcer. He kept it hidden from us, from even my mother, for many years, treating himself, wearing it under his dark suits and calm exterior until one afternoon he called us from hospital, having checked himself in because of blood in his stools. Who knows what other ailments he might have that he refuses to tell us about, or confirm with tests? He needs his rest. As I told him once, in these last ten years my sisters and I have grown up and should be taking more care of him and Mum, just as they took care of us. I thought he might snort and refuse such a suggestion, but perhaps the way I put it, avoiding any outright mention of him being old or incapable, made him accept our concern more easily. 'This is something all parents hope to hear when their children grow up.' If I remember correctly that was what he said. It was a surprise.

The father I remember more was the one who, one night, burst into my room—still pink from Ee Lin's tenancy and with one spare bed from Tim's—without knocking. I barely had time to cover the *Playboy* with the blanket and was sure he saw it. But it was not his concern. 'Ek Tim has been writing to you, Teng. What's he been saying?' My first reaction was that he knew all about our debauchery in those twenty days and was angry with me, for betraying his trust, but before I could begin my confession and defence, my father went on. 'I've just spoken to Uncle. That bloody boy has gone mad and quit university.' That mixture of shock and relief, of guilt and escape has never been repeated. 'Nothing much, Dad,' I muttered, not knowing where I found the words, 'Nothing about university.'

I heard most of what happened second-hand, from my mother or from what my father would say to her over dinner. Uncle Keong Tim flew to London immediately. He threatened to cut Tim off without a cent and then, after Tim shocked him by saying he'd just moved in with a girlfriend and was supporting himself by playing the piano and washing dishes, he reasoned with him. Tim promised to return to school after taking just one semester off. Uncle Keong Tim spoke to the university administration, got them to give Tim the time off and went home.

The months passed and he was still not back in classes. Uncle flew out again. Tim switched universities and subjects from engineering to maths. Half a year later the same thing happened and again my uncle rescued the situation and enrolled Tim in a third university, studying economics. With the repetition of this cycle, the details became less clear in my parents' conversations. 'Ek Tim's done it again,' I overheard. 'Keong Tim's got him into architecture now.' 'The boy wants to continue with his music and play in some sort of rock band. Keong Tim's blaming June for all those piano lessons.'

From Tim, I heard nothing about these changes although his letters came quite frequently around that time. He'd write about Ronnie Scotts and other jazz clubs where he'd go and listen to what he described as the Greats, the newest and wildest punk rock bands, and the drinking and jam sessions at the local pub where he and some other students would play late at night, trying to combine the two. Then about the band he'd formed— I can't remember their name—and the gigs they were starting to get in pubs and university concerts to play their punk-jazz songs.

He'd write about tennis and tell me how his game was going, but that was only occasionally, in late spring and summer when the weather was good enough. About women, he sent a scandal sheet in his second letter which he himself described in a PS to be worthy of Harold Robbins. Then in his third letter, he wrote: 'I've now decided that only those who are not getting enough of IT, talk about IT. The next blank page is intentional.'

I was finishing NS then. I'd finished only five months of active service before the ligaments in my knee cap were strained and torn in a stupid training accident. After surgery, I was downgraded and given three months' leave at home to recover. Then I was trained as a supply clerk and spent two months in dark storerooms, where anything anyone ever needed was missing, before being rescued; I joined the SAF tennis team.

Officially, I was still a supply clerk and some mornings when it rained I would help dig up whatever was needed for this or that exercise. But most of the time, I just played tennis: tournaments against local clubs and for the army against the navy or air force and social tennis against senior officers once a week, when I practised the art of pulling punches without making it too obvious. In between, we slouched around the camp and helped the officer-in-charge, a major, organize the tournaments between the different units in the army as well as national tournaments, since he was in the tennis association.

My friends told me I should be happy. If they were clerks, their desks were surrounded by the paperwork that was the routine of their lives. If they were in active service, they were in the field shouting and giving and taking orders, sweating in the rain, shitting behind bushes. My mother was happy. All my sisters were now abroad studying and the house was too empty; playing tennis meant I'd be back every evening.

I guess I was happy too but, looking back, I drifted and wasted those days. The knee injury placed a limit on the amount I could practise and that limited my improvement. I knew I'd never play in the Davis Cup, my teenage ambition. The days came and went, the yellow ball went back and forth over the net. I never had time for anything, even though I was not—according to everyone—doing anything much. I would hang around with the other players and we got on, but we were not friends; just people in the same boat, and we lost touch with each other almost immediately after leaving the army.

I bought but never got around to reading up those university books so I would be ahead of the others when I went to England. I started but never finished French lessons. As for girls, at first I went out with a few from my school days but they either went abroad to study or began to prefer the company of the older boys with them in university or the men in their office, if they were working. By the last year of NS, Saturday nights were girl-less, batang outings. I met some girls in shopping centres—sales girls, young pre-U girls—when some of the team would sneak off from training. But beyond a movie or two, nothing happened. I read Tim's letters and was all the more frustrated. My replies stopped then, but we were still inextricably linked.

My father never looked me in the eye when he said it. It was not really a conversation, although I hurriedly put together a protest; it was an announcement. In the days after, as I brooded over what I saw then as greatest possible injustice, I re-examined the words so many times. I still remember them:

'I've given it some thought, son, together with your mother. We've decided that we won't be sending you to London to study.'

'But Ee Lin, Ee Lan and Ee Cheng all went abroad. They finished and came back.'

'They are girls, Ek Teng, and I have had every confidence that they wouldn't do what Ek Tim did. You are a young man. And you might be tempted to do those sort of things too. Look at your cousin. Before he went he was so reliable, a good son.'

'But . . .'

'No more talk. I've made up my mind on this.'

I knew even then there was no point in raging on about sexual discrimination, how we men had to serve NS and lose two-and-a-half years, of the poor pay we received, of too many girl-less Saturdays, how those same faithless girls who'd been my classmates were going to be my seniors when I started work. My father's eyes were turned to a point two feet to the left of my shoulder, beyond the wall of his study.

My mother consoled me, knowing just what to say, building it up to the things that would matter most to me. My father did this because I was his only son and he always wanted a son; I had a place for accountancy and the course would take only three years; her cousin was a partner in one of the biggest firms and would be willing to take me in as long as I did well; the house was going to be renovated and I could have the first choice of the rooms; my father would give me a holiday in Europe or America; and, most convincingly, I could have a small car to take me to university, bought out of all the money they would save by not sending me abroad. I was heartbroken but hid it well under the bandages my mother applied.

The last time I saw Tim was on my first year holidays. Almost everything we did in those three weeks travelling together was just as before, as if little had happened since he left, since we met in London when we were eighteen. His father and the cycle of universities were never mentioned although they emerged indirectly. We stayed in tiny, slightly musty pensions because Tim couldn't get any money from his father and was paying for the holiday himself, out of what he had made playing the piano at a Chinese restaurant on weekends and teaching tennis to children in the spring.

When I called back home for my exam results and found that I'd finished in the top three of the class, we celebrated and after three bottles of rough Rhône wine and just before passing out, Tim toasted me as a hardworking, serious son of a bitch. Another night, after more wine, I told him that he was the reason that I wouldn't be coming to London and that he was a son of a bitch too, and he was deathly quiet. I held him by the shoulder and lied that I didn't blame him and anyway had got a car out of it. He started yelling how his father had tried to bribe him too, and threatened him, but he would die or see his father dead before just doing what he wanted. Then he threw up.

The next morning we spent the entire day trying to pick up French girls. We got two Australian travellers instead. They were going in the same direction and drank more than we did. No more was said between us. We just had fun, like twenty-one-year-olds are supposed to.

III

My sisters came back this morning with my wife, driving up early in Ee Lan's Honda so they could stay the last night and prepare for tomorrow's burial. All the children—including my two sons—have been left with my sisters' mothers-in-law. I was glad to see my wife and hear her say simple reassuring things about the children and that she missed me. It's the first time I've been apart from Susan for more than two nights since we got married. Then she was recruited by Seok to help and disappeared into the kitchen.

The last and greatest wave of relatives arrived to tax the tired and frayed nerves of Tim's mother and my parents with their half-remembered faces and well-intentioned, clumsy condolences. 'So sorry to hear . . .' a lady in her eighties said to Tim's mother, 'So young and got heart attack.' My sisters plunged in to help Seok and Ek Lam and I gladly gave them way.

In the late afternoon I went up to the old room which Tim and I used to share when I visited. As I lay down on the bed, I remembered the nights we used to sneak down the backstairs next to the room, down into the dark corridor and out through the garden gate so we could wander around the town. I slept and dreamt of Tim. Then there was a nudge and the sound of a voice which should not have been so familiar, and I woke up. In my half-sleep I made out a man sitting on the other bed, close to me. He sat with his elbows on his knees but I could still see he was big. He had black hair and a square face made round by slightly bak-pau cheeks, a face he tilted so it looked straight into mine. I thought I was still dreaming.

'Oih, sleepy, oih. If I've flown half-way around the bloody world, the least you can do is wake up.'

'Tim?'

'Who else, Eddie?'

'You came.'

'Ya. He was my father after all, I guess.'

'Your mother's downstairs.'

'Ya, I know. I saw her, together with Seok and Lam and the whole monkey show. Seven days—I could have sworn my father said he only wanted three days.'

'Your mother said you told her on the phone that you wouldn't come.'

'Changed my mind.'

I got up and looked at him, rubbing the short, deep sleep out of my eyes. He looked just as he had the last time I had seen him, a little older perhaps but not twelve years older. He had no paunch or grey hairs, he didn't wear glasses—all the fates of age which have overtaken me. He wore a cream-coloured shirt and dark pants, rather than the patched jeans and bright shirts he always seemed to be wearing when I last saw him. This, together with his quiet, solemn look, made him seem young again, closer to being the boy who had first walked into my room rather than the young piano player I'd left that last time in London, sitting in his flat, twenty-one years old, on a rusty brass bed with satin sheets, the walls behind him covered with punk rock posters, magazine pin-ups—including one which focussed completely on a blonde pubis—and a banner which said 'Louis Armstrong Lives'.

He spoke again before I could find anything to say worthy of breaking the silence.

'Eddie, let's go. Let's go for a drive or something. I've just got to get out of the house.'

He led the way down the backstairs, out the garden gate, still knowing how to ease the rusty latch open without a sound. On the corner by the side of the house, there was a rented grey BMW. We got in and drove through the narrow streets without saying anything. He drove efficiently as if each movement of the wheel and the change of the gears were the entire subject of his concentration. All the noises and the humid wet smell of the countryside were cut off. There was just the whirr of the engine and air-conditioner and the familiar scenes of the town passed like a slide show without commentary. I had hoped he would come from the first moment the phone rang and my mother told me Uncle Keong Tim was dead, but now he was here I had no idea what to say to him or what I hoped he might say to me.

As the days of the wake had passed, his absence had been noted by more and more visitors. At first, it was easy to say that Tim was in London and was having trouble getting a flight out. By the third day, I could see the visitors gossiping amongst themselves. I did not have to hear their gossip for the scenes between Tim and his father, which I'd heard about from my mother, to come back vividly. Father and son shouting at each other in the small London flat, Uncle Keong Tim slapping him and Tim punching the old man back, doubling him over, Tim yelling into the phone for more money, his father complaining to Auntie June about her son, packing his bags to fly again to London, and the final scene—three or four years ago—when Uncle Keong Tim declared to Tim that he was never going to give him any more money, or see him again or receive him in his house, until Tim finished some sort of course in a university or he was dead, whichever was sooner.

He was such a bright, polite boy. Who could have known he would waste so much money, be the greatest disappointment to his father, even hit his father and refuse to talk to him and apologize, take his father's heart from his business which suddenly went bad and make him ill from all his worries at an age when things should be easier and, finally, not even be here for his father's burial, as the eldest son, no respect—it was not right—and how can father and son share part of the same name, sure to be bad luck, told them so and now see: I didn't have to overhear the relatives to know that this was what they were saying. Especially the older ones, as if the incantation of Tim's sins was a talisman against their sons and daughters falling to the same evils. I looked at this nightmare son and he spoke first.

'Eddie, sorry I couldn't come to your wedding. I could joke that it was to pay you back for all the letters I wrote which you never replied to, but the truth is I didn't have the money at the time. Punk music had died and my brand of punk jazz with it. I was living with a girlfriend who was on the dole and making extra cash playing piano at an Italian restaurant. It was a bad time. I could have asked my dad for the money, but I'd rather have died first. Hope you understand.'

'Ya, don't think about it. I wanted you to be best man but Yew Huat was all right.'

'Yew Huat . . . old botak from Sec One? If I had known you were that desperate, I'd have sold my piano to come back! Just kidding, I'm sure he was fine.'

'OK, but you'd have made a funnier dinner speech. He was more solemn than my father.'

'Botak never had a sense of humour, did he? And I don't suppose he's improved?'

'Nope. In fact, I think everyone's lost their sense of humour in the last few years. Except you, maybe.'

'Thanks, Eddie, but if I'd come to your wedding what most people would find funniest would have been the idea that I could be any sort of "best" man.'

'Don't say that, Tim.'

'It's what they think. I could feel it when I saw them, sitting around, gossiping, chomping on snacks, playing cards: "What a bad son, I'm glad he's not mine."'

'Your mother must have been glad to see you.'

'I haven't spoken to her yet.'

'What?'

'I came in the house the same way we left, through the garden gate, without anyone seeing me. Through the kitchen windows I saw and heard my mother together with Seok, Lam and your sisters as they streamed in and out. I watched the relatives and friends and it was enough. I knew what they were thinking. So I came up to look for you. I knew you would be in the room, since I didn't see you anywhere else.'

'We've got to go back, Tim. Your mother needs you.'

'I'll go back . . . when I know what to say.'

Then our conversation lapsed and we drove on in the evening which was quickly turning to darkness.

I recognized our destination the moment Tim pulled the car off the road and parked. The river with its water slide was some twenty metres up the path. We walked there in darkness and silence, Tim leading the way. I heard the sound of the water and then, as my eyes grew used to the night, could make it out—the white curls as it licked around the rocks and gathered speed implying the darker body of the river just before it all tumbled down into the slide, which I placed by the white froth of water and its tumbling, churning noise.

Tim walked up to its edge and started to undress, down to his underwear—his winter-pale skin clear in the night. He looked across at me and I—don't ask me why—started to strip as well, as if it was the most natural thing to do at the start of the last night of his father's nightwatch. We padded across the unseen stones, our naked feet finding the secure dry footholds by the sharp edges. Tim jumped in, the water up to his waist, howling, then splashed the water at me and yelled for me to come in. I walked around to a shallower point and stepped in, ankle deep first, then walked into a deeper point, gritting my teeth against the cold.

With another howl, Tim plunged in deeper, over his head, swimming to the point where the water streamed down to the rock slide. The current had not grown weaker with the years and pulled him away quickly. Tim's head bobbed as he was swept along between the rocks and his wide grin split into a laugh which I could not hear above the water's sound. Then his body leapt into the air as he went over the slide, a white streak plunging into the pool of dark water.

I followed. The cold, certain water took over the direction of my body, making me race as it did, following Tim's path, surging round the rocks and leaping momentarily into the air before plummetting down. My feet found the deep bottom and I kicked towards the surface and the shallows. I stood there but couldn't see Tim. My teeth started to chatter. I peered into the pool but didn't see him surface. I called out his name: no answer. I plunged back in.

Hands grabbed me under the water and held me there. My lungs burnt, with the lack of oxygen, with the sudden relief that Tim was fine and the repressed laughter at his high jinks. I twisted out of his grip and grabbed him around the back, clambering over him until my whole body weight held him under.

I gasped for breath and laughed loud in the dark. Tim struggled gamely but couldn't break my hold from that position. When I let go, after a few minutes, he surfaced, spitting out water and puffing for breath.

'Got you, you trickster.'

'It's your body weight, Eddie. Your paunch gives you an unfair advantage, Fat-boy.'

'Bastard.'

'Ah Pui.'

We sat in the shallows and our laughter kept us warm.

There was always a lot to laugh about with Tim. We talked about the old times, prolonging our recollections, knowing that each extra minute of memory and laughter kept the present at bay. But it was inevitable.

'I'm sorry we lost touch, Eddie. It was a bad time for me and I just didn't want to talk or write to anyone. I heard about you though, from my mother—she still wrote. She told me all about your fast-lane promotions, your son . . .'

'I've got two sons now.'

'Oh. I didn't know. I'd given up on the music. Times and fashions change, you know, and I was left behind before I could catch up. Playing in that restaurant was just getting me nowhere. When I realized that, I also realized I didn't know why I'd done the things I had, except that I didn't want to do what my father wanted me to. I wasn't playing or teaching tennis even though I missed playing. Soho was being cleaned up and I missed it, kind of. Our favourite sex shop's been replaced by a butcher's store specializing in imported sausages, which is funny if you think about it. It sunk in that I was a failure.'

'Don't say that.'

'Everyone else does, Eddie. I know it. I knew it even before I came back. The only thing that hit me tonight was their faces: the faces of my relatives, of even my family. I felt as if everything would have been different if I'd done what they wanted. I'd be working in Singapore or KL, married, visiting every now and then. Maybe my father would still be alive and I'd still be their Number One Son. My mother wrote to me about Ek Lam, and about you, how you both were doing at work and I was so jealous.'

'No, Tim, don't . . .'

'Let me finish. I was jealous and I took a good look at myself. And you know what? I realized that I was still the same person everyone used to be so proud of and happy with. In fact I was better: more relaxed, easy going, more confident, more willing to take risks and to live life just for today, for myself. Sexier too. I knew about things I'd never thought I'd know. There's something wrong in the world, I tell you Eddie, I've realized that. When you're young and people ask you what you want to be, they mean do you want to be a doctor, an engineer, a pilot or what. If you say you want to be kinder, more knowledgeable, nicer, they think you're crazy. I wasn't what my father wanted me to be but that was all right so long as I knew what I wanted to be. It was then that I stopped being jealous of you and Ek Lam—I mean, it's OK if that's what you want for yourself, but it wasn't for me. I stopped wishing I had listened to my father. And then, with the same decision, I stopped feeling I had to do everything I knew my father didn't want me to. It's the reverse of the same thing. Do you know what I mean, Eddie?'

'I think so.'

'Well, of all the people I know, you've got the best chance of understanding. I just had to tell you. Now we can go back.'

We were quiet when we drove back, in spite of all the intervening laughter and talk. But when I looked across at Tim, I thought he might well be—as he claimed—the same person I'd shared a room with all those years back. We rolled down the windows and let in the wind, the sounds and smells. I looked forward to recognizing him. I didn't however look forward to returning to the house and the green tent of relatives. I looked at Tim as we drew nearer and nearer but couldn't see a flicker of anxiety. It was me who broke the quiet.

'Tim, don't let whatever they say affect you. It doesn't matter. Just be with your mother. She's missed you. She's never thought you were a failure.'

'Ya, I think you're right. My mother will understand. What she may have trouble accepting is the money.'

'If there are problems, I've got some saved.'

'Thanks Eddie, but it's not that.'

We'd arrived. He pulled the car off the road and parked, got out and walked to the garden gate without finishing his sentence. Only when I caught up with him did he tell me exactly what it was.

'You know what I told you at the river? After that, I got a job as a real estate agent. I got on with English sellers and Hong Kong buyers. It was a good market and I made enough money to buy houses myself. I traded them around and made a lot of money. I should have told my family earlier but I was waiting for a last deal. I closed it last week and my total gains are now a million. One Million Pounds Sterling. That's what I don't know how to tell them.'

I looked at my cousin Tim and, as he pulled back the rusty latch of the gate quietly, he turned to took at me.

I don't know which of us started first or what everyone in the house of mourning must have thought of the laughter that burst from our lungs, escaping the quiet and dark. My cousin Tim and me, we didn't care.

Tragedy of My Third Eye

Suchen Christine Lim

My third eye popped open on the evening when Linda's father spat on me and robbed me of my childhood forever.

That little tyrant lorded over us in Primary 1A because she could speak English so well. Standing in front of us, her proud little face tilted upwards, she tossed her curls, gave our teacher a sweet smile and recited, 'Humpty Dumpty sat on the wall . . .'

Her voice, clear as a bell, held me spellbound as I sat in the back row of the class, my mouth a little open. Like the other little girls, I yearned to be like her. I who couldn't speak a word of English hoped some day I too would be touched by magic and recite Humpty Dumpty and a host of other nursery rhymes.

'Doesn't Linda sound just like little Alice in "Alice and the Toy Soldier"?' Miss Wang purred.

I looked at the floor and kept my eyes down. After the first few weeks of primary school, I quickly learnt never to look up when a teacher was talking. That was one sure way of avoiding punishment. If I had looked up, Miss Wang would have caught my eye and asked me a question. Then I would be unable to answer her, and so she would have to punish me. I couldn't say any of the English words, which seemed to flow out of Linda like water from a tap. When Miss Wang pointed to any of the letters of the alphabet, say, the letter A, my entire repertoire of English sounds whooshed out of my head. How do I say it? *Air –oo-arr*? What? Miss Wang waited and coaxed. And waited some more. Then she tapped the black little squiggle on the chart.

'Come on, say it. What is it? How does it sound?'

But my mouth refused to open. I looked down at my feet.

'Come. Try. We don't have all day.'

And still no word came. My head was a dark emptiness although the sun was shining outside the window. I shut my eyes because I didn't want the tears to seep out.

'Who can tell Ping what this word is?'

I remained standing for the rest of the reading period.

I hated school. It had turned me into a dumb mutt who couldn't speak. Except during recess. And I couldn't read. And I couldn't sing. And I couldn't spell, couldn't count and, worst of all, I couldn't recite those blasted English nursery rhymes which Miss Wang inflicted upon us each morning. .

I wanted to run away. The grown-ups had cheated me. Mother had lied when she said school would make me clever. School made me stupid. I was a clever girl before I came to school. Grandma had said I was smart. My teacher in the Chinese kindergarten had also said I was smart. Why did Mother send me to a place where I am made stupid? I asked myself this question each night when I lay in bed alone after Mother had locked me up in our bedroom. Am I clever only when I'm with Grandma and stupid when I'm not with her? Did Grandma lie? Did she cast a spell on me as Mother claimed?

I could recite my Three Character classic primer from page one to the last page, in Cantonese, without once looking into the book. I could sing arias from The Patriotic Princess, Hua Mulan and Madam White Snake. Everyone listened to me in Grandma's house when I sang. I could tell Auntie Jen what to do when I waved my sword and threatened to chop off her head. Grandma called me her clever little princess. But in Primary 1A of the Convent of the Holy Infant Jesus, Miss Wang called me 'stupido'. I brushed off my tears. I would not cry. I would fight. Princesses are brave and smart like Princess Leila.

That night I shut my eyes tightly against the darkness and reached out to grasp the magic of the universe.

'Pay attention in class. Learn to speak like Linda.'

Silly cow, I thought. How could we? Linda Tan Swee Ling could even sing English songs like *Down by the station listen to the trains*. Oops! I quickly stopped the smile from spreading across my face and bent down to re-tie my shoelaces. Who was that? Who said silly cow inside my head?

My eyes followed Miss Wang all that day and the next. She asked Linda to answer questions. She smiled at Linda more than ten times. She said, 'Thank you, Linda, that was very nice.' To the rest of us, she yelled, 'Who's talking? If I catch anyone talking again, I'll send her out of the class!'

When Miss Wang was not in class, Linda took out her little blue book and pencil. She wrote our names in the book if we didn't listen to her. Then she would show it to Miss Wang and we would be punished. Because of this, everyone wanted to be Linda's friend. Everyone wanted to be part of her gang.

Well, maybe not everyone, which was why, one day, during recess, her minions made us stand in a line in front of their princess in class.

'We're playing slave and enemy. This big finger is for slave. This little finger is for enemy. Choose. Which finger?' Her Royal Highness looked at us.

We looked at one another. No one spoke. We waited to see who would have to choose first. Mugface, the biggest and ugliest girl in class and Linda's most devoted slave, singled out May Yin, my best friend.

'Touch this finger, and you be Linda's slave. Touch this little finger, and you be our enemy. Understand or not?' Mugface demanded.

I understood the words 'slave' and 'enemy'. Sister Josephine had told us stories about slaves in the Bible, like that slave, Daniel, who was thrown into the lion's den but the lion didn't eat him because, like the song said, 'he had faith in all good men, and for that faith, he was willing to die'. I didn't know what the words meant, but I could remember the music and the song, and I knew what a slave was. But why do I have to be a slave or an enemy? Why can't we be friends? I wanted to ask Linda but I didn't have the English words then and she couldn't understand my Cantonese.

'Which finger? Quick, choose, lah!'

May Yin looked as if she was going to cry.

'Choose!' Mugface barked at her.

Linda stood like a stone princess, with her two fingers pointed at my best friend's throat. Instinctively, May Yin's hands were clasped in front of her chest. Her face was flushed.

'Quick, lah! Choose!'

Like the tongue of a snake, her finger darted out, licked Linda's forefinger and retreated. Desperately, I tried to catch her eye, but May Yin refused to look at me.

'One slave!' Linda sang and moved on to the next girl.

'Two slaves!' she sang.

'Three slaves!' Mugface and the others sang.

'Four slaves!'

I began to edge away. Please God, make the bell ring. Please, please, please, make recess over soon. My heart was pounding so fast that I almost couldn't breathe, but I dared not move away any farther. Mugface had seen me. She walked to the door and stood at the doorway of the classroom. I looked out hoping that a teacher would walk past, but no one did.

'Your turn,' one of Linda's slaves poked me in the ribs. Except for May Yin, who looked downcast and forlorn in the corner, the rest of the slaves were eager for me to join them. 'Your turn, choose, choose!' they said.

Linda stuck out her two fingers. 'Which one?'

I gazed at the two daggers.

'Quick, this one or this one?'

'If I be your slave then what?'

'Stupido, you didn't hear what I said? You go and line up

and buy food for me during recess. Then, you obey me and do what I tell you.'

The girls pressed forward.

'Quick! Choose!'

The gang closed in.

'Big or small finger?'

'Quick, lah! Choose!'

Linda glared at me. 'Choose!'

My little finger touched her little one. The girls gasped. The bell rang.

No one spoke to me after recess. May Yin, who sat next to me, was dumb. I knew we were watched. I nudged May Yin. I played tap with my pencil when the teacher was not looking. I drew a funny face on a piece of paper and pushed it across my desk to May Yin. But she didn't even dare to look at it. After school, no one spoke to me.

I tried to catch a cold or fever the next day, but nothing happened even though I had covered myself from head to toe with a blanket. I dared not tell Mother. I was afraid she might cane me.

The next day, it was a little better. May Yin and I drew pictures and exchanged drawings under our desks. Linda had ordered everyone not to talk to me so I was glad when we had to recite our nursery rhymes for that was the only time I could open my mouth and say something.

On the third day, I couldn't bear it any more. I ran off to play with the Indian girls. They were lucky. There were two Indian girls in our class, and they were not included in Linda's game because she didn't like them. They could speak English better than her even though they didn't know how to sing English pop songs. Satvindar Kaur became my best friend and, together with that other girl, Param, we went out to the saga trees during recess to collect their red saga seeds to play kuti-kuti, and the wonderful thing was that Satvindar and Param dared to talk to me in class.

They weren't bothered by what Linda said or what Linda did even when Linda glared at them. When Linda saw us together, her eyes grew dark and angry. All that day, her eyes followed us and got darker and angrier whenever she looked in my direction. Several times during the day, she shot poisoned darts at me. 'Don't look!' She even scolded those who looked at me. The Chinese girls in class, even my former best friend, pretended I wasn't there.

But I don't care, I don't care! My little heart sang. Playing kuti-kuti during recess was so much better than queuing up to buy noodles for Linda Tan Swee Ling or running back and forth to fetch things for her or playing only those games that she wanted to play. I might be only six-and-a-half, and a 'stupido' in Primary 1A, but I would rather be an outcast than a slave.

Linda and I lived in the same neighbourhood, down the same row of townhouses and dilapidated shophouses. Each evening, our trishaws would drop us at the top of the lane, and we would walk home from there. One evening, I was trailing Linda and her minions. They were giggling and glancing back at me every now and then, talking loudly about lice and cow dung, but I pretended I didn't hear them. They walked, four abreast, blocking my way whenever I tried to walk past them and move ahead.

'Something white is crawling in her hair.'
'And she smells!'
They giggled and held their noses.
'Oooh! She smells!'
I ignored them. We were nearing Linda's house, and their laughter grew louder. I saw Linda's father, a spindly man in a white shirt and striped pajama pants, emerge from their house and stand in the middle of the sidewalk, waiting for her. Linda ran up to him, and, as he was bending down to take her school bag, she whispered something in his ear.

He looked up and fixed his stern eyes on me. Just as I was walking past him on the sidewalk, he spat.

'Pui! You! So proud for what? Why don't you friend my daughter?' he hissed at me in Hokkien. 'You know what kind of woman your mother is?'

I could only gaze at the dark patch on my convent blue uniform where his spittle had landed.

Out!
Out!
Out!

I scrubbed my thigh till the flesh was red and raw, but the spot where his spit had soaked through my school uniform and touched my flesh was still burning. I scrubbed harder. And harder. In desperation, I applied more soap and turned on the hose and pointed at the contaminated spot. Little rivulets of red ran down my leg where my brush had broken my skin. Soon, my socks and shoes were soaked and streaked pink. But I didn't care. His question was jangling inside my head. My ears were burning. I could feel that they had turned red and raw like the spot on my thigh.

I hated Linda's father, but I hated my mother even more. What kind of a woman was she to invite such comments from a man like Linda's father? She became my mother just two months ago! It was she who yanked me away from my Grandma, the one and only person who loved me the most in the whole wide world! Before that, she had always been Ah Koo, my Aunt. Now she was my mother, but inside my six-year-old heart, she was still the woman who'd forced me to live with her. Wicked witch! I vowed never ever to love her. Only my Grandma was worthy of my love.

'Noooooooo! I don't want to go! I don't want to live with Ah Koo!'

'Mama. Call me Mama.'

'You're not my Mama!'

She pushed me into the room and locked the door. I banged on it till she came in and caned me without mercy. She stopped only when I stopped yelling. After that, I never cried again, at least not when she could hear me or see me. She made me empty the chamber pot every morning. I had to be careful not to spill any of the urine in it when I took it out to the communal toilet down the corridor of Kim Poh's tenement house. If she were really my Mama, she'd be like Janet and John's Mummy in my English storybook. Janet and John's Mummy baked cakes for them, kissed them goodbye and good night, and tucked them into bed. In the morning, she helped them to put on their coats and took them to the baker's, the grocer's and the music school where John played the violin and Janet played the piano.

Mother never did any of these things. She slept till noon and was never awake when I woke up to go to school. Every morning, I could hear Mrs Lee in the room, across the common passageway. I could hear the murmur of her children's excited voices as she made breakfast for them while, in my room, dimly lit by a small bedside lamp, I stealthily climbed on to a chair to reach for the hot-water flask. I brought it down from the shelf and made myself a cup of Ovaltine, which I drank with a biscuit for company. After breakfast, I took our chamber pot to the communal toilet, a hut, away from the main house where we lived. No one had ever dared to go to the toilet in the middle of the night because a ghost lived there. After I had cleaned the chamber pot, I brushed my teeth in the communal bathroom before returning to our bedroom to dress for school. All these things I had to do as quietly as possible so as not to awaken the sleeping dragon, and every morning when I drank my Ovaltine tears would inevitably fall because I missed my Grandma so very very much.

'Ping! What *are* you doing? Turn off the tap! NOW! Are you stupid or what? Look at you! Dripping wet! Strip off that uniform!'

The urchins flew to us like flies to a dead cat. Watching other children being scolded or whacked was great entertainment in this house of a thousand lodgers. All the urchins loved it, which was why I despised them. I despised them all.

'What were you doing? Tell me! Did you fall down in school?'

When I remained silent, Mother yanked the blue pinafore over my head and unbuttoned my white blouse, and left me standing in my white panties. The hooligans hooted.

'What's there to laugh? Go away!' Mother yelled at them.

They fled off, screaming, 'She's naked! Naked!' I hated her more than I detested them.

'Take off your socks and shoes! Hurry!'

I pulled them off.

'Into the bathroom! Now!'

I went inside and closed the door, trembling in the dark. The sun had set by now. It was dark inside and I dared not open my eyes. What if they meet the red eyes of the goblins, which lived inside the water urn.

'Ping!'

I jumped. The light came on. I opened my eyes. A naked bulb was hanging from the ceiling. I could see the tiny strands of cobwebs clinging to it, but where were the spiders? I couldn't see any spiders.

'Bathe! What're you gaping at?'

She threw cold water over me. I gasped. I took off my panties as she poured jugs of water on my head.

'Soap.'

I scrubbed that spot again, and it started to bleed again.

'Did you fall in school? How many times do I have to tell you not to climb those rails in school, eh? Did you climb? Did you? Answer me.'

When I chose silence, she turned on the tap full blast and flung jugs of water at me. The water was cold and my teeth started to chatter. She rubbed me down with a large towel and

I followed her hands with the red painted fingernails as they went up and down my stiff little body. They were angry hands waiting for a chance to slap me if I answered back.

'Run to our room and stay there till I call you for dinner.'

Wrapped in a white towel, I raced down the corridor, past the hooting hooligans, knocked into the stools they kicked into my path and ran past all the other rooms with their gaping lodgers till I plunged into the safety of our bedroom and shut the door.

I was lying in bed in my pajamas, with my face to the wall when I heard Mother come in.

'Get up and have your dinner. Now!'

The dining table was outside our room, next to the cupboard which Mother used for storing our groceries. In Kim Poh's lodging house, all lodgers had to eat either in their rooms or in the common passageway. Mother's room was on the ground floor of the two-storey bungalow. Mrs Lee's room was opposite ours, and our dining tables shared the space in the common corridor.

'Ping! Don't just sit there! Eat! Must I feed you too? Look at her, Mrs Lee, just look at her. Food is on the table, right in front of her, and she just sits there waiting for me. Six years old coming to seven and she doesn't know how to feed herself! I look around at other people's children, her age. Like your children. They're minding their baby brothers and sisters already. Look at Ah Peck. Same age as this one here, but your daughter knows how to cook rice over a charcoal fire already. But not this one. Not that I expect her to cook. Ah no! I'd be lucky if she can eat on her own. Every evening, she sits and waits to be served. Like a helpless little princess! If this is how her Grandma has brought her up, she hasn't done me any favour. That old witch can say what she likes but this wasn't how she'd brought *me* up.'

Mrs Lee shook a finger at me.

'Ping, you better be good, eh!'

Mother pushed a bowl of soup and a plate of rice under my

nose. Then she chose the choicest part of the steamed fish and put it on my rice together with some vegetables and a large piece of pork.

'Eat,' she ordered.

I cringed. My stomach had shrunk as though it had been tied and knotted up, and there was no room for food. To appease Mother, I spooned out some rice and put it in my mouth, hoping that she wouldn't notice that I had lost my appetite. The spot that I had rubbed clean of spit still hurt, and Mother had forgotten to give me any ointment for it. My left hand moved stealthily under the table, feeling for the spot on my thigh. That part of my pajama pants felt damp so I knew it was still bleeding.

'Look at her. Just look at her, Mrs Lee! A few grains of rice at a time, chewing like a toothless old woman! Eat the fish, ingrate!'

I crammed some fish into my mouth at once, trying to swallow as fast as I could. My throat was dry as sand. I was afraid that I'd throw up again. If that happened, I would be caned. My stomach felt bloated and full, but Mother would never believe me if I told her. She always wanted me to eat more and more and more because she was fed up of Grandma always telling her that I was too skinny. 'What? Does she think she's the only one who can feed you? Am I so useless that I don't even know how to feed my daughter?' I dreaded meal times more than any other time with Mother. Every mouthful I ate was an acceptance of her and every grain of rice left on my plate was a rejection of her. I couldn't bear it. I just couldn't eat.

This evening, however, I had to try. Mother had been attacked and, even though I hated her with all my heart for yanking me away from Grandma, I still had to protect her against that spindly spider who spat on me. I tried to be extra careful as I gazed at the scoop of white rice before me. Mother was watching me to see what I would do. The hump was growing bigger and bigger, higher and higher. First, a mound, then a dune and still it grew and grew even as I spooned bit by difficult bit and crammed it into my mouth, but still the white hill grew till I couldn't stuff any more of it into my mouth.

'Eat!'

I shoved another spoonful into my mouth. Grandma, I just wanted my Grandma tonight.

'What're you crying for? I'm not dead yet. Stop it!'

Mother's eyes were burning red-hot coals.

'Drink up!' So I forced myself to drink a spoonful of soup.

'Eat your fish! Now!'

Across the aisle, Mrs Lee placed a big pot of rice and a big pot of soup on the table. Her five children pulled up their stools and held up their bowls. She ladled two large scoops of rice into each child's bowl, followed by a ladle of soup.

'More, Ma! More soup!'

'Finish what you have first.'

Mrs Lee waved away her pesky urchins, three boys and two girls; the baby was sleeping inside their room, otherwise one of the girls would be cradling him in one arm and eating with the other. The children wolfed down their rice, working their chopsticks at a furious pace, pushing the white grains into wide open mouths and slurping up their noodle soup noisily. I envied their hunger. They looked so happy.

I tried to smile at Mother, but she barked, 'Swallow what's in your mouth. Eat your fish even if you can't finish your rice.'

I swallowed hard even though I was afraid the lump in my mouth might choke me like it did the night before.

'Is there a bone stuck in your throat?'

I shook my head vigorously.

'Mrs Lee! How I wish I'd no eyes to see! I just can't stand the way she scoops up her fish. Little bit, little bit at a time! You think the fish will bite you? Eh?' she screamed at me. 'You think you're doing me a great favour by eating! Don't eat! Starve!' Mother turned to Mrs Lee again. 'I know she's doing this deliberately to anger me!'

'Aiyah, Ah Lien! Children are like this. You don't care, they'll eat. You scold, they don't eat. Look at my brood. They know. If they don't eat now, tonight, no more food.'

'I know, Mrs Lee, I'm impatient, but she's the death of me. Am I going to let this six-year-old lump control me? I could've just left her with her wretched grandmother. Let her be brought up a prostitute. Like my sister. But my heart wouldn't let me do it.'

'Then blame your heart,' Mrs Lee laughed.

'Aye, I blame my heart.'

'Aiyah, Ah Lien, a few nights of going to bed hungry will cure her.'

Mother got up immediately and reached for the plates of fish and vegetables.

'Then I hope you don't mind leftovers. Your children can have these since this one here doesn't want them.'

'Thank you so much, thank you!'

'Ma, give me some, I want some!' her three boys plunged their chopsticks into my fish.

'Hey, no manners, ah! Say thank you to Auntie Ah Lien first!'

'Thank you, Auntie!'

I kept my eyes on my plate, pretending to be oblivious to the noise and laughter at the next table. I was hoping that Mother would leave me alone now. She cleared the table except for the hillock of rice still in front of me.

'Eat up!'

I was about to put some rice into my mouth when she grabbed my hand and took away my spoon.

'Open your mouth,' she hissed and shoved a spoonful of fish and rice into it. 'Now chew quickly. Don't you dare to cry.'

She was staring at my lips, which were threatening to tremble. I bit hard and tasted blood.

'Open your mouth! Now!'

She shoved another mouthful of fish and rice into me.

'Chew and swallow quickly!'

I thought I was going to faint. She grabbed my shoulders

and shook me.

'Don't shut your eyes. Swallow your food.'

I swallowed but the lump was hard and dry as stone.

'Drink some soup.'

She pushed the bowl towards me.

'Drink up!'

When I hesitated, she held the bowl to my mouth.

'Open up! Wider! No! Wider! Now drink!'

I coughed and gasped for air. Warm soup splashed on my arm. Mother pushed me away from her.

'Don't you dare puke on me! Go to the bathroom, you little devil! I feel like smacking her hard, Mrs Lee! Just to wake her up!'

In the bathroom, I splashed cold water on my face and tried to clean up my pajamas as best as I could.

'You're not going to bed in those filthy pajamas. Go and change!'

I looked at the time. Seven-thirty.

'Hurry! Get into bed.'

The phone in the hallway rang.

'Ah Lien! For you! It's the Millionaire!'

'Coming!'

Then Mother's sweet voice floated towards us, in the passageway where Mrs Lee was helping me to mop up the spilt soup.

'Aiyah, Darling, hhmmm, don't be like that, lah! Just half an hour more only, then I'll be with you. Give me half an hour more, I'll be dressed and ready.'

AWOL

Umej Bhatia

Chocolate goldfoil on his navy-blue trousers. He smiled at the sight, despite himself. The chocolate bar was still in his right hand, a nugget of dark brown. Such colours, pure concentration for his eye.

Agamemnon Raja Tan reclined on the four-star Dunlop mattress, half-listening to the toil of rain outside. 'She will be here soon, a matter of minutes.' He repeated this to himself, every quarter-hour or so. In this position, this frame of mind, for four hours. Paralysed by the blows of his dependence.

His books were strewn around the room. Easily digested, rice packets of knowledge, a hawker centre of wisdom. Mills and Boon, Sidney Sheldon, historical romances, Changi airport fiction. Cigarette butts heaped in an impossibly small ash bowl, filter tips scored by the extinguishing glow of a neighbour.

A room in Yishun New Town. As anonymous as they come. Tagged blocks of nameless flats, washed in Yishun-yellow. It was a deadpan tincture, the colour of numbers. Street 21, Block 372—Yishun-yellow. For Agamemnon Raja Tan, it brought pangs: it was the colour of industrial crying, the effluvia of the city smeared on the walls of its residential prisons.

Sorrow and regret. Agamemnon Raja Tan was full of borrowed sorrow and regret. His books were strewn around the room, cigarettes heaped, chocolate in hand, the rain was working hard, ignored but refusing to submit. And the chocolate goldfoil.

Agamemnon smiled. He wondered, marvelled. Somehow, *this* makes me smile, he mused.

The clock registered five-thirty, plain as day, right as the rain. He stared at the digital figures, five-thirty . . . thirty-one. The change startled him, in the gloom of a room that functioned like an inverse sundial. A shadow flitted across his eyes and changed his point of view. 'She's not coming . . . bitch.'

The bitch was close to howling, but she let the sense of helplessness collapse in a silent sob. To Ranita Ismail, it all looked the same. The endless horizon of void decks, raised above street level, punctuated by the occasional convenience shop run by dark little men in bed-sheet white. Cadbury's, Marlboro kechil, sem-bway, *Her World* magazine—the sum of her demands to the mamas. 'Mama', it always made her laugh. Kavita, her Indian friend, wasn't so amused. 'Mama means uncle, bodoh!'

But Agamemnon saw no contradiction. The mamas were baby-sitters for all the latchkey kids, mollifying them with their impressive array of sweets, chips and expiring chocolate with frayed wrapping, laid out in their line of vision to deter the light-fingered. And the mamas didn't know it—but they were invisible helpers in the kitchen. Stocked with instant noodles, Maggi-mee was a harassed housewife's perfect recourse.

This was the void-deck view Agamemnon shared with Ranita, going steady, an intimate assortment of hare-brained theories about the world around them. The same theories they had to deny when confronted with the rational, linear-thinking Singaporean.

Ranita dragged her feet, jaded by the dullness and drabness of her surroundings. She longed for a beach with pearl-white sand ringed by a sapphire-blue sea. Anything but the noodle-yellow blocks that oppressed her. 'Fast to cook, good to eat.' The insistent chant began to play in her head. 'Maggi-mee, fast to cook, good to eat.' The terse, happy sing-song of noodle ads became a march-beat in the rain. 'Myojo noodles, so good to eat . . .' She carried the commercial mantras in her head, stopping every few minutes to crane her head and squint at another wrong block-number sign. She was famished but the walls offset her hunger, yellow like freeze-dried noodles. And the colourless whisper of rain was cold and diligent.

Her umbrella failed to open after the last block, already weathered and old and now the spring mechanism failing with the relentless rhythm of snap and shut, snap and shut, shut, shut, 'shit!', between open air and cover. Soggy and lost, Ranita froze, trapped in an invisible circle of helpless fury. She screwed up her small, heart-shaped face, her dainty foot kicking at the cemented ground, three times till her gnarled toes hurt. She invariably performed this little routine whenever she was feeling frus and it always made Agamemnon laugh and tease, 'You are like some horse!' She'd shoot back in a hurt voice, 'You drive me around the bend, Agamemnon Raja!'

Ranita had squared many circles for Agamemnon, whatever that means. It was significant that in the tight geometry of their relationship she had never once forced him to see that he was a paradox better left alone. 'Too much, too much,' she would sigh, reflecting on her sacrifices as she thought about the boy with the dark eyes and the crooked smile that formed deliberately under the sharp nose whenever he saw her. She had joined him in an underground life, a series of dotted lines broken by his unwillingness to leave Singapore. She was his double in the staccato dance of his daily inexistence. Agamemnon was AWOL.

She recalled her sweet naiveté when he first told her, 'Girl, I'm AWOL.' It did not strike her as particularly significant. Just another Singapore acronym. 'Absent while on official leave?' she asked innocently, her light fringe touching her inquiring eyes.

Now she was saddled with the meaning, like the partner of an AIDS patient. It bore down on her, implicating her. But she had never thought of leaving him or suggesting that he surrender himself. It was a decision he would have to make on his own. But, today, here, rain-streaked and despondent, the thrill of courting danger in an otherwise sterile environment long over, Ranita finally began to question her acceptance.

'Too fucking much, over and over again, this house, that room, can't call, can't say where I am going, just doing it, cleaning up and then leaving. What are you doing Ranita? Are you gila? He's just like sitting or running or calling you. This is madness. One year already, shit, like one long wait for a pregnancy test. Shit, shit, shit.' Ranita headed for the nearest bus shelter and waited for the first bus to the Yishun terminal, massaging her sore feet and blowing her stringy wet hair out of her eyes.

Lighting another bent cigarette, Agamemnon looked at the digital desk-clock. His uncle would be back soon. He was a laid-back, *relak one corner* kind of guy who was rarely at home. He spent most of his time in and around various gambling dens in KL where he had moved his bookie operations since the crackdown in the Turf Club. As much as they got along, both fugitives of a sort, discussing the psychology of 4-D numbers and analysing *Punter's Way*, Agamemnon was not sure if he had anything to say today. It would be OK if Ranita was around. She managed the silences. This was only his third visit here. He preferred staying in Johor Bahru with his cousin, where he had first headed after going AWOL. Those were good times. Ranita had finished her first year in the poly and they had a fabulous month free, locked in each other's soft and odoured weaknesses. Malaysia inspired them to grant an unrealistic immortality to their intimacy. Of course, it was impossible to keep this up once Ranita returned to the poly. Her weekend visits barely dulled the intense ache he felt for her in between Sundays.

Back in Singapore, having stolen in with his brother's restricted blue passport, he paid a short visit to his father. Linus Tan was a retired arts undergraduate. He had been a card-carrying Communist and an associate of the infamous Tan Wah

Piow. The wash of history was already against him when he was finally forced to quit the bad undertow of his allegiances. Linus Tan had been swept along by a force he barely understood, drawn to Communism because he favoured the Marxist approach to novels. He had spent several months in detention without trial but was finally released when it was recognized that his contribution to the ill-fated student-worker activism of '74 was minimal. And because he agreed to confess. He had little to say to his sons, except to commiserate with them on what he saw as the conspiracy to destroy him. 'I should have left, boys, I'm so sorry. We would have done OK in Perth. But your ma left and all my energy was gone,' he would say by way of explanation, sigh heavily and then return to his neurotic reveries of the past.

Agamemnon never said much to him. All those diamond hard ideals had gone soft in his head. He did not have the character or the strength to sustain all those fancy ideals: freedom, democracy, and equality and brotherhood of man. His father was someone who would have failed in another time and place, a casualty of history wherever and whenever. Here in Singapore he had tripped on his ideals, broken his nose and cursed his sons with ridiculous names that belonged to a myth and a culture they barely understood. Agamemnon's brother was called Menelaus Shah Tan; both were named after the two brothers in Greek legend who started the Trojan war to save Helen of Troy. Their middle names were laughed at by their Pakistani mother, whom Agamemnon remembered as the woman in an orange salwar kameez who never smiled.

Desertion was in Agamemnon's blood. His mom had deserted them when Agamemnon was about five and he hadn't seen or heard from her since. He had two memories of her: buying him chocolate and buying him chocolate.

In school everyone called the brothers by their middle names. He recalled his short, intense bestfriendship with someone named Troy, when he was in Sec 2. But that ended when Troy burnt up during his exams and had to go to vocational school. They had a name for it—'pressure'. Your resistance to this uniquely Singapore virus would determine the kind of car, the price of the country club and the number of rooms in the flat you eventually owned.

National service taught Agamemnon to polish boots until he caught his drill instructor's stern eye on his toecap, salute until he mastered it with a ritual bounce, and strip and assemble an automatic eye, stripped and assembled by thousands before him and to be stripped and assembled by thousands more. He learnt survival skills in the army, for example, how to report sick and convince a young medical officer, fresh out of his houseman's lab-coat, that his back was killing him. Never raise your legs above a certain level, claim debilitating pain, come in stiff in gait and expressionless, like the outcome doesn't matter, just the pain.

Then he was nabbed by his RSM in a well-known nightspot, *Zouk*, while still on medical leave. He had half-expected it, but not so soon. He had been out nearly every night, partying with a vengeance. He wasn't apprehended right away, but took orders the next day. He remembered being marched into the CO's office by the RSM. He was all wrong-footed, in his head, the house music from the previous night still pounding away, 'boom-boom-boom-boomboomboom-boom-boom . . . 73911314H . . . Lance-Corporal . . . Agah-Menon . . . caught . . . while on medical . . . MC number 73984 . . . ke-kanaan pusing . . . boom-boom-boom . . . Rani, oh God, I love you.'

Ranita coolly inserted her stored-value card into the validator and selected a sixty cents bus ticket. Wherever she went, always sixty cents. What were occasional ticket inspectors to the diluted clandestine existence she shared with Agamemnon. It inspired her sometimes. However, today, she felt like returning to the machine and seeking forgiveness with the right ticket. 'Don't even know the correct fare, forget it.' She rolled up the ticket from one of its corners until it produced a sharp end. At every red light, she felt herself prick the skin between her thumb and forefinger, next to Agamemnon's rosary ring, and missing his body.

Agamemnon descended in the lift and headed towards the void-deck coin-phone. Receiver, ten cents, dial 4745656, ring-tone, *kring-kring, kring-kring, tooooooooot*. Ranita wasn't at home. Agamemnon spoke anyway. It was a form of cheap therapy that would cost New Yorkers much more than ten cents. 'Hello, hi, yah, sorry to bother you, not busy, right? It's just these dreams. No, not dreams exactly but the sort of trailer dreams you have, yah, preview before you get to the main attraction, akan datang kind of thing before you get to sleep? Yah, I don't know why, some nights it's good; I think of myself chopping at trees or skiing or falling from a plane with silk blossoming from my back, all man things of course. I usually fall asleep, because I can't remember any redwoods falling on me or hitting pines or getting stuck in a large rainforest tree. But recently I've always been a soldier in some war, like the Gulf war, and I'm stationed there with the Singapore medical team and I got my little flag sewn on, big time and all, yah and then the Iraqi Republican Guard come and slaughter everyone in the hospital with their fierce mustaches and gleaming eyes but I'm there firing away, *budda budda budda budda budda,* get some, get some, or sometimes pretending to be wounded hiding under the bed and then coming out and blasting away, I get medals, not just the long service courteous shit but the real thing, promoted, airborne wings, all the real soldiers there, the American SEALs, the British Special Air Service, looking at me like I am some Gurkha killer from hell, they're congratulating me, slapping me on my back . . . '

He felt someone touch his back and slammed down the receiver suddenly. He whipped around and faced the intruder of his fantasy, a boy in uniform. 'Excuse me, do you've ten-cent change?' The soldier's voice was small and apologetic. Agamemnon glared at the chubby young face with nervous eyes behind square frame black spectacles and porcupine shock of hair. The camouflage colours were still dark and jungle-green and stiff looking. His sleeves were rolled up to regulation length, four fingers above the elbow. His skinny arm peeped out, looking absurdly unsoldier-like. He had no rank insignia and was just screaming to be teased xin-chiao. In BMT, this guy would be the ultimate blur-fuck and blanket-party candidate.

'Ten cent, you got ten-cent change?' the boy repeated.

Agamemnon studied the dull twenty-cent coin in the open palm and the boy's raised eyebrows and hanging jaw, waiting for a response. Agamemnon wanted to punch him very hard and break his jaw. This guy probably cried when he had to do bayonet practice.

'Sorry, no change, but, eh, you know I'm AWOL?'

The boy stared back at him, nonplussed, with a *huh, le kong si mi* or *huh, what you talking* look. His jaw hung a little lower and his eyebrows were raised a little higher. He looked like Munch's 'Scream', frozen there. Agamemnon leaned over the boy, his wavy black hair standing up and accentuating the height difference. The boy leaned back. Even Agamemnon was surprised by his sudden revelation. It hit him—*O I am actually doing it, heights, man!* He reflected that this was the first in a short line of dominoes. He pictured the last domino—himself, falling into a Detention Barracks cot after a long, hot afternoon of Sisyphean struggle ferrying bricks in a field pack.

'Oi, what unit you from?'

The boy told him.

'Close to my camp. Pass the message, I'm AWOL and I'm waiting.'

The boy began to turn away, refusing the unexpected assignment.

'Oi, they'll give you some off days you know,' Agamemnon urged.

The boy started to walk away briskly with a look of frozen terror.

'My name is Raja Tan, Agamemnon Raja Tan and I am AWOL!'

The boy looked back one last time nervously, then quickened his pace, almost tripping as he gripped his twenty-cent coin.

Agamemnon slapped his forehead and cursed out loud; he felt his adrenaline pumping, incredulous at what he had done. He wasn't sure what would happen now that he had come out into the open.

He waited by the phone, toying with the idea of calling the camp himself. But he stopped himself, dialling instead Ranita's number every ten minutes or so. He had no one else to call. Finally, at about seven, he heard her familiar bubbly voice gone flat.

'Girl, what happened? You got lost again, ah?'

'Huh . . . Memnon shit, shit, shit, what do you expect? I'm damn sick of it, can't tahan, OK. Always moving, always running here and there . . .'

'What's up, girl? What's wrong,' Agamemnon asked and said.

This is wrong, that is wrong, aborted silences, painful breaks, fumbling for more coins, machine wants competing with her wants, balancing this, balancing that, soothing words fractured by a harsh accusation, having it out, letting it out, right-punch, left-hook, verbal fallout of lovers, out for the count, *sorry-to-say-this-buts*, who suffered more, emotional balance sheets, why, it was becoming an inquiry into a long and shell-shocked private war until Agamemnon ran out of coins.

He dashed over to the mama shop at the next block, the phone receiver swinging uselessly like a pendulum without a clock, and asked to borrow two ten-cent coins, 'very urgent, very urgent'. Coins pressed into his hand, he ran back. He called her again, smiling with the certainty of a decision.

'Rani, I am going to surrender myself,' he said breathlessly, holding up the receiver like a smoking revolver.

Long silence.

The revolver was cocked back again next to his ear as he hissed, 'But I'm not going in, they can come and collect me.'

Agamemnon's last stand.

Short silence.

'Memnon, I'm coming now, OK, please . . .'

Ranita's first stand.

'No, it's OK.'

'Please don't spoil everything. I'm coming, meet me at the terminal?'

'Oh, the terminal, the end right?'

'Huh, Memnon, yah, OK?'

'No,' he said for the sake of being stubborn as he felt his throat tense up.

Her voice began to break. Then, Agamemnon couldn't contain himself: he started babbling. She was silent with her tears. He stopped when she said, 'I can't take it, please,' her voice small and stretched although she was feeling stronger already. Agamemnon could play man now, feeling weak in the role of strength.

'OK, I'll see you there.'

He brought her up to the flat. His uncle had come and gone, smoking what was left of the extra pack of cigarettes. The ashtray had been cleared. She ate some of the chocolate in the goldfoil.

They made love.

Slowly.

Goldfoil on his navy-blue trousers.

Books strewn. Mills and Boon covers mocked them.

They held each other. Kissing with teeth and mouths. Scrape of skin, aroma of insides, leaving quantum traces on each other. Mascara run on her face in dark dull tears, hint of lipstick on his neck. He lay next to her softly murmuring '*ROD loh*', the national serviceman's ritual chant of finishing up, Run-out date. They were running out of time. He joked about it, some time before, after they reached a peak together, bodies pressed like hands in prayer. Then, they had rolled away laughing. She smiled a little. They stared at each other for a long time. The music helped as they took in each moment, minds photographing each flicker of body.

'Memnon, you know I love you right?'
'No, you love me wrong.'
'Stop playing.'
'Yah, let's get serious. I'll call them now.'
'No, let them come. Lie down for a while.'
'Uncle will be back soon.'
'So?'
'Knock-knock.'
'Who's there?'
'BOO!'
'Boo-hoo?'
'BOO who surprised you.'

The military police took a week to find the Yishun address. By then the crying was long over and neither of them was surprised. Agamemnon was apprehended at the void deck, buying chocolate for Ranita. He held up the Cadbury's bar; he had pulled the goldfoil pin and counted to three, waiting for the explosion.

There was none. Ranita went home. She washed her hands, plunged a block of freeze-dried noodles into boiling water and watched as the stiff strands softened and separated. The memory of freeze-dried Yishun and Agamemnon began to blur. And soon she began to wonder. Agamemnon wasn't AWOL, she thought. She finally figured, '*I* was AWOL, Always Waiting Or Leaving.' She giggled once, and then cried out the memory of Agamemnon, before re-joining the legions of the living and the shopping.

The Move

Wena Poon

Perhaps I should take the pomegranate tree with me, she reflected. There is still time.

Madam Teo, seventy-one, was leaning against the parapet of the corridor outside her flat. It overlooked the car park a floor below, with its canopy of angsana trees. The boys said they'd be here at nine in the morning, but already at seven she had been ready, packing up the last bits of her thirty-year existence in apartment unit 02-04, Block 14.

'Ma, you are not taking those footstools!' Tommy had wailed. 'They have to be retired! I've sat on them since I was a baby!' On the faded leatherette tops, faint blue drawings from a ballpoint pen, from Tommy's boyhood when he was really into depicting Ultraman battling Godzilla.

Jimmy had suggested she donate her wedding chest of drawers to an antique shop in Orchard Road. 'Ang mohs like this kind of thing,' he said, fingering the worn teak exterior.

Florence, one of her granddaughters, had tugged one of the drawers open and shrieked in delight to find that her baby toys were still kept in the same place. The bottommost drawer, for her young hands to reach, back in—was it 1976? Out of the corner of her eye, Madam Teo saw Florence, now an air hostess, pocketing some old strings of pink 'princess' beads and a wind-up tin chicken that pecked at imaginary rice on the ground. *Rat-at-tat-tat.*

They had spent a pleasant afternoon yesterday, fingering the flotsam and jetsam, deciding which to bring to the new flat (Tommy's—she was moving in with him after Jimmy moved out). The bed went to Third Aunt's daughter. The sofa went to Second Uncle. The coffee table, to the neighbours who had 'choped' it. Everything else she could take with her to Tommy's new flat. Everything except her plants.

The old lady was vaguely irritated for the first time. It's always the plants that get left behind. Why?

'The new flats don't have big corridors like these for you to lay out the potted plants, Ma,' explained Tommy. 'I mean, you could take some of the small ones, but those big potted palms and trees—I think you'd be blocking people's way.'

So all that evening the old lady, by the cool breeze after the humid day, when it was kindest to plants, cautiously gathered cuttings. Cuttings from the palm with its lingering fronds, from the 'water plum' with its upside-down white blossoms, from the bougainvillea—that easy-blooming friend, so generous with its colour—which had always reminded her of those can-can girls in the New World Amusement Park, back when she was dating her husband.

'Too bad the pomegranate has grown so big,' said Florence, putting her arms around the girth of the dragon vessel at the base of the tree. 'Remember how Melissa and I would wait forever for the first pomegranate of the year to turn red? Did you really have this since before we were born?'

Indeed she had; it was a cutting she took with her when the Government offered the family, along with tens of thousands of islanders, a real proper flat back in 1971. The original pomegranate tree was over six feet, planted in the corner of her old kitchen garden. Well, not her own, she shared that little plot of dirt with six other families off Serangoon Road. The six families lived together on one floor above a two-storey shop house, and the Teos lived in one bedroom, with a screened-off cubicle for Mum and Dad and three sponge mattresses for five kids.

Madam Teo had been a seamstress then, the kind who transformed ready-cut fabric patterns into five-pocket denim jeans for a famous Chinese family-owned department store. She did it from her sewing machine at home, at night, after the kids went to bed. Every morning, her third son, Eric, who was about seven or eight, would be responsible for shouldering a bundle of jeans she had sewed the night before to the drop-off point and picking up a new bundle of cut patterns for her. She can still remember his little form struggling under the bundle of cloth, weaving through traffic. She will repay him in her next life, she always thought.

Eric's daughter Cynthia was now a lecturer in a law school in America. Every now and then Cynthia would call her grandmother from that strange land whose night-time was Singapore's daytime, and whose daytime was Singapore's night-time.

'Ma,' she would joke, 'I'm lecturing today on labour laws to protect immigrant textile workers in New York's Garment District. I thought about you.'

The old lady would protest gently. 'Oh, in my time it wasn't that bad. They paid about fifty cents per pair of jeans. That was good money then. Of course, nowadays people deserve better. Nobody should be doing that kind of work.'

'They still do!' said Cynthia. And proceeded to tell her about Mexicans, about Chinese workers in America. Their hopes, their sacrifices. Cynthia was a bit of an activist. Madam Teo was very fond of her. She never could understand why Cynthia studied so much just to help illiterate people in a foreign country, but she was glad that the girl did. Madam Teo didn't know how to read. She knew that all she could do was to contribute to life the labour of her hands, the fertility of her body. She knew very well what was fuelling the souls of these immigrant men and women in faraway America, even though she had no idea what a Mexican looked like.

Beneath her, the coffee shop was bustling with the breakfast trade. She could smell steam from char siew bao and the occasional humid waft of nasi lemak coconut rice from the Malay stall. She wondered if the boys would be hungry when they arrived with the lorry. All they and their wives and kids ate these days was food out of cans and boxes. They even drank out of boxes. Like astronauts.

In some ways she was not sorry to leave her old housing estate. The wet market had been scaled back. They'd stopped selling live chickens on the premises—the Government said it was unsanitary. And Ah Goh of the famous beef ball kway teow soup had retired. His stall had been rented out to a young, churlish hawker whose rojak was quite rubbery. Thrown together like fast food, the chilli from a supermarket-bought squeeze bottle, not home made. He didn't know the real stuff. (Madam Teo's father had been a street hawker. And a rubber planter. And a durian picker.)

Just as she was wondering how to fill her sons' stomachs when they arrived, her wok having been shipped off to the new flat two days ago, an open-back lorry turned into the parking lot. Someone honked and waved a bare arm wildly out of the window. She watched Tommy disembark, followed by Jimmy, and Tommy's two teenaged sons.

They were talking about soccer when they slapped their flip-flops up the stairs. 'Ma! Ready for some action?'

First went the dining table, carried upside down like a strange beast shouldered off for slaughter. Then a couple of spare chairs, folded up. Then bags and bags. And boxes upon boxes. A seemingly endless stream, all carefully tied with string. At the end of the parade came an odd assortment of things she threw together at the last minute after she ran out of boxes. Slippers. Bamboo poles for clothes drying. Shower curtains (still damp).

To each of the boys' questions, 'Why take this?' she answered, 'Then you don't have to buy a new one.'

'Ma, this cheapo ash tray is only a couple of dollars at the most. You can leave it behind, no? We've had it for forty years!'

squeaked Jimmy, showing it to his nephews.

'No, no, keep, keep!' said his brother. 'Antique! Antique!'

The four men made short work of the move. Within an hour the lorry was loaded to the brim. It was curious to see her belongings in the full light of day, pulled from the blue darkness of her two-room flat, like mushrooms unearthed and exposed to air. Exposed to the eyes of curious passers-by (every move is interesting, arouses the same feelings in everyone); to the eyes of breakfasting old men in the coffee shop, who followed the progress as if it was something on television.

'Ah So! You are finally moving!' called out the Ah Pek who sells coffee (hence, 'Kopi Pek'). 'Take care in those newfangled housing estates! I heard they have those new types of automatic trains that go above ground on sky bridges—with no drivers! Scary if you ask me!'

Madam Teo blushed and murmured that she was proud to move with the times. 'The Government must have tested them to make sure they were OK before they let us ride them!' she said.

Tommy's elder son, Boon, handed her his mobile phone. 'Ma, Aunty Florence on the phone.'

Florence apologized from the airport for not being there on the big day. 'I'm scheduled to fly back from Sydney on Thursday. I'll come see you all in the new place then!'

'OK. Be careful in the air,' said the old lady, who distrusted airplanes.

'Are you sad, Ma?' asked Florence. 'After all these years?'

The old lady did not expect the question.

She thought about it for a while. No, no. They were just relocating from one housing estate to another. They were getting a new flat. How could this be sadness? Sadness was war, was famine. Sadness was seeing your father-in-law in China lose all his rice fields when the Communists took over. Sadness was watching your father crawl home after being bayoneted by Japanese troops in 1942. Sadness was watching your pregnant mother succumb to malarial fever in occupied Singapore, not having any drugs to allay her fever. Sadness was waking up in the darkness finding her not in her bed, going out to the rubber plantation to search for her, fearing, as she had threatened, that she would take a cold bath in the nearby pond. Sadness was finding her drowned pregnant form by moonlight, and knowing that you had to be the one to run home to wake your father and tell him the news. Sadness forever after was the funerals of mothers that her friends and cousins lost, which she could never attend, because they reminded her of how she lost hers.

They told her the other day, on television, that Singapore was celebrating its thirty-sixth year of independence the following month. Someone—one of the younger grandkids—had remarked how short that time was. To her it didn't feel short at all.

Carefully, while the boys were waiting, while the lorry's engine was panting in the rising heat of the afternoon, she snapped off a branch of the pomegranate tree, wrapped some moist tissue around its base, and put it in a plastic bag with the other branches. Which would someday be green saplings potted in new soil. You take what you can with you.

She locked up the old flat for the last time. Smiled a little when she saw that one of the boys had prised the metal door number plate—02-04—off the front door as a souvenir. 'History, man!' she could just hear Tommy saying to his sons.

Then she made her way downstairs to the waiting lorry and the laughing boys (for they will always be boys to her) and they began trundling northward up the island to a new life.

Hamid and the Hand of Fate

Zuraidah Ibrahim

That morning, Hamid wondered how he could make love to a woman equipped as he was with only one hand.

Would his stump not seem hideous in the silhouette of two bodies curled around each other? Would she recoil or cringe if he held her with it? Would one hand make a good enough embrace? Would he pay for this in another life?

The questions hurt his head for he had no answers. How could he? He had never held a woman, not even when he had the use of his right hand.

His cigarette drooping from his turned-down mouth and a weary look etched on his face, he stared emptily at the stream of thick-waisted housewives waddling home from the market with their swollen bags and baskets. His mind's eye lingered over Salmah's own soft doughy body. He breathed in her talcum scent, sweet yet faintly laced with sour sweat.

Pak Ali was grumbling. It's already so late and you've not touched your breakfast. Stop it with the silly daydreaming and eat, Mid. What, you don't like my food anymore? It's rezeki— Hamid heard him unleashing a volley of words, as if from behind a wall.

Hamid pulled out the cigarette, now limp with saliva, squashed it with his fingers and aimed it at the metal ashtray. He took a swig of his cold glass of coffee. The condensed milk sat at the bottom of the glass unstirred. He looked at the banana leaf packet. He lifted his stump slowly to press down one end of the leaf, and with his left hand unwrapped it. The mound of nasi lemak and the smell of fried fish, muted and made almost pleasant by the fragrant leaf, tumbled out of the packet. On any other day, his mouth would water and he would polish off the stuff with such speed that sometimes he'd wave his stump to Pak Ali to signal for a second packet before he was halfway through the first.

Today, he could barely finish a few mouthfuls. He slipped his stump through the arm of the washing kettle and poured the water over his left hand. He was done.

'You want something else to eat?' asked Pak Ali, who was tossing used glasses of coffee into a bin of murky water.

Hamid shook his head and lit another cigarette.

It was almost ten. Pak Ali's makeshift stall of red folding chairs and tables, on the side of the road, was deserted. A couple of taxi drivers on their mid-morning break sat on their haunches a few seats away, plotting high strategy with their plastic pieces of checkers.

Pak Ali stole sidelong glances at Hamid as he swished the glasses about, drained the water out of the bin and tipped over a pail of fresh water. The boy's not well today, he concluded.

Pak Ali had known Hamid, or Mid as everyone called him, since he was a baby. Their two families lived in the village almost a mile deep from the main road, beyond the clearing where he had set up his stall, a middle ground to attract the villagers slipping in and out of their enclave and the human traffic by the road.

In the village, tamarind and coconut trees grew rampant in between blankets of undergrowth rolling out here and there next to cultivated patches of lawn grass in front of wooden loud-hued houses. The homes were laid out organically. Bedrooms sometimes faced neighbours' side porches that in turn were built at an angle to avoid looking into outhouses. Extensions had an impetuous ill-considered look, cobbled as they were by flimsy clapboards and zinc. All in all, Kampung Air Laut was a study in defiance against the oncoming orderliness of modernization.

It was wedged in a triangular patch of land and so stood as if with its arms folded, fending off the encroachment of amenities like tarred roads, street lamps and concrete homes. On one side of the wedge were the clearing and the main road, and on another, swampy malodorous mangroves. On the east, huge aluminium sheets boarded off the beach.

It was at a spot on the blocked beach that Hamid's life changed one afternoon. Looped like a necklace around the coast were construction sites. Their main activity was to bury the sea with sand to claim more land for the insatiable needs of the city.

Hamid had been one of the hundreds of labourers roped in for the task. He was not skilled in the heavy dredging and machinery work, or even in the building of rock and sand bunds to block off, section by section, the sea. He was limited to more menial duties, hauling sacks of cement and helping his supervisor man the mixers to make grey concoctions that would be used to fill up parts of the reclaimed spots.

People in the village loathed the work at the dusty construction sites. Hamid's older brother, Hamdan, and his other village buddies preferred clacking away at their Olivettis in offices in the city, sneaking off for smoke breaks every chance they had and watching the clock strike five like it was announcing the Toto results. At the end of the day, all they wanted was to be back in the village's embrace, feeling and looking almost as fresh as when they left in the morning.

Hamid was not qualified for such a job. He failed his Senior Cambridge in the Malay secondary school and he was embarrassed about his English.

He found the construction site job satisfying. He rather enjoyed the sheen of sweat on his face, neck and back and he was thrilled that gut-spilling labour had hardened his body and made him look more imposing than his short height afforded him.

He had a pancake-shaped face, a thin spindly nose that seemed lost in the pudginess and soft, almost meek, eyes. He was plain and knew it. So, early in his youth, like many other average-looking, filial sons in the village, he entrusted his prospects with the opposite sex to his mother, Cik Aminah.

Apart from reeling in a wife who would be dutiful, perhaps even pretty if his mother scoured around hard enough, the only other ambition he harboured was to go on holidays and put away enough to send his parents to Mecca.

He accomplished both sooner than he had planned. He did not earn the money through brute force though.

He had brutal fate to thank for that.

The day it happened would often play in his mind long after, especially when everyone else was at work. It would creep up on him like a ghost slipping out of a locked cupboard and scare his spirits into submitting to despair. Then he would lapse into silence for days and he would not leave the house, not even to loll about at Pak Ali's stall.

Hamid was mixing cement when the hand and four inches of his right arm came off. After grinding the gravel stones and pouring in the dry powdery cement, he sometimes thrust a wooden stick into the mixer to stir the liquid about to get a sense of its viscosity even though this was not a required step. He had seen some other workers doing it and thought it helped.

That day, he shoved the stick in before the machine had stopped. The wooden pole broke and the spiralling of the liquid pulled his hand in. The blades seared his flesh. He thought he let out an unending scream as he yanked his hand out but it was a short shriek of shock before he collapsed to the ground. His right hand was covered in blood and lay hanging to the rest of his forearm by twisted slivers of flesh, skin and white splintery bones.

The other workers lifted him up. A crowd ringed him in.

The foreman came running, his safety boots clunking noisily. They bundled him into a lorry and drove him to the hospital cradled in someone's lap with his bloodied arm covered in swathes of striped and Good Morning towels.

When he came to, Hamid saw his mother seated by his side, the edges of her scarf mottled with tears. The doctor told him matter-of-factly that they could not sew his right hand back. His co-workers should have packed it in ice.

'Mid, sabar, Mid,' said Cik Aminah. Sabar.

'Mengucap Mid, mengucap,' she said.

Hamid did as told. He recited his declaration of faith. He told God he accepted what had happened to him.

He told himself he would be sabar. When he was young, his ustaz told his madrasah class that sabar was not mere acceptance. It meant acceptance and submission melded into serenity. Sabar, the ustaz intoned, rolling the *r* at the end, was a virtue that constituted half of faith. So what could he do but be sabar?

After a week in hospital and a stream of visitors, Hamid went home.

Representatives from his company, a Japanese conglomerate, drove their Datsuns through the sandy lanes of the village to his house. The Japanese official bowed in apparent contrition. Cik Aminah, her husband back from his sailing job in Palembang, Hamdan and Hamid nodded back stiffly. He handed Cik Aminah a hamper filled with foodstuff and a dozen bottles of Essence of Chicken. She thanked him in as gracious a tone she could put on, even though no one in her family could possibly drink the fortifying but non-halal drink.

The representatives were also armed with papers. His father and brother listened. Cik Aminah brought in sugary tea and kueh. Hamid flipped through the reams of papers and said nothing. He did not understand most of it. He felt he should present a composed look of *sabar*, so he mustered a smile.

He couldn't sign with his left hand. Someone whipped out an inkpad and pushed his left thumb on to it and then pressed it on to the papers.

A month later, the cheque arrived. Stamped on it was $80,000, a lump sum payment for the loss he suffered. He was also to receive free medical treatment for the rest of his life. Plus, he could go on a paid holiday to any destination in South-East Asia, subject to a cap of $2000, to help him recuperate.

In return, he would neither sue the company nor ask for any more money.

He studied the cheque and decided that being sabar might have its rewards. Cik Aminah gave away the Essence of Chicken to the Chinese egg seller at the market. The holiday, he took with his village friend Isa. They flew to Java for body rubs with herbal oils to revive the nerves in his shortened arm.

Back in his village, news about his new fortune bounced from one mouth to another. Long-forgotten friends called on him. Relatives from as far away as Malacca wanted to visit. Mothers re-appraised his son-in-law worthiness, debating whether his stump could pass for a minor defect. Cik Aminah tolerated the friends and the relatives. But she knew her kind well. 'Hamid is such a good boy,' she would say at the market. 'He keeps saying he wants to live with me until I move on. He doesn't want to get married. No, not my Hamid, he won't know what to do with a girl.'

Whenever someone ventured that she would be better off without him on her hands, she would say: 'No, no, every child is rezeki from God, no matter what his condition is. He's no trouble at all.'

This part was true. Hamid was never home in the mornings, her busiest time of day when she needed to cook, sweep, dust and clean without a man about the house demanding to be served. Hamid filled his mornings at Pak Ali's stall.

'Pak Ali, if you had a choice, would you like being married or being a bachelor? Would you get married if you had this?' Hamid asked, raising his stump. The end of his forearm was a rounded ball of crumpled papery skin covering an uneven clump of flesh.

'Mid, I can see it, you don't have to wave it about like that. Marriage is in the hands of God. Just leave it to Him. If it happens, it happens, if not . . . then it's God's will.'

'God's will,' Hamid echoed.

The struggling hawker and the soulful handicap shared long, fractured conversations about everything: from the ongoing reclamation and whether their village would be swallowed by its expansionist ambitions to the news on TV and the local goings-on as Pak Ali alternated between chatting and attending to his chores and customers.

Every day, Hamid smoked his cigarettes, downed glasses of milky coffee and dragged himself home around noon.

Lunch would be waiting for him at the kitchen table. After that, he would try to read the paper, half-listening to the community-building rallying calls on the Malay radio station.

Each afternoon, while the sun was still lashing out strong rays and only the reckless children would run about outside kicking scuffed footballs, Hamid would walk out to his backyard and lift the iron bar bells he had bought from an ageing body-builder in the village. His skin would glow from his perspiration after a while and a sense of sweet satisfaction would follow.

Once or twice, he joined in the kids' game. But his shortened forearm flailed about and swished their ears and necks whenever he tackled them. He stopped after a while. Now, the most he did was to buy them ice cream whenever he was in a good mood, when the ghosts of his accident did not spring out of the cupboard.

Hamid wondered whether the village children would be out playing football that afternoon. 'Pak Li, do you think it's for my money? And what it can buy? I mean, if a girl likes me?'

Pak Ali told him he could tell a white lie to the girl and say his money was all gone or that his mother kept it or he could give it to Pak Ali himself. 'Then, if she is after your money, she'll have to deal with me. I'm your banker, tell her, hahaha!'

Hamid gave a stiff laugh and took another swig of his coffee.

When he was whole, he had flirted in a half-hearted fashion. He chatted up a few girls at the bus stop and at the mama shop where he bought his cigarettes but felt like fleeing when any one of them warmed up. His confidence would desert him for no reason and he would run out of things to say.

He had tried being friendly with Salmah. But by then she had her sights on Hamdan, his older brother with his trendy shaggy hair, a guitar attached to his chest and a swagger to match.

When they married, Hamdan strummed his guitar and in a much-practised wispy voice unleashed a Bee Gees song at their dinner reception. He thanked his guests in Malay and English. Salmah sniffed as mascara dribbled down her cheeks.

By the time they had their fourth child, Salmah had grown from slender, adoring bride to a sad cellulite-encrusted housewife. Her husband had had his guitar prised off his chest and his shaggy hair clipped short. The swagger though was still detectable. He was a clerk, but dressed well, like so many of his type who wore their pants too tailored and their shirts too smart, as if hoping by appearance alone they could be talent-spotted for managerial positions.

Beneath the façade of professional success, Hamdan was crumbling under the growing weight of hire-purchase loans for the household appliances his young family had acquired. He had also not paid his parents a debt for a dubious investment in a music studio. As for Salmah, the heady romance of their marriage had bubbled over and calcified into regret. She saw that her life was not going to be much different from her parents' or other friends' in the village. They were not moving up or out. She was trapped in the triangular embrace of their lowly village life.

Hamid had witnessed from the periphery of his vision Salmah's growing slovenliness. He thought of her faded, mismatched blouses and sarongs and her hair in a burnt frizzy perm and he thought of her soft hands. Only the last reminded him of how she was once.

'Pak Li, I ask you, it's not wrong to accept gifts if people show you they are grateful for your help, right?' he said.

What strange questions is the boy asking me today, thought Pak Ali. He's really not well. 'Mid, you ask me questions like I'm some wise old man. I haven't even gone on haj. Who are you helping anyway?'

'Nobody. I was just thinking, that's all.'

'Well, Mid,' offered Pak Ali, 'the way I look at it is this: if people want to thank you and you've been well-meaning, nothing wrong with accepting. Accept graciously. Be thankful you've been able to be of help.'

Hamid decided he could not tell him all, could he? Pak Ali would ask him to mengucap and spout out religious sayings to calm himself down. Anything Arabic-sounding would unnerve Hamid and remind him of his madrasah teacher and how he was not being sabar about his circumstances.

He could not tell Pak Ali, could he, that, Salmah was repaying him in deeds he had neither desired nor demanded but all the same enjoyed now.

He was at his mother's kitchen table, eating his lunch with a spoon because Cik Aminah disapproved of him from using his left hand to touch food. It was unclean and ungodly, she said. Pak Ali thought the rule could be bent. 'I don't think God will mind,' he told Hamid.

Salmah had appeared at the kitchen door that first afternoon as if out of nowhere and teased him about how she had spotted him at Pak Ali's stall using his left hand.

He gave her a tight smile.

She needed to borrow a pair of scissors from his mother, she said.

'She's gone to Geylang. She said she'll be back after four,' he replied, his stump stuck close to his side. Salmah could look in the sewing machine in the front room, he suggested.

OK, but she had also been meaning to talk to him alone, she said.

That was how the money-lending business began. Salmah complained about Hamdan, moaned about her children's unceasing demands and cried about how she had neither jewellery nor nice new outfits to wear.

She had dreamt her whole life of living in a concrete house with modern amenities, a handsome smart husband and bright children who would go to university and be featured in the newspapers for being top students. She even wanted to work but Hamdan would not have it.

Would he lend her some money? But could he keep it a secret? Just between them because Hamdan would never forgive her if he knew and Cik Aminah would disown their four children and she already had enough problems on her plate? Would he? She would pay him back, she promised. Every single cent of it, she added.

'Yeah, OK,' Hamid replied.

He pulled out his wallet. 'Take whatever you want.'

Salmah fished out two $10 notes and stuffed them into her bosom.

Hamid stared at his rice. She was standing behind him. He could almost feel her belly brushing his back. She ran her fingers over his stump. He felt so scared, he wanted to jump out of his seat and run. She placed her hand on his face and held it gently. Then she was out of the door.

He remembered her when she was younger. In school, she never looked his way. She was two years ahead of him. Her clothes were starched and her white long blouse was pristine even on Fridays when everyone else looked like their clothes were more than ready for their weekly wash. She told friends she would either be an air hostess or an art teacher.

Their kitchen encounters now had fallen into a routine. Salmah would appear only when Cik Aminah was out of the house in the afternoons to the shops in Geylang or to visit her relatives in other villages.

Conversation preceded all transactions, physical and

financial. She would open with her mental bag of woes. Her children who were terrible in school upset her. Her waning beauty and the brown patches on her face that were darkening by the day depressed her. Her strutting husband whose notion of ambition and ability was confined to dressing stylishly angered her.

Hamid did not say much. He nodded, added a word here and there and kept his gaze down. By then, she did not ask for the money. He would pull out his wallet when she grew quiet, her signal that she was ready for it. And she would lean closer and help herself. First, it was $20, then $50 and sometimes even $100. He always made sure he had enough in his wallet to satisfy her, going to the bank almost every week now.

As always, she would walk to his seat, wrap her arms around him and give him a squeeze. Sometimes, she would plant a kiss on his forehead. Several times, she would slip her hand into his shirt and let it linger on his chest. Once, she tried giving him a brief peck on his lips but he leapt up and fled out of the kitchen. She laughed and left. By then, she had spruced herself up, her burnt perm had its frizzy edges trimmed and she had on gold bangles and earrings and a silver watch, he noticed.

He appeased his conscience with thoughts of his accident, sometimes even willing the ghosts to come and haunt him. He had paid his dues for this life, surely. Anyway, the money was for his sister-in-law, his nieces and nephews. His own flesh and blood. Charity did begin at home. His religious teacher did say that, he remembered. He was not doing anything wrong. He was just accepting of what was happening, he told himself.

The last time they met, she was distracted, in one of her moods.

She had heard his mother was planning to marry him off, she snarled.

'Uh, I don't think so. You know her, she's very protective,' Hamid told her.

Well, he should be careful. Because you never knew who was

after your money, she said. Young women these days, she warned, cared only about working in fancy, vain jobs like being air hostesses and splurging on themselves. Young women these days ought not to be trusted.

'Can I trust you?' he asked and surprised himself at his bluntness.

Her voice rose and he noticed her neck. So he did not trust her? So he did not think she would pay him the money someday? So he was going to marry some young girl and cut her off? She was going to pay him back, she said, her eyes rimmed with tears.

Hamid's eyes stayed fixed on his food, his mouth glued by fear, his feet too leaden to move.

She was going to pay him back, she repeated. She would show him, she said. He would not be disappointed. Then she was gone. Gone without transacting in any tenderness or legal tender.

'Pak Ali, does your wife get jealous when she sees you talking to all your female customers?' Hamid opened up again.

The hawker made up his mind. He was visiting his charge's mother that very afternoon. The boy is dying to get married and Cik Aminah should get serious about it and not worry about losing her cash cow, he felt.

'Mid, you're a real busybody today. It's time you went home, OK. Your mother will be asking for you. It's almost one,' he said.

'Yeah, I'm going. I'm sorry to have been such a pain today Pak Ali. It's just one of those days. See you tomorrow.'

'OK, go straight home. Don't you go wandering about now.'

Hamid shuffled past the coconut and tamarind trees and thought about his dumbbells. He had lifted them for almost two hours the afternoon before.

At home, lunch would be waiting for him at the kitchen table. Cik Aminah had said that morning she was going out to visit.

Notes on Authors

Che Husna Azhari is professor in the Department of Mechanical and Materials Engineering, National University of Malaysia. She has written two collections of short stories, *Kelantan Tales: An Anthology of Short Stories* (1992) and *Melor in Perspective* (1993), and a novella, *The Rambutan Orchard* (1993).

Gopal Baratham has written three books of short stories and three novels. The stories are collected in *Love Letters and Other Stories*, *People Make You Cry*, and *Memories That Glow in the Dark*. The novels are *A Candle Or the Sun*, *Sayang* and *Moonrise, Sunset*. He is a neurosurgeon and lives in Singapore.

Umej Singh Bhatia was born in Singapore in 1970. At Cambridge, he won the Rylands Prize for his poems and short stories, which have been published in anthologies in Singapore and the UK. A Singapore Foreign Service Officer, he is currently serving in New York as an Alternate Representative to the United Nations Security Council. He is married and has a daughter.

Kee Thuan Chye has been wearing many hats in his life—as an actor, playwright, stage director, literary activist-promoter and journalist. His best-known plays are '1984 Here and Now' and 'We Could **** You, Mr Birch'. He has published *Just in So Many Words* (a collection of his writings in the press) and *Old Doctors Never Fade Away* (a biography). His poems have been published in numerous anthologies and journals at home and abroad. Currently Associate Editor of *The Star*, he is in charge of 'Mind Our English', the newspaper's campaign to help improve the standard of English among Malaysians.

Chuah Guat Eng was born in 1943. Her published works include a novel, *Echoes of Silence* (1994), *Tales from the Baram River: A Collection of Sarawak Folktales* (2001) and numerous poems and short stories. A dramatic monologue, *Pandora's Box*, was performed in Kuala Lumpur (1996, 1999) and in Pakistan (1999). She lives in Kuala Lumpur, where she runs creative writing workshops for adults.

Lloyd Fernando has written two novels: *Scorpion Orchid* (1976) and *Green Is the Colour* (1993). He has also published works on literary criticism and edited a number of anthologies. He was formerly professor in the English Department, University Malaya.

Zuraidah Ibrahim was born in Singapore. A journalist by profession, she has been writing for *The Straits Times* since graduating with a degree in political science. She wrote *Muslims in Singapore* (1994) and contributed to an edited volume, *Lee's Lieutenants* (1999). *Hamid and the Hand of Fate* is her first foray into fiction. She lives in the San Francisco Bay Area with her husband.

Catherine Lim was born in 1942 and is a writer in Singapore. She has published sixteen books, mainly collections of short stories and novels, which have been translated into many languages. She is an active social and political commentator for newspapers and journals.

Shirley Geok-Lin Lim has published five books of poetry and three collections of short stories. Her first book of poems, *Crossing the Peninsula and Other Poems* (Heinemann Press, 1980), won the Commonwealth Poetry Prize. Her memoir, *Among the White Moon Faces: An Asian-American Memoir of Homelands* (Feminist Press, 1997), won the American Book Award. Her first novel, *Joss and Gold,* was published by the Feminist Press, New York, and Times Books International, Singapore in 2001. She is working on a second novel and a new collection of poems.

Suchen Christine Lim was born in 1948. Her novel, *Fistful of Colours* (1993), was the first novel to be awarded the Singapore Literature Prize. Her other novels are *Ricebowl* (1984), *Gift from the Gods* (1990) and *A Bit of Earth* (2000). She is currently International Writer-in-Residence at the University of Iowa.

K.S. Maniam was born in 1942. His short stories have been widely anthologized. His first novel, *The Return,* was published in 1981, and his second, *In a Far Country,* in 1993; he has just finished his third novel. Formerly an associate professor at the English Department, University of Malaya, he now devotes his time fully to writing. He lives with his wife, son and daughter in Subang Jaya, Malaysia.

Wena Poon was born in Singapore in 1974. She lived in New York and Boston for ten years, where she has published essays on film criticism, women's issues, and Asian American culture. She is a graduate of Harvard-Radcliffe and Harvard Law School. She currently lives and works in Hong Kong with her husband.

Karim Raslan was born in 1963. He is the author of *Ceritahlah: Malaysia in Transition* and *Heroes and Other Stories.* He is a graduate in English and Law from St. John's College, Cambridge, and is now a practising lawyer in Malaysia.

Alfian Bin Sa'at was born in 1977. He has written two collections of poetry: *One Fierce Hour* (1998) and *A History of Amnesia* (2001). His collection of short stories, *Corridor* (1999), won the Singapore Literature Book Prize Commendation Award.

M. Shanmughalingam's short stories and poems have been published in anthologies in Ireland, Malaysia, Singapore and the UK and in university publications in Harvard, Malaya, Oxford and Singapore. Along with Professor K.S. Maniam, he compiled *An Anthology of Malaysian Poetry* (Dewan Bahasa & Pustaka), Kuala Lumpur.

Kirpal Singh has written and edited many books. His most recent book, *Monologue,* was launched at the First Hong Kong International Writers Festival in May 2001. In 1997 he was Distinguished International Writer at the Iowa Writers Program. He currently teaches at the Singapore Management University where he is also Director of the Centre for Cross-Cultural Studies.

Hwee Hwee Tan grew up in Singapore and the Netherlands. She published her first novel, *Foreign Bodies* (Penguin, 1997), aged twenty-two. Her second novel, *Mammon Inc* (Penguin, 2001), was on the WH Smith Top 20 Bestseller list for over two months. Her short stories have appeared in *PEN International* and *New Writing 6*. She now lives in Singapore, where she works as a journalist in the Executive Lifestyle section of the *Business Times*.

Simon Tay is a writer and a professor of international law. His books include *5* and *Stand Alone,* both of which received national awards. He is widely published and quoted in the international media on international and Asian issues, especially concerning the environment and human rights. From 1997 to 2001, he served as a member of the Singaporean Parliament, nominated by the public and confirmed by the President.

Ovidia Yu was born in 1961. She has written plays, short stories and novels, all set in Singapore, which is where she lives today. Her plays have been performed in Singapore, Hong Kong, Kuala Lumpur, Glasgow and Edinburgh.